DEATH OF A
SABOTEUR

AN AMOS LEE MAPPIN MYSTERY

DEATH OF A SABOTEUR

AN AMOS LEE MAPPIN MYSTERY

HULBERT FOOTNER

COACHWHIP PUBLICATIONS

Greenville, Ohio

CONTENTS

CHAPTER ONE

WHEN OUR COUNTRY went to war, Mr. Amos Lee Mappin's habits, like those of most of us, underwent a change. With this difference: that while other people became more serious-minded, Mr. Mappin appeared to turn frivolous. Some of his friends shook their heads sadly over the change; others, who knew him better, merely smiled. Little Mr. Mappin, bald and chubby, who looked so much like Mr. Pickwick on the outside and was so unlike him temperamentally, had always enjoyed good talk and superior food, but he was choosy. Nor would he blunt his appetite for society by indulging in it too freely. To appreciate company, he said, a man must be acquainted with solitude.

Now, suddenly, he began to seek out the glittering, featherweight stratum of life in New York, the darlings of the gossipers, the brilliant moths who live by and for publicity. Since Mr. Mappin for years had enjoyed unlimited publicity himself, he was very much of a Name and, as such, was welcomed by the Name worshipers. He laid aside his big book on the psychology of murder, and was to be seen daily and nightly in the smartest restaurants and the most exotic night clubs. You did not hear of his being engaged in war activities or civilian defense work. There were some who hinted that his way of life at this time was positively disloyal.

In such circles he was bound to run into Prince Alexis Lenkoran, a leader among the gayest, the most sophisticated and the most publicized. Not that the Prince was a featherweight; far from it; a man of obvious ability and an iron will, he nevertheless insisted upon being regarded only as a playboy. Having been around New York for eight or nine years, he had become a fixed star in the social sky. Not yet fifty, magnificently set up and savagely handsome in the virile Cossack style, young men admired him tremendously and tried to copy his elaborate Continental manners, and his hard, masked stare. And naturally he had everything that attracts women, including a suggestion of refined brutality. In respect to women he was said to be very difficult to attract—then insatiable! Women, even though they were not kidded by his title, loved to address him by it. Lenkoran was not one of the titled sponges that have infested New York during recent years. He paid his own way and more. Among the young men who had attached themselves to him in the beginning were some who now occupied positions of wealth and power, and through their aid, it was believed, the Russian had accumulated a handsome fortune of his own.

The first meeting between Mr. Mappin and Prince Lenkoran took place at El Morocco late one night as two select little parties met and decided to have their tables pushed together.

"For years," said Mr. Mappin to the Prince, "we have been traveling in concentric circles, and now at last we meet!"

"This is a great pleasure to me," the Prince. His English was as good as Mappin's—better, perhaps, because as a foreigner he could take no liberties with it. "I have followed your career as well as I could in the newspapers, but, being such an idle person myself, I didn't expect to have the privilege of your acquaintance."

It was the start of a beautiful friendship. Mr. Mappin and the Prince seized the occasion while the ladies were on the floor with other partners of taking a drink together at the bar. Later, since they were both stags that evening, they left their parties and taxied to Prince Lenkoran's apartment over the Tsarkoe Selo restaurant in East Fifty-third Street.

This apartment, which Lenkoran referred to slightingly as "my little flat," had been much talked about around town. The Prince also had a charming *pied-à-terre* near Tuckahoe in Westchester County. Mr. Mappin looked at the living room of the apartment with the appreciation of a connoisseur. With its heavy carved furniture, black with age, the gleaming brass which included a lordly samovar, and the rare antique rugs from the Eastern provinces, it was a bit of old Russia. On the walls hung a collection of ancient ikons, small paintings on wooden panels, exhibiting a touching, primitive piety.

"I have heard much about this room," said Mr. Mappin.

"Anything a little different from the usual quickly wins fame in New York," said Lenkoran shrugging. "It's not very grand but it suits me. All this Russian stuff is not queer to me, but homelike. My own home in Russia was burned to the ground by the Reds with everything in it—including my mother and my father."

Mr. Mappin murmured sympathetically.

"So, as I could," Lenkoran continued, "I have picked up objects here and there which reminded me of my home and my people. I have lived in this house ever since I came to New York. The restaurant downstairs was started by my friend, Prince Yarenski. He wasn't doing very well and he was glad to rent me the two upper floors of the building. Yarenski, as you may remember, finally married a rich widow and sold out to the two American women who are now running the place. The restaurant has lost its true Russian character, but the widow didn't care for Russian cooking and the old cook of the Yarenskis is still employed below. I don't have to eat the so-called Russian messes he cooks for the customers; he prepares the old dishes for me and sends them up. We will sample his wares a little later."

"Did you come from the Don Cossack region?" asked Mr. Mappin.

Lenkoran smiled scornfully. "All tall Russians are called Cossacks in this country. I let it go at that. As a matter of fact, my family has been established in Trans-Caucasia since the seventeenth century. We are a savage race, so distant from the rest of Russia, they will scarcely admit we are Russian.

"You don't look savage to me," said Mr. Mappin politely.

Again Lenkoran smiled grimly. "You don't know me. Of course, as an officer of the Imperial Guard in my youth, I received a social education in St. Petersburg . . . Let me get you a drink."

"Thanks," said Mr. Mappin very willingly.

"I noticed that you were drinking Scotch and soda all evening. I would like you to try my Scotch. It's a private importation. My man sleeps out so I shall give myself the pleasure of waiting on you."

"Let me go with you when you fetch it," said Mr. Mappin. "Your apartment inveigles me, as George Moore would have said."

"By all means."

They went through a short passage to the foyer. Said Lenkoran: "When this old-fashioned dwelling was altered into modern apartments, there were two self-contained flats on this floor, each having one large room with a foyer, kitchen and bath." He indicated a door on the right. "This was the bathroom of the front flat which I left as it was. It now serves as a powder room when I have guests. The two foyers I threw into one, closing off one entrance door, and the two kitchens I transformed into a bar opening off the foyer. My bedroom and another bathroom occupy the rear of this floor."

"Didn't you say you took two floors?"

"Yes, but that was to save myself from possibly undesirable neighbors. I didn't care to have people passing up and down the stairs outside my door. I have no need of the rooms upstairs. There are two small apartments. I locked them up and left them."

"As things go in New York, I would call that a princely gesture," said Mr. Mappin.

"Ah, I'm afraid you're pulling my leg, Mr. Mappin!"

"I like princely gestures. Unfortunately, I have not a suitable figure to make them myself."

There was nothing Russian about the bar off the foyer. It was pure Manhattan, period 1890, with its mahogany bar, brass rail and fiber-ware spittoons. As a touch of verisimilitude the old-fashioned mirror behind the bar, surrounded by gingerbread work, had been soaped and the design of a full-rigged ship drawn in with a forefinger on the soapy surface. The floor was covered with sawdust.

"It gets tracked through the rooms," said Prince Lenkoran, "but my man doesn't mind sweeping. I picked up the fittings down in Bleecker Street during prohibition."

He set out the makings like a regular bartender. When the drinks were mixed, they toasted each other across the mahogany.

"This is all right to make the ladies rave," said the Prince, indicating the fittings; "1890 is considered so cute! But let's carry our drinks into the living room. It's really more comfortable."

As they went back, Lenkoran carrying additional supplies on a tray, Mr. Mappin noticed that his host had the habit always of closing a door behind him. There was a door from the bar into the foyer, a second door opening into the short passage, and a third door from passage to living room. In the living room one of the most conspicuous objects was a remarkable old chest, carved, inlaid and painted with scenes of a primitive wedding. It stood against the wall at the other end of the room from the fireplace. When Mr. Mappin admired it, Lenkoran said:

"It's the oldest piece I've got. The dealer said it came from Byzantium, but perhaps I was swindled."

"I should say certainly Byzantine," said Mr. Mappin. "Is there another painting on the inside of the cover?"

"No," said Prince Lenkoran.

"There usually is in wedding chests of this type. The lock is modern, of course."

"Yes. I had that put on. I keep my papers in there. They are of no value to anybody but myself, but I don't want to have servants rummaging through them."

"Quite," said Mr. Mappin.

The chairs were American and extremely comfortable. Mr. Mappin sat by one open window, Prince Lenkoran by the next. There were three windows looking down on the street. It was a night in May and the air was deliciously fresh. At two o'clock in the morning the roar of traffic was subdued to a far-off hum broken by the occasional bustle of a taxi below. The two men presented an odd contrast. Mr. Mappin was frankly envious of the nobleman's superb physique. Lenkoran had bright brown hair and ice-blue eyes. His willingness to make friends was flattering because he had the reputation of never putting himself out for anybody. Even in his courtesy there was a suggestion of contempt. Hundreds claimed his friendship but nobody knew him.

"What are you engaged on at present?" he asked.

"Nothing," said Mr. Mappin blandly.

"What! No interesting case?"

"No case of any sort. I have always tried to avoid engaging in cases. It is the psychology of murder that interests me, not the practice."

"But you have solved a number of baffling cases. I have followed them in the newspapers."

"I know. I got dragged in one way or another, but never again! I have laid aside my study of murder, too. The times are too distracting. I can't concentrate."

"Then how do you occupy yourself?"

Mr. Mappin produced his snuffbox, offered it to the Prince, who declined, and took a luxurious pair of sniffs himself. "I drift! I have taken for my motto: Eat, drink and be merry for tomorrow we die!"

"A good motto, too," said Lenkoran, with his smooth voice and glittering eyes. "I have been acting on it for twenty-five years." He refilled their glasses and raised his. "To a short life and a merry one."

They drank.

Later Mr. Mappin happened to use the phrase: "In your country," and Lenkoran quickly corrected him.

"America is my country now. I became naturalized at the earliest possible date. Why, after twenty-five years, I can no longer speak my native tongue with any freedom."

"Your position must be a difficult one now that we are allied with the government of Russia."

"It is," said Lenkoran grimly. "I will not deceive you. I love the Russian land and the simple, brave Russian people, but I hate the present government. They destroyed everything that was dear to me. Let me tell you briefly what happened."

"If it is painful . . ."

"No! I wish to tell you. It will enable you to understand me. I was twenty-four years old at that time. I fought through the war. I was twice wounded. After the humiliating peace of Brest Litovsk, I made my way home in disgust. I arrived to find my father's house in flames. A shrieking, drunken mob danced around it, waving revolvers and inviting my father and mother to come out and run the gauntlet. I was recognized, seized, bound and forced to look on. My parents did not come out; they preferred to perish with their house. Later, with the aid of an old servant, I got away and escaped into Turkish territory. That's all."

"It is too terrible!" murmured Mr. Mappin.

"But understand me," Lenkoran went on, "America is my country now and I am heart and soul with the United Nations in this war. I am not so idle as you might suppose. I have made it my work to raise money for Russian Relief. I have found the means to send it into Russia secretly, because I cannot support the present government even in a work of mercy without appearing to betray all my Russian friends in exile."

"I understand perfectly," said Mr. Mappin.

Their talk was interrupted by a ring at the door of the apartment. Lenkoran went to answer it and came back followed by a waiter bearing a cold supper on a tray. The waiter, whose name was Elias, was a strange being, thin, hollow-eyed and intense. He arranged a small table and set out the delicious appearing food as if the fate of nations depended on his getting everything just so. Mr. Mappin observed that his glance at Lenkoran was anxious and terrified. When they were ready to sit down Lenkoran sent him away.

The different delicacies were named for Mr. Mappin, who had difficulty in remembering the Russian. Caviar he knew, but this was such caviar as he had never tasted.

"My private stock," said Lenkoran. "I have a way of getting it."

"I'd like to give a Russian dinner," said Mr. Mappin. "I mean real Russian, not New York Russian. Russians are so popular now."

"Not my kind of Russian," remarked Lenkoran grimly.

"Do you think they would furnish the food from downstairs?"

"The ladies would be delighted to get the order. You should, however, leave the menu entirely to Pavel, the cook. I'll speak to him myself. Elias could bring everything to your house in a taxi. He knows how it should be served."

"Elias looks as if he had been drawn through a knothole," remarked Mr. Mappin with an innocent air; "or as if he had been
through hell."

"He has," said Prince Lenkoran coldly.

He did not volunteer any further information, and Mr. Mappin
did not like to ask too many questions. The subject of Elias was
dropped. "Will you come to my dinner? I have a Chateau Puy
Ducasse of 1874 that I would like you to sample. There will never
be another such wine in our time. I shan't offer it to the other
guests. In fact, I am selfish enough to keep it for myself when I
feel low-spirited. It has a rare lift."

"I should be delighted. With or without the Puy Ducasse."

"I'll let you know the date."

MR. MAPPIN LEFT about three-thirty and walked across town to settle
the caviar and the celestial vodka while he thought over what he
had heard. Under a street light on Park Avenue he paused, while
the details were still fresh in his mind, to draw a sketch plan of
Lenkoran's "flat" on a page of his notebook.

At home he found a report waiting for him from George Welby,
who was working for him at the time. It ran:

> P. L. came out of his house at 9:30 this morning,
> early for him. He hailed the first taxicab that came
> along and Richardson, who was watching the house,
> got the next one. Unfortunately, P. L., as he has done
> before, was able to shake him off. As you know, it's
> uncertain trailing a man through the streets in an
> automobile. You never know what the chances of
> traffic may be; sometimes the lights work for you,
> sometimes against you. I cannot say if P. L. knows
> he's being watched, or if he's just taking general pre-
> cautions. He's a slick one!
>
> He returned at one o'clock and had his lunch sent
> up from the restaurant. Service for one. At 3:15 a
> man called; tall, thin, gray, gaunt features, scrawny

neck; about sixty years old; had the look of a respectable, Americanized foreigner, fairly well-to-do. He
stayed forty minutes; came out with a long face as if
he had been bawled out. Richardson tailed him over
to Brooklyn where he found that for three months
past he has been occupying a small service apartment in a high-class house on Montague Street, a
block from Borough Hall. Is known there as Paul
Estevan. I have assigned men to watch his further
movements and will report later.

Meanwhile, I took up post across the street from
the Tsarkoe Selo restaurant. P. L. came out at 5:30
already dressed for the evening. I tailed him in a cab
to the Plaza bar where he ran into three men friends
and drank with them at a table. These three were
well-dressed, important-looking American men; the
conversation was just about this and that; nothing
worth reporting. At 6:45 he went back to the St.
Regis where he met a lady who was giving a small
dinner in the Iridium Room. The lady's name was
Mrs. Anderson Willard. At 8:30 they all took cabs
for the Shubert Theatre to see the musical *By Jupi-
ter*. Fifth row to the left of the left center aisle. After
the show they went on to El Morocco, the night club
in East 54th Street. In El Morocco I saw them join
the party you were with. I saw you and P. L. drinking at the bar and afterwards you left with him. So I
judged it was unnecessary to watch him further tonight and I went home.

Mr. Mappin went to bed.

CHAPTER TWO

HE GAVE HIMSELF less than three hours sleep that night. Up at seven, he telephoned to Jermyn in the kitchen to serve breakfast at eight and proceeded to dress himself with particular care. When he entered the dining-room, the correct, leathery-faced Jermyn took note of his costume.

"Going out of town, sir?"

"I'm taking the nine o'clock plane for Chicago. If all goes well I'll be back tonight. If I'm delayed I'll wire. This is confidential. I'm booking under the name of Cephas Watson. If anybody inquires for me during the day, say that I'm attending the Arnold-de Grasse wedding in Baltimore. My name will appear in the list of guests, so nobody can prove you a liar."

"Very good, sir."

Arriving in Chicago in the early afternoon, Mr. Mappin looked over the rank of taxis at the airport and picked out a driver whose face he liked. There were objections from other drivers who claimed precedence, but Mr. Mappin sat tight, and in the end drove away with the man of his choice. A right taxi driver always taught him something about life, he said. From his address book he read out a street and number, and on the way to North Chicago they discussed the war as one reasonable man with another. The address proved a blank; they were sent on to another address and from that to a third, then a fourth, in different parts of town: a good hotel, another not so good, an inexpensive furnished apartment, another in a poorer street. On their fifth try, a rooming house of the better

16

sort, they struck pay dirt; in this case it was a lady named Miss Jocelyn D'Arcy. What was more, she was at home.

"Third floor rear; you can go right up," said the landlady.

In answer to Mr. Mappin's knock the door was opened wide by an agreeably full-fashioned young woman with naturally curly black hair. At the sight of her visitor a cry of delight broke from her. "Lee Mappin!" Seizing him by both hands, she yanked him into the room and kicked the door shut. "How long have you been in Chicago?"

"About an hour and a half," said Lee.

"And you came directly to see me! You duck! I am touched to tears!"

"A mere figure of speech!" said Lee. "Tears are strangers to those beautiful eyes."

"You don't know the half of it, darling!"

She was not a girl, but time as yet had laid no finger on her. The first thing that struck an observer was the directness of her gaze and the brilliance of her black eyes. Later he would discover that her lips were full and seductive, her skin like white velvet (which is not a dead white); and that she moved and stood as if she owned the world.

"Sit down! Sit down!" she urged Lee. "I haven't a thing to drink here."

"We can go out for that. Let's talk first."

"What has brought you to Chicago?"

"You!"

"You're kidding! An important little duck like you! I didn't think you would even remember me!"

"You are not so easy to forget!"

"I am stunned! How did you find me? I have moved . . ."

He finished the sentence for her. "Five times in the last three years." He looked around the room. "And not always for the better."

"What you mean is, with my looks I ought to be living in splendor." She glanced in the mirror over the bureau and roughed up her hair. "It's true. I'm immoral enough to live high, but not sufficiently mercenary. I can't take money from a man who doesn't interest me."

Lee laughed. "The same old Joss!"

"That's why I'm generally broke," she went on. "And at the present moment stony."

"Your luck is about to change."

"What are you getting at, duckling?"

"I have come to get you to work for me."

She looked anxious. "Oh, Lee, I couldn't do your work. I'm not the type. I'm too damn natural. I can't play a part."

"For this job the only part you have to play is—yourself!"

"What do you want me to do?"

"Make a certain man fall for you."

She was disappointed. "Is that all? I'm fed up with men!"

"This is an exceptional man."

"Every man thinks he's exceptional. As a matter of fact, there are only about five different kinds of men and I'm sick of them all!"

"Exceptional was *my* word. This is a new kind."

"I can't attract a man unless I am attracted by him."

"You will be."

"How do you know?"

"My child, I am supposed to be a psychologist. In my mind I have gone over my whole female acquaintance, and for this job I must have you or nobody."

She looked more hopeful, but continued to bring up objections. "There are only two sorts of men that fall for me, duckling; both extremes; the great mass of average men don't like me; they think I'm unwomanly."

"Their mistake," said Lee.

"The near-Nancys," she went on, "they are fascinated by my hardness because they're so soft themselves. They follow me around all but begging me to tread on them. I can't stand the type."

"You're no mean psychologist yourself," remarked Lee. "What's the other type?"

"The really hard man. He can't rest until he's mastered me." She smiled reminiscently. "Sometimes it's fun to be mastered."

"This is one of the hardest men I have ever met," said Lee.

"Gosh! Already I'm beginning to be thrilled!" She looked anxious again. "You realize, I suppose, that I'm not the siren type. I can't sway from the hips and look into his eyes as if he was my God. In fact, I can't do anything. Either he falls for me or he doesn't."

"That is perfectly understood."

"How old is he?"

"Forty-eight."

"An interesting age! Who is he?"

"When you were in New York did you ever run into Prince Lenkoran?"

"A prince! Golly! I might have known you'd be after big game. No, I never met him. Heard of him, of course."

Lee slapped his thigh. "Good! If he had already been exposed to you, it probably wouldn't work. I want you to be sprung on him."

"What for, Lee?"

"I can't tell you that."

"I didn't suppose you would, but I had to ask."

"I can't tell you because I don't know myself . . . yet. It's your job to find out what he's up to. I don't want you to act on my suspicions. You must start with an open mind."

She nodded. "I will have to have plenty of clothes. Not necessarily the most expensive because I know how to choose for myself."

"All the clothes you want and I don't care what they cost."

"No jewels. It's better style not to wear any in wartime."

"All that is left to you . . . Just one word of warning, Joss. You mustn't go all out for this man. For your own sake."

Her chin went up. "Don't worry, duckling. I shall only be thrilled . . . How am I to be introduced to my prey?"

"That must be left to you, too. You'll be provided with everything you consider necessary, but obviously I can't have any hand in bringing you together. I don't even want to make a suggestion for fear it might be recognized as mine. We will consult, of course. The telephone is safe if you dial your number. Later, I will arrange a place where we can meet and talk in safety."

"When do I start?"

"The sooner the better."

"Okay. I'll fly to New York tomorrow."

"Good girl! Call me up when you get there. . . . What about your pay?"

She turned quickly. "Please, Lee, I'd rather leave that to you. You're a straight-shooter. Pay me according to the value of my services."

"Very well. You won't be disappointed. Whatever may happen you'll be well paid, and if we are successful, there is scarcely anything you may not have for the asking!"

She traced a pattern in the rug with her toe. "Lee," she said diffidently, "if it's a fair question, *please*, who is our employer?"

Lee looked at her searchingly; made up his mind. "The United States," he said.

Color flooded in her pale face. "Thanks for telling me."

He took out his wallet. "Now for expense money. Have you any debts in Chicago?"

"Picayune," she said disgustedly. "A hundred and a half will cover."

Lee began counting out crisp, new, hundred-dollar bills.

"Stop! Stop!" she said with a broad grin, "or you'll tempt me to abscond to Mexico!"

"We have a reciprocal agreement with Mexico for the return of absconders," Lee retorted without cracking a smile. "Here's two thousand," he went on. "You have clothes to buy. Don't buy too much in one shop. It might start gossip. If it seems advisable to furnish an apartment, you shall have more for that."

"I shouldn't appear to be *too* well provided," she put in dryly. "It discourages a man's generosity."

"You don't have to account for this penny by penny," Lee continued. "Just give me a general idea of where it goes."

"Okay, duckling!" She clasped the bills fondly. "How delicious to have money to spend!"

"This is important," said Lee. "The first time we meet in New York when he is present, greet me as a former, slight acquaintance. That is safer than trying to make out we are complete strangers."

"I get you, wise duck!"

Lee drew a small silk bag from his breast pocket. Upon being opened, a dangerous-looking little black automatic was revealed. "This is going to be a dangerous job, Joss, and I have brought you this. It is small but sufficiently deadly at close range. I carry one of the same model. I would like you to have it on you at all times, but Lord! with women's clothes as scanty as they are, how can you?"

"I'll find a way," she said, taking it with a smile.

Lee arose. "Now let's go out and have that drink. I want to catch the five o'clock plane."

"Can I drive out to the airport with you?"

"Surely! But you mustn't get out of the cab at the airport. God knows whom I may find as fellow-passengers. I have a philosophic taximan waiting downstairs who will edify you with his conversation on the drive back."

CHAPTER THREE

Upon reaching home that night, Lee found Welby's daily report. As on the preceding day, it detailed Lenkoran's movements. It told Lee nothing new because it was apparent that when Lenkoran had serious business in hand, he always took the precaution of shaking off his shadowers. At the end Welby wrote:

> I have taken a top floor rear apartment at — East Fifty-third Street, rent $105. This was as close as I could get. Richardson has found a small front office across the street and we can communicate by telephone.

In the middle of the following afternoon, Lee had a telephone call from Welby. He said:

"The slick foreigner with a mustache is with P. L. in his apartment. You told me to let you know if he turned up again."

"Sure," said Lee, "I want to have a look at that gentleman. I'll be right over. Where are you calling from?"

"The office that Richardson has taken across the street. It has a dial phone. I sent Richardson down to the street in case the two should come out while I'm telephoning."

"All right, let him stay there and you remain where you are. I may get a chance to signal you. Which is your window?"

"House directly across the street, second floor, front hall room. I'll be just below you."

22

"Okay. Watch for signals without exposing yourself at the window."

From Lee's apartment overlooking the Fast River it was about half a mile across town to the Tsarkoe Selo, or five minutes in a taxicab. When Lee got out in front of the restaurant, he saw the small dark figure of young Richardson strolling by on the sidewalk opposite. Richardson had a passionate enthusiasm for the profession of detective. He was a promising boy, whose principal fault as yet was that he looked too elaborately unselfconscious while on duty.

Fifty-third Street was originally lined along both sides with dignified brownstone dwellings, the town houses of the rich sixty years ago, all precisely alike. They had now undergone various transformations to suit the changing neighborhood. All had little luxury stores in what had been the basements, and some had stores on the parlor floors as well. The upper stories were rented out to all sorts of little businesses catering to the rich, and in small apartments occupied by bachelors of both sexes. It was still one of the most desirable addresses in town and rents were correspondingly high.

The Tsarkoe Selo restaurant had started in the basement of such a house and now took in the parlor floor and the second floor. The original brownstone steps, stoop, and front entrance were still at one side, and the front door was always open for the convenience of the restaurant. Lee ascended the steps, walked in and started up the stairs. The restaurant was empty at this hour. The second floor was devoted to private dining rooms, large and small, and Lenkoran's "flat" was above that.

When he reached the third landing, it occurred to Lee that this was as good a chance as he would get of taking a look at the top floor. He kept on until his head rose high enough to see. If he was surprised, he could always make out that he had mistaken his floor. The stair well was lighted by a skylight in the roof. On the top landing there were two doors side by side in the middle of the house. Not a thing else to be seen. Lee noted with a slight smile that, in addition to the ordinary lock, each door was fastened with a padlock run through two staples. He returned to the third landing.

His ring at the door was answered by Lenkoran's man, whose name was Vassily. He was a dusty blond young man, of much the same indeterminate color all over. His manner of innocent servility stamped him as a foreigner, but of what race Lee could not decide. Russian perhaps, but it was doubtful. Vassily was born to be a servant.

Lee announced his name: "Mr. Amos Lee Mappin. Can I see Prince Lenkoran?"

Vassily was flustered. He had not the face to say that his master was out, because Lenkoran's voice, raised in anger, could be heard through two doors. Moreover, Vassily had undoubtedly been told that Mr. Mappin was an important man, and he didn't know what to do with him.

"Prince Lenkoran is engaged at the moment," he stammered.

"I'll wait," said Lee cheerfully.

This increased the servant's distress, for the natty little Mr. Mappin was obviously not a person who could be asked to sit down in the foyer. Moreover, he was doubtful if his master wanted these two visitors to meet. Lee helped him out by suggesting:

"Shall I sit down in the bedroom?"

"If you please, sir," said Vassily gratefully.

He led the way through a short passage toward the rear. This was the part of the flat that Lee had not seen. Through an open door on his right, he had a glimpse of a luxuriously appointed bathroom. The bedroom occupied the whole width of the house with three windows overlooking the roof of an extension below and across back yards to the rear windows of the houses on Fifty-fourth Street. It was furnished solely with a view to comfort; nothing Russian about it except an oversize bed.

Lee planted himself in an inviting chintz-covered chair beside a window and Vassily softly retreated. "I will announce you," he said as he disappeared.

Lee had not to wait more than three minutes before the military figure of Lenkoran came striding in. He had the effect of making any ordinary room look stuffy. Though his lips were smiling courteously, the lines of anger still showed around them. His eyes were dangerous.

"So glad to see you!" he cried. "That fool Vassily, to bring you in here!"

"It was my idea," said Lee. "You were engaged."

"Just an old friend," said Lenkoran, with a wave of the hand. "Vassily should have brought you in to us. I cannot beat any sense into his thick skull! Come, I want you to meet my friend."

They went through to the living room. The friend stood in front of the fireplace with his hands behind him. Lenkoran introduced them.

"Mr. Scharipov . . . Mr. Amos Lee Mappin. You two should have much in common."

At first glance, Scharipov looked like a prosperous, conservative, American businessman; smooth, squarish face, neat mustache, an adequate head of hair, rimless glasses. He was about fifty-five years old and beginning to spread through the middle. Not quite American though; Welby's instinct was sound in terming him a foreigner. He spoke perfect English, but not as one who had learned it in infancy. He had the manner of a man accustomed to authority. In his eyes, too, there was a sparkle of anger. If Lenkoran had been bawling him out, he was not taking it meekly.

Now everything was smiles and politeness. "Scharipov and I are old Russians together," said Lenkoran. "He is working for the cause I told you about, and has brought me a very handsome contribution from the Coast."

"Not as much as I should like to have brought," said Scharipov.

He mentioned that he had been in business in San Francisco for nine years as a coffee importer. It appeared that he knew practically everybody on the Coast, and he and Lee spent a pleasant five minutes in matching their common friends. As soon as Scharipov had registered his identity and his connections with Lee, he took his departure. Lenkoran left the room with him.

"If you think of anything else, call me up at the hotel," said Scharipov as they went through the door.

"The Biltmore as usual?"

"Yes."

The door closed. There was further low-voiced conversation outside. Lee turned quickly to the window. Without, difficulty he

found Welby standing a little back from a window across the street
watching for him. Lee's glance swept the neighboring windows.
Satisfied that nobody else was looking out at the moment, he swiftly
telegraphed in the sign language of the deaf:

"Scharipov of San Francisco. Now at Biltmo . . ."

Hearing the outer door of the apartment close, he broke off and,
leaving the window, picked up one of Lenkoran's Russian cigarettes
and lighted it. When the Prince entered, Lee said:

"I feel I ought to apologize for dropping in without warning.
It's not done nowadays."

"Not at all!" said Lenkoran with assumed warmth. "It was a
friendly thing to do. You're right, nobody does it any more, and I
miss it." He picked up a cigarette and lighted it, obviously waiting
for Lee to explain why he had come.

"I will have my Russian dinner on Thursday night of next week,"
said Lee, "if that is convenient for you."

Lenkoran consulted a little pocket notebook, scratched out an
entry, and wrote in Lee's name in place of it. "I will make it convenient," he said.

"I came to order the food," Lee went on. "Since it was the first
time, I thought it might be troublesome to make myself understood
over the phone. Of course I needn't have bothered you, but you
were good enough to say you would recommend me to the chef
here."

"Surely," said Lenkoran. "And this is the best time of day to
talk to him." He pressed a button beside the fireplace and Vassily
presently entered. Lee noted how the servant's pale eyes cringed
when he stood before his master. "Ask Monsieur Pavel to be good
enough to come up," said Lenkoran. To Lee he added: "Even Russian
cooks have to be addressed as Monsieur. It's their title of office."

Vassily disappeared and they sat down. "How many are you
going to have?" asked Lenkoran.

"Eight only," said Lee. "You at one end of the table, I at the
other; four pretty women."

"And the other two men?"

"I haven't asked them yet. They hardly matter."

Lenkoran took a fresh cigarette and puffed it thoughtfully. "I am thinking what you ought to have," he said. "You must allow me to furnish the caviar. This must be an unforgettable dinner!"

"It is good of you to take so much trouble," said Lee.

"I wouldn't do it for anybody else," said Lenkoran with a steely smile.

SHORTLY AFTER LEE GOT HOME, Welby called on the phone. He said: "I tailed Scharipov back to the Biltmore. He is known there. I mean he makes frequent visits to New York and always puts up at the Biltmore. When he returned to his suite, he telephoned to the office for a ticket and berth on the afternoon plane to Frisco. I tried to get you on the phone but you had not returned. I took the responsibility of purchasing a berth on the same plane and sent Linder out with him."

Lee smiled dryly. "Linder will report that Mr. Scharipov is a well-known businessman," he said, "who lives in good style, belongs to the best club, and is highly regarded by all!"

"Did I do wrong in sending Lindner?"

"You did exactly right. For all that, Scharipov is one of the key men in this situation and must be kept under constant surveillance."

"I'll see to it, Mr. Mappin."

CHAPTER FOUR

Young Richardson was living at one of the huge and busy hotels near the Pennsylvania Terminal. Upon reporting to the desk that he had lost the key to his room, the price of it was entered on his bill, and a new key given him. The first key was conveyed to Lee Mappin, who thereupon made an appointment with Jocelyn D'Arcy to meet him in Richardson's room in the early afternoon. She was not to send her name up but to proceed directly to the room and enter without knocking. This was five days after her arrival in New York.

At the sight of her Lee said: "Bravo!" and her pleased eyes looked around for a mirror. She was wearing a deceitfully simple, black-and-white street dress with white doeskin gloves that must have been a yard long, wrinkled over her forearms. Attention was focused on her little white hat, which was simple, too, but different from every other woman's hat in New York that day. She gave the effect, not of following, but of creating style. She commanded attention without having to rig herself out like a freak. She sat down.

"What will you have to drink?" he asked, extending a hand toward the telephone.

"Wait until after I have made my report, duckling."

"So you have a report to make."

"And how! I hope I haven't put you out by bringing you here. It could have been done by telephone."

"Why deprive me of the pleasure of looking at you?" said Lee.

"Thanks, darling. Even though you know the phone is safe, it's hard to confide things to a soulless transmitter."

"Go ahead!"

"I took one of the cheaper suites at the Ambassador. I mustn't appear to flaunt myself. Each of the leading hotels in town has its special character and for this the Ambassador best suited my lay."

"I get it."

"My first act was to look up Lily Dardan. I went to school with her in the dim past, and she is one of the few women who really like me. She's married to an executive in the Bowling Green Trust, she's fairly well in the know around town, and a great gossip."

"What did you tell her about yourself?"

"Simply that my luck was out in Chicago and that I'd come to New York in the hope of bettering it. That was enough for Lily."

"Go on."

"I let her run on for half an afternoon before I began to steer her toward the subject of Lenkoran. She didn't know she was being steered. As soon as his name came up, I got an earful. Lord! that guy has got the women of New York locoed! Lily doesn't know him but she would like to. I won't bore you with all she told me because it's only what everybody knows. There was nothing in her talk I could act on, but I picked up a couple of leads that I followed later, and, to make a long story short, I learned that Lenkoran would certainly attend the ball in aid of refugee children at the Ritz night before last.

"I bought a couple of tickets and asked a man I know to take me. His name is Jack Langford, not that it matters, because I shan't need him again. He didn't know Lenkoran. I got somebody else to point him out to me. Gosh! what a man! Terrific, duckling!"

"Do you want to resign?"

"Not me! Naturally, I ignored him but I took care to give him opportunities to notice me. He couldn't help but see me, for I was wearing a little rag that would put a man's eye out, duckling—that is if he appreciated the finer points of clothes."

"I believe you," murmured Lee.

"Everybody was asking who I was. When I danced past, out of the tail of my eye I could see Lenkoran asking this person and that, and nobody could tell him. Later I saw him making his way toward me and I sent my escort away on a make-believe errand. 'Haven't we met before?' he asked. 'Not that I can remember,' I answered sweetly. 'I am Prince Lenkoran,' he announced, as if he were the Angel Gabriel. I bowed without saying anything. 'Will you dance?' he asked. 'Sorry, I am engaged. My escort will be back directly.' 'Later, then?' 'I'm afraid not.' His eyes flashed blue fire. 'Whom do you know here who can introduce me to you?' he demanded. There was a woman I had met in Chicago, a Mrs. Donlon, and I pointed her out. Jack, who had been instructed to return in ten minutes, turned up, and I danced away with him, leaving His Highness standing."

Jocelyn was a good mimic, and Lee had to laugh at her rendition of Lenkoran's towering manner. "The moment we paused, Lenkoran dragged that woman across the floor and introductions were made," she continued. "'Will you dance?' he again demanded. I accepted indifferently and we started out on the floor. His body is like steel. Meanwhile, Jack had picked up a pretty girl, and all the time we danced I was trying to follow them with my eyes. I bit my lip to register jealousy. I asked the Prince who she was. He didn't know and made it clear he didn't give a damn. I'm sure he would have enjoyed strangling me right out there on the floor.

"However," Jocelyn continued, "that sort of thing can easily be carried too far, so when the Prince took me for a drink I melted a little. He asked me a few questions about myself. I told him I had been married; had been divorced in the state of Illinois and granted the right to resume my maiden name; that my ex-husband had died last year. So far that was true; then I embroidered it by mentioning that my former husband had unexpectedly left me a sum of money that enabled me to live in a larger way than I had, and so I had come to New York. This was to account for my fine clothes and the suite at the Ambassador. It doesn't matter whether he believes it or not. He's hooked.

"He only asked a few questions, because he's so arrogantly sure of himself—damn him!—and it would never occur to him that a woman could be dangerous to him. His talk was all about the dizzy people he plays around with in New York. These people are his window-dressing; they have nothing to do with his real business here, whatever that may be. This kind of talk was to let me know that if I was nice to him I would be introduced to this sooper-dooper kind of society. I let on that it was okay by me.

"My escort had instructions to pick me up again in an hour, and when I left the Prince he asked me to come for cocktails at his place the next afternoon; that was yesterday. 'Will it be a party?' I asked. He got it. 'Surely, the usual crowd,' he said. 'And I'd be happy to meet any friend of yours you might care to bring.' So I said I'd come. I took Lily Dardan with me. She was transported to the seventh heaven of delight. It was a weird joint, duckling . . ."

"I have been there," put in Lee.

"Then I can skip the description. I took care to be rather late in arriving. Every woman was presented with a corsage of orchids, not the common kind, but rococo blossoms that we had never seen before. I drew a green and black spray, rather poisonous, but extremely becoming. There were about twenty people there, all of the sort who get their names in the paper every day of the week. His Highness paid no particular attention to me—yesterday that was his game, see?—but there was a Mrs. Baskerville who acts as a kind of stooge for him. She introduced me to all the celebrities and I was made to feel that anybody Lenkoran smiled upon was one of them. It was the usual gin klatsch, duckling; everybody shooting the gas at once. The only thing different was Lenkoran's intent glance. In that there were overtones . . ." Jocelyn's face sobered. ". . . overtones of mystery and terror!" She shivered slightly.

"Are you afraid?" asked Lee.

"Certainly I'm afraid," she sharply retorted, "but don't misunderstand me. I adore it. I wouldn't back out for anything, but . . ." She hesitated again.

"But what, Joss?"

"It's only fair to warn you that I'm not going to succeed in this."

"You have already succeeded beyond my hopes."

She shrugged. "Oh, it was a simple matter to hook the man, but that isn't going to do you any good. I shan't be able to earn my pay. Because there are no chinks in his armor. He will never give himself away. Not even when he sleeps!"

"I'm prepared for that," said Lee cheerfully. "What I hope for is, that while you are associated with him, someone among those who surround him or visit him will give him away, perhaps with a single word. I want you to listen for that word."

"Okay! I've warned you." She pulled a droll face. "They say that emotion makes a woman doubly alluring. I'll be busting with emotion. He won't know that it is merely fright."

"If he did know it would please him. He's a man who likes to be feared."

"Sure, wise duck!"

"Anything else?"

"Yes. As I was leaving his apartment he asked me to dine with him, go to a show and, if I cared to, on to a night club afterwards. That's what awaits me tonight. I have another dream of a dress that will make the town look up. I shall be seen with the Prince and tomorrow I'll be famous!"

"Fast work, Joss!"

THAT EVENING at the time when Jocelyn would be arraying herself, Lee had a call from Welby. Welby said:

"I have just had a wire from Linder in Frisco. He says that Scharipov took a sudden resolution to fly back to New York this afternoon. Must be important. Linder didn't try to get on the same plane because he thought it likely Scharipov had spotted him on the flight out."

"That's all right," said Lee. "Let Linder get on with his investigation in Frisco. We'll take care of Scharipov while he's here."

"He'll arrive in the morning," said Welby. "The listening post is ready. There seems to be little danger of discovery."

"Keep me informed," said Lee.

At noon next day, Lee received a written report from Welby.

Scharipov came directly to P.L.'s apartment from the airport. Time of arrival 9:50. I was waiting with the ear-phones on when they met. The microphone isn't satisfactory. I'll try to get a better one. I could hear P.L.'s angry voice all right, but some of Scharipov's answers escaped me. Scharipov spoke at first in some language, strange to me. I don't think it was Russian. "Speak English!" said P.L. angrily. "I can't follow your uncouth tongue!" I took down what followed verbatim.

"What the hell brought you back?"

"Bad news," said Scharipov.

P. L. cursed him. "Bad news! Bad news! When did you ever bring me anything but bad news! Bad news is only the excuse for weakness and incapacity! We are not interested in your bad news. We want action!"

Scharipov started some kind of explanation that I couldn't hear. P.L. shut him up angrily. "Do you dare to suggest that our plan must again be postponed?"

"It must be, your Excellency."

This seemed to put P.L. beside himself with rage. He roared so that I couldn't make out all the words. Scharipov begged him to be quiet. Warned him that the servant would hear. P.L. shouted:

"I'm not giving away any secret when I call you a fool! God! how I am cursed with fools. Six weeks ago you should have been ready. What was it then? I forget. Three weeks ago you found some traitors in the crew and when they were liquidated you allowed the owners to send men aboard that we couldn't trust!"

"We could act no differently, your Excellency."

"Bah! why couldn't the new men be liquidated at sea? What matters a few more bodies fed to the sharks? Boldness is necessary to carry out so intricate and far-reaching a plan. Boldness will overcome every obstacle! You all lack boldness!"

What Scharipov said in answer to this I couldn't hear. P.L. broke out again:

"Twice I have had to call it off because of the weakness and folly of others. It is too much! The enemy is always growing stronger and warier. Soon it will be too late. And now a third time! Why? Why? Why?"

"Diehl has come down with a fever. He's in hospital."

"Why did the captain allow him to be taken to hospital? Is there not a doctor aboard?"

"It was taken out of the Captain's hands, your Excellency. The health officers removed him from the ship."

"God damn it! What's a purser's health to me when victory hangs by a hair! Replace him! Replace him! Promote the Assistant Purser. He's one of our men."

"We can't do that. Diehl is our contact with the Customs Inspector. For a year Diehl has been cultivating his friendship. The Inspector wouldn't trust anybody else."

"Then delay the sailing of the ship until we can arrange something."

"Your Excellency forgets that we have no control over the movements of the ship. To attempt to exert control would immediately arouse suspicion."

"Suspicion! The way to avoid suspicion is to act boldly! When does the ship sail?"

"Tomorrow."

"And I must sit twiddling my thumbs for three weeks until she returns? I must cancel all my orders! God! this is bitter! This is bitter!"

He launched out in a fresh stream of cursing. Scharipov is no tame cat. As soon as he could make himself heard, he said coldly:

"This is getting us nowhere, your Excellency. I will return to my hotel to await your further instructions. Should I not hear from you by four o'clock, I'll take the plane for San Francisco."

"Get out and be damned to you!" roared P.L.

I'll call you up as soon as you have had time to read this.

Welby.

Later Welby said over the phone: "The conversation I took down doesn't seem to add up to much, Mr. Mappin. I hope you can decode it."

"Not very far," said Lee. "However, it provides us with several leads. Whatever may have happened, it is good news for us. Their plans have miscarried. We have gained time. It is most important to discover what Lenkoran had in mind in saying he would cancel all his orders."

"I don't believe he's Russian at all!" said Welby.

"I'm sure he isn't," said Lee dryly.

"Richardson is watching the house," Welby went on. "I'll relieve him when I get out on the street, and Richardson will take the earphones in case Lenkoran sends for Scharipov."

"Telephone Linder in San Francisco to find out what Scharipov's interest is in shipping. Does he own any ship or ships, or charter any? Does he own stock in a shipping company? I must also have, quick, a list of ships now loading in San Francisco, and particularly what ship or ships are sailing tomorrow, and a full account of them. Linder must also find out if a purser called Diehl has been admitted to a San Francisco hospital. He may call himself something else. Any man who has been hospitalized from a ship. Let Linder know that this is of the most extreme importance."

"I'll take care of it, sir."

CHAPTER FIVE

THE GUESTS HAD BEEN INVITED for half-past seven on Thursday night, and dinner was to be served at eight. At Mr. Mappin's you dined at your ease, without being snatched away to the theater, and after the theater whisked to some other place. Good talk was the main stay of the entertainment, and every guest was expected to contribute to it.

At seven, Elias, the waiter from the Tsarkoe Selo, arrived in a taxicab with his various containers, bottles, and a satchel full of assorted aids to the culinary art. He immediately went into consultation with Lee's man, Jermyn, in the kitchen. A third man had been engaged to assist Jermyn in serving. Jermyn thought two would be sufficient, but Lee didn't want Elias to come into the dining room. That gaunt and tragic face of his might take the edge off his guests' appetites, he said.

The guests began to arrive. First came Miss Delphine Harley, the actress, on whom Lee could always depend for beauty and wit at his table. She was followed by the famous Mrs. Nick Cassells, whose income in normal times was said to be a million a year. Mrs. Cassells was not a young woman, but she had the means to arrest time. Slender, exquisitely dressed and jeweled, she was ageless. The other two women were Miss Marjorie Denmeade, the eminent foreign correspondent and commentator, who was good-looking to boot, and Lee's own little Fanny Parran, who contributed youth and a delicious blonde prettiness to the gathering. The red-headed Tom Cottar, an ace on the *Herald-Tribune*, brought Fanny and had eyes for nobody else. The other man was Mr. Sologub of the Soviet Embassy, who had come all the way from Washington to attend this dinner. He was a pleasant man with an open manner and a willingness to look facts in the face.

Miss Harley, glancing around, murmured to Lee: "I foresee a good party."

While waiting for Prince Lenkoran, they had cocktails out on the balcony overlooking the East River far below. They sat in shadow. The westering sun was hidden behind the apartment house and the whole scene before them was flooded with golden light. Even the ugly factories of Newtown had their moment of grace.

"How I miss the broad-beamed Fall River liners that used to waddle upstream every evening at this hour!" said Lee.

Eight o'clock arrived and Lenkoran had not appeared. The ghost of a smile was hovering around Lee's lips. Presently Jermyn appeared in the French window opening. Catching Lee's eye, he shaped the word: Telephone.

Lee went in. "Who is it?" he asked.

"A message from Prince Lenkoran, sir."

Lee's smile broadened.

Over the wire he heard a man's voice that was strange to him saying: "Dr. Westcott speaking. I am speaking for Prince Lenkoran. A little while ago I was called to his apartment and found him suffering from an attack of acute gastritis. He is in great pain."

Lee's smile was at its widest then. He might have pointed out that gastritis attacks a man after eating, not before, but he did not; merely he said that he was very sorry.

"Prince Lenkoran deeply regrets that he cannot come to dinner," the voice went on, "and that he was unable to notify you earlier."

"That's quite all right," said Lee. "Tell him not to distress himself on my account and that we'll have another dinner as soon as he feels able."

Jermyn was standing by to hear the outcome. "Remove his place," said Lee. "Jermyn, did you tell anybody that a gentleman from the Soviet Embassy was coming to dinner?"

"No sir! No sir!" cried Jermyn in distress.

"How could he have found out?"

Jermyn had an idea. "Elias has had an opportunity to look at the place cards, sir."

"Ha!" said Lee. "Has he used the telephone?"

"Yes, sir. Called the Tsarkoe Selo for something that had been forgotten."

"Did you overhear his talk?"

"No, sir. I was busy in the dining room."

"That explains it, then." Lee shrugged philosophically. "Oh well, there are more ways than one to skin a cat. . . . You may serve the dinner."

Lee told his guests what had happened and led the way with Mrs. Cassells to the dining room. Lenkoran provided a good conversational opening. Everybody had something to contribute.

"I like to look at him," said Delphine, "but I never fall for a man who is in such demand. Puts me off, somehow."

"He's extremely rude," remarked Mrs. Cassells.

"That's a part of his attraction, darling," said Lee. "Rudeness is so *soigné!*"

"Anybody can be rude," put in little Fanny. "It's no distinction."

"When I was in Europe, I never met anybody who knew him," remarked Miss Denmeade.

"He's God's gift to the gossip writers in this country," said Tom Cottar.

Only Mr. Sologub had not spoken. "What do you think?" Lee asked.

"I have never met your prince," said Mr. Sologub, smiling.

"He's not my prince; he's yours."

"In Russia we used to have a swarm of princes. Where are they now?"

"His family is known, I suppose?"

Mr. Sologub shook his head. "Not to me. There were so many noble families."

"He was an officer in the Imperial Guard."

"They all were," said Mr. Sologub dryly. "I wouldn't know."

"The family seat was in Trans-Caucasia."

"Very far away, Mr. Mappin. On the Turkish side."

The talk passed to other matters.

LUNCHING AT HOME ALONE on the following day, Lee looked out of sorts. Linder in San Francisco had reported again. Scharipov had no interest in any ship or shipping business; no ship was sailing that day; no purser or other seaman by the name of Diehl or any other name had recently been carried to a hospital.

"Jermyn," said Lee, "I believe I'll crack a half-bottle of the Chateau Puy Ducasse. It may change my luck."

Jermyn, suitably impressed by the occasion, went to fetch it from the closet in the main corridor where Lee kept his wine. He returned with the precious bottle reclining in its little basket. Nobody but the master was permitted to draw the cork of this wine. Placing the basket beside Lee and laying down a corkscrew, Jermyn stood by anxiously watching the operation. Lee removed the cap and prepared to insert the corkscrew. Suddenly his glance of pleased anticipation hardened.

"Fetch me a magnifying glass," he said in a changed voice.

Jermyn flew.

Lee, examining the cork, said very dryly: "This is not one of my corks. This is not my bottle."

Jermyn began to tremble. "Oh my God, Mr. Mappin, you don't think that I . . . ."

"Nonsense! In what position was this bottle in the rack?"

"It had been drawn forward out of the rack, sir. I thought for some reason or other you wanted this one used first."

"Naturally you would. But I did not change the position of any bottle. . . . Who else has had access to the wine closet?"

They looked at each other and the same name occurred to both.

"Elias?"

Jermyn nodded wretchedly. "I was obliged to leave him alone in the kitchen while I was serving."

"And the key was hanging in its usual place?"

"Yes, sir. Very careless of me, I . . ."

"Never mind that now. We'll be more prudent hereafter," Lee lifted the bottle from its cradle and stood it aside. "Fetch me another. I really feel the need of it now."

The second bottle had not been tampered with. Lee drank it with relish and insisted on giving the shaking Jermyn a small glass.

After lunch Jermyn was sent down to Bellevue Hospital with the suspected bottle and a note to Lee's friend, Dr. Hatchett.

Dear Hatch:
Will you please have one of your chemists analyze the contents of this bottle immediately. Do not under any circumstances tell him or anybody else that it came from me. This concerns a matter of supreme importance and I know I can depend on you to keep it quiet.

Yours,
Lee.

At five o'clock the bottle came back with an answer:

Dear Lee:
This wine is loaded with the bacteria of bubonic plague. For God's sake what fiend did this? Take care of yourself, old man. They might get you in some other way. We will keep the secret.

Hatch.

Lee showed this to Jermyn, who turned ashy. "Oh, sir, if you had drunk the wine!"

"Well, I didn't," said Lee cheerfully. "Have the lock on the wine closet changed and keep the key in your pocket hereafter, as I keep mine. He forced the cork into the bottle as far as it would go, wrote "Poison" across the label, dated it, and after signing it, had Jermyn sign it, too. "This may be needed for evidence later. Tie Dr.

Hatchett's note to the bottle and put it on the top shelf of the closet, where I keep my exhibits. Here's the key to it."

Lee sat thoughtfully smoking in his living room. When Jermyn came back he said: "Let us see if we can't turn this to our advantage. At six o'clock call up the Tsarkoe Selo restaurant and say that Mr. Mappin has had an unexpected guest for dinner. Say that I enjoyed the food so much last night, I want to give some Russian food to my friend. Say that you realize there isn't time to prepare something special; get the woman to read you the menu and order something from it, it doesn't matter what, because it's going into the garbage pail, anyhow."

Jermyn repeated this. "Shall I say that Elias is to bring it?"

"Don't say a word about Elias. He might smell a rat. If Elias happens to answer the phone, so much the better. Elias has got to bring it. It's his job to deliver food outside. They haven't any other male waiter."

Jermyn lingered.

"What's on your mind?" asked Lee.

"Shouldn't I notify the police, sir?"

Lee shook his head, smiling. "I'm after bigger game than a waiter, Jermyn."

AT SEVEN O'CLOCK, when Elias again arrived at the Mappin apartment with a smaller outfit of containers and accessories, Jermyn brought him into Lee in the dining room. Lee was seated at the table with a bottle of Puy Ducasse before him and two glasses. At sight of the label on the bottle, Elias' long, death's head face turned ghastlier still; his eyes widened; his mouth kept opening and shutting. Behind the polished glasses, Lee's glance was hard. He said pleasantly:

"Good evening, Elias. My guest has not come yet. I want to thank you for your services last night. Everything was perfect. You may sit down."

"Thank you, sir," the servant stammered. "I would rather stand."

Lee removed his glasses, polished them, put them on again. Watching the waiter intently, he said in his mild voice: "Drink a glass of wine with me. Elias. This is wine that a man doesn't get every day."

The man's eyes were fixed in horror on the bottle. "You are very kind, sir," he stammered. "I never drink liquor."

Lee poured a glassful with care. "This isn't liquor; it's bottled sunshine."

"Doctor's . . . doctor's orders, sir. I'm not allowed to touch it."

"You appear ill, Elias," said Lee, slowly and smiling. "You are sweating; your hands tremble. Drink this. It will buck you up."

Elias, unable to speak, could only shake his head. He looked around wildly for a means of escape. Jermyn, as grim as stone, stood between him and the door.

"Well, I'm sorry you won't join me. I drink to you." Lee lifted the glass.

Elias, with a strangled cry, staggered forward and knocked the glass from Lee's hand. "Don't drink it!" he yelled. The wine spread like blood over the table; the glass fell on the rug.

Lee's smile warmed. "I knew you'd do that," he said. "You have not the look of a murderer."

Elias seemed about to fall. Jermyn shoved up a chair behind him and he dropped on it, covering his face, sobbing and shaking uncontrollably.

"This is not the bottle you put in my wine closet yesterday," said Lee. He filled the other glass. "I drink to you quite safely." He drained the glass.

There was a silence broken only by the man's sobbing.

"Of course, I know who sent it to me," said Lee presently. "What did you do with the bottle you took away?"

"I gave it to him," said Elias brokenly. "As proof that I had done the job. He drank it."

Lee laughed silently. "Adding insult to injury! . . . Do you know what was in that bottle, Elias?"

Elias shook his head. "He said . . . he said it was a wine of a better vintage than yours and he wanted to surprise you."

"That was his little joke . . . Did you believe him?"

The wretched Elias shook his head.

"I had the wine analyzed," said Lee. "It was loaded with the germs of bubonic plague."

Elias moaned.

"What was the price?" asked Lee.

"My wife, my two little children," murmured Elias. "We are Belgian. They fled into France in advance of the Germans. I was already in this country. They are in Paris now . . . starving. They could be smuggled into Vichy-France, they could get to America if I had the money. Where is a waiter to find so much money? He promised to bring them safely to America if I did what he told me."

"Ah!" said Lee. "How   like him! . . . You're an American citizen, aren't you?"

Elias nodded.

"Wouldn't you prefer to work for your own country?"

"Only give me a chance!" groaned Elias.

"It can be arranged. . . . What do you know about the man's activities?"

Elias hung his head. "Nothing, sir. Nobody knows. Not even his own servant. He's a devil!"

"I believe you," said Lee cheerfully. "Have you ever done a job for him before?"

"Never! I swear it!"

"By continuing in your present job you could learn something about him."

Elias raised a despairing face. "If you do not sicken and die he will have me killed."

"Nonsense!" said Lee. "I will tell him a story that will protect you. He will soon come to you with some other scheme for getting me."

"I dare not face him again!" groaned Elias.

"That's up to you. If you are frightened of him, it won't give you away. He expects servants to fear him and he enjoys it. . . . As for your wife and children, I shall make that my business. I have connections in Paris and a sure way of communicating with them. It shall be started at once."

Elias clasped his hands and the tears began to flow again. "Oh, sir! . . . Oh, sir, I will be your slave!"

"I don't want a slave," said Lee briskly. "I want a good American . . . Jermyn, fetch me a sheet of plain paper and a pen from the study."

He made Elias drink a glass of the wine to steady himself. When the writing materials were brought, he said:

"I am going to write a confession of your part in this business of the wine. You are to sign it and Jermyn shall witness it. This paper is to remain locked in my desk so long as you serve your country faithfully. Should you try to betray us, you will be arrested."

"I'll sign! I'll sign!" said Elias eagerly.

The paper was duly written, signed and witnessed. Lee put it in his pocket.

"I am dining out," he said, rising. "I have to dress now. You and Jermyn may as well eat the food you have brought. If you want a friend, Elias, I recommend Jermyn. He's as firm as a rock! When you have finished eating, carry the containers back to the restaurant and go on as if nothing had happened."

Elias began to stammer his gratitude.

"Skip it!" said Lee, waving his hands. "Let your actions speak for you!"

When Lee was ready to leave the apartment, Elias had gone. Jermyn, with an anxious face, said: "Dare we trust him, sir?"

"We've got him pretty well sewed up," said Lee, smiling. "It's obvious, other things being equal, that he would rather serve on our side. But he's weak and he might cave in under pressure. He'll have to be watched. Try kindness, Jermyn. From the look of his woebegone face he has never known it."

Late that night, Lee, cruising around town on his own, ran into Prince Lenkoran supping with a party of friends at Fefe's Monte Carlo. Left alone with him for a few minutes while the others were dancing, Lee got Lenkoran started on the subject of wine. The Prince was an enthusiast and widely informed. Lee let him run on for a while, listening and sagely nodding his head. Finally when he saw an opening, he said:

"You must come and sample my Chateau Puy Ducasse. There's a wine! Come and dine with me informally some night, just the two of us, and we'll kill a couple of bottles. There is too little of it left to serve at a party."

"Nothing would please me better," said Lenkoran. "Any night you say."

"I'll call you up."

"Does the Puy Ducasse keep well?" asked Lenkoran casually.

"Perfectly. Of course, I keep a sharp eye on the corks. By the way, speaking of that wine, I had an unpleasant little experience today."

Lenkoran raised his highball glass to the light and looked through the amber fluid. "What was that?" he asked.

"I felt a little down at lunch time and I asked for a bottle of Puy Ducasse to buck me up. As I was about to pull the cork, I noticed that it was not one of the corks I had used in recorking it. A very close imitation; I had to look at it with a magnifying glass to make sure. This bottle had been emptied and refilled."

"Good God!" said Lenkoran coolly. "Your servant?"

"I'm afraid so, though I hate to believe it. He never served me so before."

"The servant is not yet born who can be trusted," said Lenkoran. "What do you suppose was his idea?"

"Oh, I take it he drank the wine and filled the bottle with some cheap stuff."

"Did you taste it to see?"

"No indeed! I made him pour it down the sink."

Lenkoran was silent for a moment. The knuckles of the hand that clutched his glass whitened, but his smooth, hard face concealed every sign of disappointment. "Have you discharged him?" he asked.

"No," said Lee. "He's a good servant. It was partly my own fault. I have bragged so about that wine, that I suppose he looked on it as some wonderful elixir of life. I said nothing about it. It's enough that he knows I have discovered the trick. I'm going to give him another chance."

Lenkoran swallowed his drink. "The only way to govern servants is through fear," he said harshly.

"Very likely you're right," said little Lee. "But look at me! I couldn't make out to be a fearsome figure!"

CHAPTER SIX

Prince Lenkoran is a very liberal spender. He has already made me several handsome presents; I accept them without a qualm because I feel that otherwise the money would be spent in some way to injure my country. He always carries a great sum of money in crisp new bills of high denomination and ever since I entered the apartment I have been wondering how he replenished them, since I never see him writing a check or sending to the bank. Last night I found out. As we were going out to dinner he sent me ahead of him out of the living room. I left the door open behind me and I distinctly heard him unlock that strange old painted chest that stands against the wall and afterwards lock it again. That's where he keeps his money.

This afternoon he added to his store. I got to the apartment before he did and was admitted by the servant. While I was waiting in the living room, Alexis came in carrying a big suitcase that I could see was very heavy. I instantly suspected that there was something special about the suitcase because Alexis never carries anything himself, and when he sent me out of the room I was sure of it. He said:

"Your nose is shiny; better go to the powder room and titivate." I said: "I can do it without moving," indicating my pocketbook. His eyes glittered like blue steel. "You can make a better job of it in the powder room," he said, and I flew. But I didn't stay long. When I came back the door to the living room was locked. When he opened it I said: "What on earth did you lock yourself in for?" He just didn't choose to answer me and of course I didn't repeat the question. The suitcase was then empty and of course whatever was in it must have gone into the painted chest. There wasn't any other place. And duckling, my nose wasn't shiny.

A WRITTEN REPORT from Welby:

AT 9:20 THIS MORNING a man came to see P.L. that we have not seen before since we started watching the place. He is a small, thin man, dressed in a dandi-fied style; wears a black derby; might be either an American or a foreigner long resident in this coun-try. His most noticeable feature was his eyes, brown in color, larger than you expect to see in a man's face, with a sort of hot, irritable expression. He looks about 37, but is so particular about his appearance, is probably older. Was carrying a bulky brief case.

I had a good look at him in the street and then proceeded to the listening post. In this way I lost a few minutes and the man was already engaged in conversation with P.L. when I adjusted the ear-phones. As usual it was in English. P.L. addressed him as Tashla. Tashla was in the middle of reading a list of names to P.L. but he spoke so low I could only catch a word here and there. Sounded like a list of newspapers with a sum of money written alongside each name. The amounts were not large, $500 being the highest. It ran something like this: Willoughby Bee, $50. Taneyville Witness, $75. Wentworth Herald, $50—and so on. Must have been between forty and fifty in all. Sorry I can't make a complete report of the conversation; however, I enclose a copy of his list.

Judging from the sounds, P. L. was pacing up and down the room while Tashla read. I could always hear what P.L. said. He occasionally interrupted the reading.

"How the hell do I know what return I am getting for these sums I pay out?" I could not hear Tashla's reply. "God damn it, I'm not going to read their tripe! I've got something better to do!" Another inaudible explanation from Tashla. "Sure. Sure!" said P.L. sarcastically. "You read it and in your distinguished judgment it's worth the money. What I have read is unbelievable. Such a collection of asses I have never met with. Half the time they don't print the stuff you send them, or if they do print it, it is unrecognizable as expressing our ideas. Yet you go on paying them!"

I can't give you the various answers made by Tashla because I couldn't hear them. After one of Tashla's explanations, P.L. burst out: "The hell they'd suspend the paper if you didn't pay on the nail. Running a newspaper is like a drug in a man's veins. Once he starts eating it he can't leave off. You'd be perfectly safe in taking a sharp tone with them; print my stuff as it is written, or I withdraw all support. You'd have no further trouble then. Send them more stuff to replace the incredible rubbish they write themselves."

After another mumbled explanation from Tashla: "Sure, I know they're crackpots. That was the idea. There is a crackpot in every small town. He always has a great flow of verbiage without saying anything. He is always crazy to own a newspaper. You were ordered to search them out and when you found one to make believe you were a kindred spirit; help him to buy a small newspaper to express his so-called ideas, or if there wasn't any, to start one and pay part of the running expenses. He would then be obliged to print your contributions. The reason for choosing crackpots was that a crackpot wouldn't grasp the meaning of the stuff we were feeding them, but you were ordered to direct and control the crackpots, not let them run you!"

After all his grousing, P.L. paid Tashla in the end, for he said: "Seventeen thousand dollars for a very doubtful return! Here it is." Tashla must then have offered him the list, for P.L. said: "God, no! What would I do with it? In this business we don't require vouchers. Burn the paper and keep everything in your head! And after you have read their damn newspapers, burn them too! These Americans are soft-headed fools, but we must always act as if they were as hard and clever as we are. Keep it in mind that the police may visit your rooms at any time and be prepared for them."

After Tashla had received the money, he must have made some request on his own account. P.L. turned on him angrily. "This is no time to bring that up! Take care that you are not suspected of disloyalty. You serve as I serve without asking anything for ourselves. We submerge ourselves in the Cause! Individually we are nothing!"

This made me laugh, considering how well P.L. does for himself.

Tashla left after that. Nothing was said about any further meeting. Richardson picked him up in the street and tailed him to Grand Central, where he retrieved a suitcase from the parcels room and proceeded through the subway passage to the Hotel Roosevelt. He registered as Nicholas Tashla, Cleveland, Ohio, and was assigned to a room. From his room he telephoned to a Miss Clara Moore at — East Forty-seventh Street and made an appointment to meet a woman in her apartment in half an hour's time.

Richardson telephoned me. I went to the Roosevelt and showed my credentials to the manager. He admitted me to Tashla's room himself without telling any employee, and I searched Tashla's bags. The suitcase contained nothing but his personal effects. In the brief-case was the list of newspapers, also a copy of each of the newspapers named. There was also a ticket to Cleveland and a Pullman ticket for a room on the 7:30 train tomorrow night. Just on the chance that Tashla might return, I took the list to the manager's office and copied it myself on the typewriter. I did not take the newspapers, because I assumed you would want time to act before Tashla took alarm. I have entered the date of each paper on the list so that you may obtain copies if you want to read the kind of stuff they print, or need it for evidence. I left everything in Tashla's room exactly as I found it.

Richardson phoned me again to say that Tashla had come out of Clara Moore's apartment with a woman and had taken her to the Astor for lunch. As it was clear from what Richardson said, that this was just a private adventure of Tashla's, I called him off. I will have a man on the 7:30 train tomorrow to tail Tashla back to Cleveland.

Welby.

Another report from the same, two days later:

LENKORAN'S BROOKLYN AGENT, the tall, thin, respect-
able-looking foreigner, seems to lead a solitary life
in his apartment on Montague Street, where he is
known as Paul Estevan. To Lenkoran he is known as
Anton Goroshovel, and I shall so refer to him hereafter. He has occasional visitors but they do not appear to be personal friends. He patronizes the best
restaurants and eats enormously, thin as he is, but
always alone. He drinks considerable, but never
shows any effect. In the afternoons he goes to the
movies, always by himself, and he patronizes the
public library just like any ordinary citizen. His reading is confined to detective stories. He is such an
ordinary, harmless, middle-class-looking individual,
nobody would ever suspicion him. He is very polite
to his neighbors when he meets them in the hall.

Nights when he is not expecting a visitor, he is
generally drinking alone in one of the saloons along
Sands Street, which are frequented by sailors of the
Navy and workmen in the Navy Yard near by. He lis-
tens to the talk without appearing to, and sometimes
joins in it in the most natural way in the world. He
speaks without any accent.

His apartment consists of parlor, bedroom and
bath, second floor front, in one of the fine old con-
verted dwellings on Montague Street. It is a walk-
up building. A visitor rings Goroshovel's bell at the
street level and G. opens the door by pressing a button in his apartment. Thus visitors can come and go
without being seen by a hall man or elevator boy.
Since we have been watching the house, seven different men have called in the evening. Three of them
we have succeeded in following home and learning
something about them. It is significant that all three

are employed in the Navy Yard. They are foreign-born American citizens; all bear a good reputation in the Yard; if they didn't, they would have been fired before this. (Welby gave the names and addresses of the three men.) (A) is a pattern-maker; (B) a riveter; (C) the foreman of a small yard gang. I shall make no effort to contact these men unless you instruct me to do so. This is a delicate situation. If they are doing wrong, they will be very much on their guard.

It is possible that these fellows are merely stringing Goroshovel along or feeding him false information. Just the same, that is too dangerous a game to be allowed to go on and I recommend that these three be quietly arrested. They should just disappear without a word being said to anybody. It should be just too bad if there was an accident at the Navy Yard while we were waiting for conclusive evidence.

At 3:15 this afternoon (this seems to be his regular hour), Goroshovel appeared in 53rd Street on his way to report to P.L. Richardson tipped me off and I had the earphones on when he came into P.L.'s living room. I'm sorry I can't give a better report of their talk. Everything worked against me today. P.L. seems to have more confidence in this man than the other two; he didn't bawl him out, but for the most part listened in silence to what he had to say. As for Goroshovel, he was sitting at the other end of the room from the mike, and like a true conspirator he scarcely raised his voice above a whisper. All I can give you are the occasional remarks that P.L. put in.

"Yours is the second most important task that has been entrusted to us, Goroshovel. You have a post of honor and danger. You cannot fail!"

"Naturally, you must not spend money in a manner that would attract attention to yourself, but you

can have any sum that may be necessary. Offer anything you like for the information we are after. If it
turns out not to be worth it, we won't pay. A traitor
has no come back."

"You are quite right. They will not install the
appliance amongst all those thousands of workmen
in the Yard. We can assume that it is being manu-
factured in some other plant, and will be installed
on the carrier when she goes to sea for her trials. At
the same time, there are certainly men in the Brooklyn Yard who know the nature of it, and there must
be a blueprint among the other blueprints. It may
take time to get a sight of that blueprint. Meanwhile,
make it your business to discover the principle of
this new device and we'll forward it to our engineers
and let them work on it."

P.L. paid money to Goroshovel—the amount was
not named, and Goroshovel got up to go.

Here is an idea that has occurred to me; I pass it
along for what it may be worth. In a newspaper
correspondent's report of the Battle of the Coral Sea,
I noted this statement:

"One by one the planes lighted like birds on the
deck of the carrier and were quickly stopped by that
wonderful new gadget which is the pride of the Navy
and its most closely-guarded secret."

Perhaps this is what our enemies are after.

As Goroshovel was leaving, I heard something
that gave me a shock. P.L. said with a laugh, "I'm
going to ask Amos Lee Mappin here to dinner on
Monday of next week and I want you to be present."
I couldn't hear Goroshovel's reply, but he laughed
in an ugly fashion. Good God, Mr. Mappin, if this
gang is on to you, you are in very serious danger!
You mustn't attend this dinner.

CHAPTER SEVEN

PRINCE LENKORAN CONVEYED HIS INVITATION to Lee by telephone. In the course of their beautiful friendship they had now reached the stage of addressing each other as Lee and Alexis.

"Lee, my dear fellow, you have shown so much interest in my unfortunate country, I'd like to have you come to dinner on Monday night to meet some of my Russian friends; Scharipov, whom you already know, and a couple of others. It will be a stag affair—that is, I have asked a beautiful lady to act as hostess at the table. She has an engagement later and that will leave us men to talk in perfect freedom."

Lee drew a long breath. He answered with seeming heartiness: "Why, I'd be delighted, Alexis! At what hour?"

"Say half past seven. Earlier if you like. Black tie."

"I'll be there."

ON MONDAY AFTERNOON Welby called Lee on the telephone. "Both Scharipov and Tashla have returned to New York," he said, "apparently for the purpose of attending P.L.'s dinner tonight."

"I knew it," said Lee.

"Evidently something against you is cooking," said Welby earnestly. "You're not going, are you?"

"I certainly am," said Lee.

"Mr. Mappin, this is too dangerous!" protested Welby. "Once you're inside the place, how can we protect you?"

"I shall not be liquidated in P.L.'s apartment," said Lee. "Too many people know that I am going there. He means to get me when he can, but it will be in some place and in some manner that could not be traced back to him."

"What is his purpose in giving this dinner, then?"

"That's easy, Welby. It is exactly how I would expect him to act. He has guessed or he has discovered that I am investigating him. He is a supremely self-confident man. He thinks himself so much cleverer than I that he is not at all alarmed. He believes in acting boldly. Therefore, in case my suspicions may have fallen on these lieutenants of his, he is presenting them to me in this open fashion in order to pull wool over my eyes. It's a kind of challenge."

"Shouldn't I place men within call?"

"Absolutely not! Not even in the street below. P.L. will certainly be watching from his windows."

"Well, I suppose you know best," said Welby reluctantly.

"I want you to be listening throughout the dinner," said Lee. "P.L. has no dining room, so I assume the meal will be served in the big front room. I will need your report of what is said in order to refresh my memory."

"Just as you say, sir. But, oh God! how terrible it would be if I heard danger threatening you and was unable to reach you!"

"You can make your mind easy about that. P.L.'s own flat is the safest place in the world for me."

PRINCE LENKORAN HAD INVITED HIM to come as early as he liked; therefore, walking across town in his deliberate fashion, Lee was planning to arrive about seven-fifteen. At Third Avenue he met newsboys running past, shouting an extra. The Attorney General of the United States had caused the arrest simultaneously of thirty-five editors of small newspapers throughout the country. They were charged with printing seditious matter. Lee frowned. Somebody had slipped up somewhere. The news was breaking too soon.

Five minutes later he was climbing the stairs of the Tsarkoe Selo. As luck would have it, just as he was extending his hand to press the bell beside Lenkoran's door, the door opened and Elias, the waiter, came out with an empty tray. The haggard, white-faced Elias was obviously in a bad state of nerves. To give him a little courage, Lee murmured: "Everything is going splendidly," and, passing into the apartment without having to ring the bell, closed the door after him.

The foyer had been turned into a makeshift pantry for the evening, and Lenkoran's man Vassily was arranging some dishes at a side table. Lee handed him his hat and gloves with a smile, saying: "I'll go right in," and started for the front room. He could hear Lenkoran's voice raised in anger. Evidently he had read the extra. Lee opened the first door and, closing it behind him, paused in the little passage to listen. Lenkoran was shouting:

"He stole your list from you! He struck unerringly. Every newspaper! Every one!" Another voice spoke but Lee could not hear the words: Lenkoran went on. "You don't see how he could? Where was the list? . . . In your brief case! Did you ever let it out of your hands? . . . You left it in the hotel room while you attended to private business! Oh, my God, what a fool you are, Tashla. One would think you were playing pussy in the corner instead of holding the fate of your country in your hands!"

There was a silence, then Lenkoran broke out afresh: "The loss of the newspapers is nothing. I suspected we were wasting our money on them. But to be shown up by these dim-witted Americans! That endangers our vitally important work. It puts them on their guard! And to be mocked in their flatulent newspapers. That I cannot bear! God damn you, Tashla! And God damn that smooth-faced little owl with his innocent ways. For this I must kill him with my own hands! I shall not leave it to anybody else!"

For the moment the man was out of his mind with rage. The listening Lee put out a hand against the wall to steady himself. He started back toward the foyer and paused irresolutely. Rapid steps could be heard approaching the other door. Then there was only one thing for him to do. Quickly stepping forward, he opened the door and faced the blazing Lenkoran.

Lenkoran almost instantly recovered himself. It was an extraordinary transformation; it was too quick to be natural. "Lee!" he cried with exaggerated heartiness. "Welcome, my friend!" Seizing Lee's hand in a grip of steel, he pulled him into the room. Meanwhile his glittering eyes were fastened on Lee's face, trying to discover how much he had overheard.

Lee from long habit was able to smile blandly in the presence of the man who had just sworn to kill him, but he was sweating gently. "I'm afraid I'm intruding," he said.

"Intruding!" shouted Lenkoran. "Nonsense, man! You're the guest of honor tonight! . . . This is my friend, Nick Tashla. Mr. Amos Lee Mappin."

They shook hands.

"I didn't hear you ring," said Lenkoran.

"I didn't ring. The waiter was coming out and so I walked in." Lee wiped his face.

"You find it too warm in here?" Lenkoran asked with a sudden terrible quietness.

"Not at all. I walked across town and I have overheated myself a little."

Lenkoran burst out again: "You must have a drink! Come on! I hate to wait for my dinner in the same room where it is going to be served."

A table in the middle of the room, set for six, was laden with flowers and antique silver.

Lenkoran led the way out through the little passage into the foyer, thence to the bar, Lee and Tashla at his heels. The latter was a skinny little man with big emotional eyes set in hollow sockets, a sensual type. He was dressed too young for his years.

Lenkoran went behind the bar. "Vassily and Elias are busy with the dinner," he said. "I'll be bartender. What shall it be, gentlemen?"

"Something long with ice in it for me," said Lee. "Cocktails can wait."

"The same here," said Tashla.

"A planter's punch?" suggested Lenkoran. "I have limes picked ripe in Cuba and flown north by plane."

"The very thing!" said Lee.

While Lenkoran was mixing the drinks, he was studying Lee's face with stabbing glances. "You caught me in a vile temper," he said with a deprecating laugh. "I hate to lose my temper. The old Tartar in me comes out, savage and murderous!"

"I didn't notice anything," said Lee.

"You are too polite, my friend! When you came in I was roaring like the bull of Bashan!"

"Well, I did hear a noise," said Lee carelessly.

"Just before that," Lenkoran went on, "Tashla had told me that a little owl of a Bolshevist had been caught spying on us. Those jackals won't even let us perform a work of mercy without interference!"

"I never had much use for Bolshevists myself," said Lee blandly, "though now they have become the fashion."

It was impossible to tell from Lenkoran's face whether or not he was deceived by Lee's casual air. Probably not, for this man was always on guard. However, having said all he could, he let the matter drop and started questioning Lee about the famous Letty Ammon case, which had so exercised the public just before the war. Lenkoran's air of courtesy and friendliness was perfect, but his icy-blue eyes glittered. That was something he could not control. Lee disliked talking about his own cases, but on this occasion he did so in order to keep things going smoothly.

They were presently joined by Mr. Scharipov of San Francisco, dignified and conservative as always, with expressionless, slate-colored eyes behind his rimless glasses. He looked like a gilt-edged banker. He and Lee had met before in Lenkoran's rooms. After him came the tall Goroshovel, gaunt and gray, with a disarmingly awkward air. Of Lenkoran's three lieutenants, he was the best actor. After the long drink, Lenkoran stirred a pitcher of cocktails and kept their glasses full. All the Russians had this in common, that they could put down considerable amounts of liquor without showing it. Lee alone appeared to become a little high. Perched on a stool in front of the bar, he chattered happily about nothing in particular.

The bell rang again. The door into the foyer stood open, and when Vassily answered the bell they could all see the black-haired vision in silver who entered. She was wearing a close-fitting lamé evening coat that made her look taller and slenderer. Lenkoran went out to greet her. She tossed the silver coat to Vassily and was revealed in a cunningly-draped white satin gown without any ornament whatsoever. Her vivid face was sufficient. Lenkoran swung her into the bar within his arm.

"Miss Jocelyn D'Arcy, gentlemen. Mr. Goroshovel, Mr. Scharipov, Mr. Tashla."

"Hi-ya, fellows," said Jocelyn. "I'll never be able to remember your funny names."

"I'm Tony," said Goroshovel with his Adam's apple working up and down.

"I'm Sergei," this from the dignified Scharipov.

"I'm Nick," said Tashla, whose hot brown eyes were snapping.

"And this," said Lenkoran, coming to the last stool, "Is Mr. Amos Lee Mappin, the celebrated author and criminologist."

"Hello!" said Jocelyn with her friendly air, so like a boy's. "We've met before."

"Have we?" said Lee. "Surely I couldn't forget that."

"Yes, we have and I'll tell you where it was. Wait a minute! Now I remember! It was three years ago when I came East to see the World's Fair. It was at a dinner in the French pavilion, looking down on those marvelous fountains. I forget who gave the dinner."

"Surely, I remember," said Lee. "What exquisite food they served at the French pavilion."

"Is that all you remember!" said Jocelyn, pouting.

She climbed on a stool in the middle of the bar and Lenkoran went behind to mix a fresh cocktail for her. Lee no longer had to chatter. Jocelyn took care of that with Messrs. Goroshovel, Scharipov and Tashla hanging on every word, all ready to laugh. Not only was she an extremely attractive woman, but she was the Big Boss's girl of the moment and it was up to them to make good with her. It had every appearance of a good party but Lee could see by Jocelyn's face that she was aware something was wrong.

This was how she knew it; there she sat in front of Lenkoran looking as lovely as she had ever looked in her life, and he was thinking of something else.

"You look like the father of five," she said to Scharipov.

Her effect on that dignified man was to make him simper. "Only two," he said.

"And you," turning to little Tashla, "are certainly not married."

"How can you tell?" he asked conceitedly.

"You have not that roped look. I suspect that you're a buccaneer among women."

Tashla was charmed. "You flatter me!"

"You," she said to Goroshovel, "were romantic when young."

"I still am," the ugly old fellow said with a killing smile.

"Of course! I can see that you were married when still a student. Your wife has been dead for a long time; your children are grown up and scattered."

"That is exactly right!"

"What about me?" asked Lee.

"Oh, you're a confirmed old bachelor. You see through women far too well. That's why you never married."

"Wrong!" said Lee. "Woman is the number one mystery!"

"That's what they try to make men think," she said. "I tried marriage once," she went on pensively. "I didn't care for it particularly. Men, as tame as they are, still claim savage rights. I mean, what attracted my husband to me when we met, made him furiously jealous after marriage. Jealousy in a modern man is so ridiculous!"

Her candor charmed them. They did not know that Jocelyn, like other outspoken persons, was perfectly capable when it suited her of using her outspokenness as a cover.

When Lenkoran suggested that they go in to dinner, Tashla said he'd like to brush up a little. Goroshovel and Scharipov expressed a similar desire. While Lenkoran was opening the door for them that led to the rear of the apartment, Lee and Jocelyn had one minute alone together.

"What has happened?" she murmured swiftly. "There is something grim and frightening about this party."

"Lenkoran's in a bad humor," Lee lied smoothly. "He has discovered that some Bolshevist is spying on him. It has nothing to
do with us."

"It feels like something worse than that," she said somberly.

"Forget it, my dear."

Lenkoran was beside them again. "Like my dress?" Jocelyn
asked offhandedly.

"Perfect, my dear! Only an exceptionally lovely woman can wear
unrelieved white."

"Sorry I couldn't put on your flowers. Tonight, you see, the effect was to be stark."

"You did right to leave them off."

Later Jocelyn sat enthroned like a queen at the foot of the dinner table with the faces of all five men turned toward her as to the
sun. Lee was placed at her right with Scharipov opposite; Goroshovel and Tashla flanking Lenkoran at the head of the table.
Jocelyn kept them all in play. Lenkoran appeared to be enjoying
the success she was having, but the unchanging smile seemed to
be etched in his face and his eyes had no part in it. The food was so
good Lee couldn't help enjoying it in spite of all he had on his mind.
The talk mostly revolved about the ever fascinating subject of men
and women.

"Men are delicious creatures," said Jocelyn, "and utterly comi-
cal. Nearly every one of them approaches a woman as if he were
the first man born on earth. He reels out the old tripe with such an
air of novelty. It never seems to occur to him that an experienced
woman has heard it dozens of times before. If only they wouldn't
talk so much! The man who doesn't bother to talk but takes the facts
of life for granted is therefore devastating. That's why women fall!"

"Tell us more about what women like," said Tashla. "Our only
aim is to please them!"

"I'm not going to give away the secrets of my lodge," retorted
Jocelyn. "I can tell you this, though. Women are not so different
from men after all. But men are bigger and occupy the key positions. Consequently women have to get around them. You can't
blame women for lying to men."

Lenkoran said with his fixed smile: "Be careful, my dear, or you'll tempt us to use our superior strength."

When they had eaten dessert, which consisted of a delicious confection of pastry larded with nuts and spread with honey, they rose from the table. Coffee and liqueurs were to be served on small stands alongside the comfortable chairs and sofas. Section by section, the two servants carried out the dining table. In the general movement which was taking place, Lee and Jocelyn came together again. The other four were grouped around Lenkoran's cigar humidor at the moment. Lee and Jocelyn smiled at each other as one smiles at a casual acquaintance. Jocelyn said:

"I caught you looking at me so strangely. What's on your mind?"

"I am anxious about you," said Lee. "I know you can handle anything civilized in trousers, but can you cope with a savage?"

"Don't worry," she said. "There are ways of taming them. . . . You're the one I'm bothered about. Alexis hasn't said anything, but I can feel that he hates you poisonously. You are in danger."

"I know it," said Lee. "Consequently my eye is peeled."

When she had drunk her coffee, Jocelyn rose to go. All the men protested but she stuck to it. "I made this date before Alexis planned his party," she explained.

Lenkoran went to see her out.

When he returned, a supply of Scotch, soda and glasses was brought in and the servants were dismissed for the night. The five men grouped themselves in easy chairs within the open windows.

"Now we can talk freely," said the stiffly smiling Lenkoran.

He started a conversation about old Russia in which his three followers joined in fond and reminiscent vein. To an attentive ear it had the effect of something rehearsed. It sounded as if they had prepared for it by reading old-fashioned Russian novels. Lee rubbed his upper lip to iron out a smile. At first he affected a deep interest in their anecdotes and asked many questions, but after a while he got restive under the heavy-handed attempt to impress him. If he left them the listening Welby might hear something real.

It was about ten when Lee rose to go. All expressed polite regret. Lenkoran made no real attempt to detain him.

About an hour later, as he opened the door of his own apartment, the telephone rang in the pantry. When he took down the receiver he heard Jocelyn's terrified voice:

"Oh, Lee, something terrible has happened!"

"What is it, my dear?"

"Alexis has been shot."

"My God! is he dead?"

"He has just died in my arms."

"Did he say anything?"

"He was unable to speak."

"Where are the other men?"

"They beat it at the sound of the shot."

"Is anybody with you?"

"Only Vassily."

"Keep him with you. Have you notified the police?"

"No."

"Do nothing until I get there."

CHAPTER EIGHT

WHEN LEE'S TAXI let him out in front of the Tsarkoe Selo, the stocky, dependable figure of Welby was waiting on the sidewalk. The two men exchanged a grave glance without saying anything. The after-theater patrons of the restaurant were driving up. Some entered by the basement door, others mounted the steps to the first floor entrance. Lee and Welby went in among the latter without attracting any attention, and kept on up the stairs.

The door of Lenkoran's apartment was a little open and the ghastly face of Elias could be seen inside, watching. He let the door swing open and the two men entered. Lenkoran's stalwart body lay on its back in the narrow, oak-paneled foyer. His white shirt front was crimson and wet. Two coins had been placed on his eyelids to keep them closed. Jocelyn stood leaning against the wall at the other end of the foyer, watching with distended, hysterical eyes. She was still wearing the lovely white dress. There was now a hideous red smear across the bodice. Welby closed the entrance door and stood with his back against it. Lee looked down at the body. The force of evil was stilled. Only the handsome shape of clay was left.

"What a damned unlucky chance!" Lee murmured bitterly. "With my work only half done!"

Nobody else spoke.

"Is that the spot where he died?" asked Lee.

"Yes," whispered Jocelyn.

"Good! he is not to be moved. Who closed his eyes?"

"I did," she faltered. "He was staring . . . staring. I couldn't bear it!"

"Should I remove the coins?" stammered Elias.

"Don't touch them!" said Lee.

"Oh, Lee! . . . Oh, Lee . . . !" wailed Jocelyn.

She swayed forward, and Lee was just in time to catch her. "Pull yourself together!" he said sharply. "You mustn't fail me now!" He placed her in one of the antique carved chairs standing against the wall. "Get water for her," he said to Elias.

Elias went into the bar. Lee said to Welby: "His desk is in the bedroom. Search it. You know what we're after." Welby hastened to the rear.

Lee dropped to one knee beside the body and touched the clothes here and there to judge what his pockets contained. Covering his hand with a handkerchief, he drew out Lenkoran's wallet and went through the contents hastily. He put everything back and restored the wallet to Lenkoran's pocket. From the left-hand pocket of his trousers, he took another little leather case which, upon being opened, revealed a line of keys. Lee detached two keys and transferred them to his own pocket.

By this time Jocelyn, having drunk some of the water Elias brought, felt better. She began a confused and half-hysterical account of what had happened.

"Never mind that," said Lee sharply. "There's no time. Just answer a few questions. Did you hear the shot?"

They both nodded. "Muffled," added Elias.

Lee addressed Jocelyn. "Where were you when it was fired?"

"In the bedroom."

"What brought you back to the apartment?"

"I never left it. Alexis said he was sick of the party and that I was to wait in the bedroom until he had got rid of you all."

Lee turned to Elias. "Where were you when the shot was fired?"

"Coming up the stairs, sir. Madame had telephoned for a whiskey-soda and I was bringing it. I was frightened by the sound. I stopped on the stairs. The three men came running down. They passed me. Afterwards I remembered that Madame was up there alone and I went on up. The door was open. Prince Lenkoran was leaning against the wall holding his breast. Madame entered from the rear. The Prince said: 'I'm shot' and slipped to the floor. She dropped beside him and supported his head on her arm."

"That's all I need to know now," said Lee.

"Should I return to the restaurant?" asked Elias nervously. "I'll be missed."

"You'll have to be missed," said Lee grimly. "Let the police find you here."

Welby returned. "The desk wasn't locked," he said. "It contains nothing of any interest to us."

"I didn't suppose it would," said Lee. "Come into the front room."

All three followed him. Lee went direct to the antique painted chest and, unlocking it with another of Lenkoran's keys, threw back the cover. The other three gasped in amazement. The big chest was lined with steel. It was nearly half-full of crisp, new United States treasury notes, in packets of one hundred, each packet strapped with a band of manila paper. Those that were visible were of the one hundred dollar denomination.

Even the impassive Welby was overcome. "Good God! a great fortune!" he exclaimed.

"What did you expect?" said Lee sharply. "Hummingbirds? . . . Don't stand there gaping! Quick! Has Lenkoran any hand baggage in the apartment?"

"In the bedroom closet," stammered Jocelyn.

"Fetch it! Fetch it!"

Jocelyn and Elias returned to the living room bringing four elegant suitcases marked A. L. Two were of the largest size, called Pullman cases; the others smaller. Lee opened them on the floor and signed to Welby to help him throw in the packets of money. The other two watched with staring eyes.

"Lee . . . ! Lee . . . !" protested Jocelyn in distress.

"Be quiet!" said Lee. "I know what I'm doing."

As the cases were filled and the chest emptied, Lee said to Jocelyn and Elias: "I want you two to go through the pockets of all of Lenkoran's suits that are hanging in the closet."

They went away.

The four suitcases held all the money. As they closed the cases, Lee said: "Can you handle them?"

"Sure, if I take my time."

Lee handed him the two keys he had taken from Lenkoran. "I don't know which is the right one," he said.

Luckily Welby was a sturdy specimen. Carrying one of the big suitcases in each hand and with the other two tucked under his arms like a red-cap porter, he made for the door of the apartment. Lee let him out and closed the door after him. Jocelyn and Elias returned from the bedroom.

"Nothing in the pockets," said the former. She looked through the two open doors leading towards the living room. "Where's the man?" she asked.

"He's gone," said Lee.

She noted that the suitcases were gone, too. "He'll be seen!" she said hysterically. "This will ruin you!"

Lee smiled. "I'll take my chance of that . . . I'm going now," he went on. "Give me time to get out of the house and then telephone for the police."

Jocelyn's hands went to her head. "The police!" she cried. "Oh God! how can I face that?"

Lee took both her hands. "You cannot fail me now, Joss!"

She quieted a little. "But what am I to tell them? How can I remember what to say? I'm all unstrung!"

"Listen! You are to tell them the simple truth about tonight. That requires no study. The truth right up to the moment when you telephoned me."

"Am I to say you were here to dinner?"

"Certainly. Why not? But you are not to say that I came back afterwards, and you are to say nothing about the money. Nothing about our previous arrangements, naturally; nothing about my suspicions of Lenkoran."

"I'll have to put the sound of the shot later," she said.

"Don't do that. Others may have heard it. Account for the lapse of time before calling the police by telling them you fainted, and that Elias was trying to bring you to."

"Oh, Lee! if you could only stay here to back me up!" she moaned.

"I shall be back in a very short time," he said with a dry smile.

Before leaving he restored the little leather key holder to the dead man's pocket.

CHAPTER NINE

As he re-entered his apartment, Lee glanced at his watch. Not more than twenty minutes had elapsed since he left it. In about half an hour the telephone rang. Lee waited a little before answering it. This was the voice of his friend, Inspector Loasby, chief of the detective force of the New York police. Loasby said:

"Sorry to arouse you at this hour, Mr. Mappin, but it's important."

"What's the matter?" said Lee.

"Prince Lenkoran has been found shot dead in his apartment."

"Good God!" said Lee. "I was with the Prince about two hours ago."

"That's what I was told."

"Who did it?"

"I don't know for sure. We found a woman in his apartment but she denies shooting him. The gun is missing. There was also a waiter on the premises. Would you be good enough to come over and tell us what you know?"

"Why of course!" said Lee. "Anything I can do to help. Just give me time to dress and find a taxi." He let ten minutes elapse and started out.

When he got back to the Tsarkoe Selo there was a crowd in the street. Officers stood at the two entrances to keep out all who had no business within the house. Some of the patrons of the restaurant had left; others remained at the tables, enjoying the excitement. Lee, whose name was known to every man on the police force, was admitted to the house without question. Another officer was posted at the bottom of the stairs leading to Lenkoran's apartment, still another at the door. The third landing was filled with newspapermen waiting for their story. Lee was bombarded with questions.

"What has happened, Mr. Mappin? . . . Give us your angle. . . . How come you are interested in the case?"

"Nothing to say!" said Lee, waving his hands. "I don't know what the situation is myself."

Inside the apartment, Lenkoran's body was lying in the foyer just as he had last seen it. A police photographer was taking pictures of it, while the Medical Examiner stood by with an assistant waiting to begin his work. Detectives and fingerprint experts were everywhere. Lee made his way into the living room. Jocelyn, with a stony-white face, was sitting in a straight-backed chair with her hands in her white satin lap. She was guarded by a uniformed officer. At the other end of the room sat Elias, similarly guarded.

"Oh, Mr. Mappin!" she breathed. "It's so good to see a friendly face!"

"My dear!" said Lee, patting her hand. "This is truly a terrible situation!"

"They think I did it!" she said wildly. "They accuse me! Mr. Mappin, I swear to you that I am innocent!"

"I believe you!" said Lee soothingly. Lowering his voice, he murmured: "I will have to ask you to submit to arrest and imprisonment for a while."

"I trust you," she whispered. Raising her voice, she went on: "They say it must have been either me or Elias."

Lee glanced at the ashy Elias, who looked actually as if he were about to die from terror.

"Maybe it was Elias," Jocelyn said, low-voiced. "Maybe it was! He was already on the scene when I got there!"

The policeman stepped forward. "I am sorry, Mr. Mappin, but I have positive orders not to allow anybody to speak to the young lady. She is under arrest."

"Where is the Inspector?" asked Lee.

At that moment Loasby, handsome and troubled, entered the room with a sheaf of papers in his hand. "Here you are!" he cried.

"They told me you had come. I was in the bedroom. I have kept out as many people as I could, but the place is swarming! Where can we go where we can talk quietly?"

"How about the bar?" said Lee.

Loasby stationed a detective at the door of the bar. "While I'm talking to Mr. Mappin, I am not to be interrupted unless it's important." They went in, closing the door after them.

Lee was his usual bland and composed self. "Is there any reason why we shouldn't have a drink?" he said.

"It wouldn't look very well," said Loasby longingly. "But, damn it, I need it!"

Lee went behind the bar and set them up. Loasby climbed on a stool and laid his papers on the mahogany. Lee joined him on the next stool.

"This is an ugly business, Mr. Mappin!"

"I believe you," said Lee.

"How well did you know Lenkoran?"

"That's hard to say," answered Lee. "He was a friendly man, but secretive."

"Well, how long have you known him?"

"I've been hearing about him around town for the past eight or nine years, but we did not meet until a month ago. It was at El Morocco. He was a picturesque, colorful sort of character and he appealed to me. I collect characters, as you know. He appeared to like me, too; consequently I have seen a lot of him during the past few weeks. I know nothing about his private affairs except what is gossiped in the night clubs. All that is exaggerated, I am sure, and much of it completely untrue."

"What did he do?"

"If you mean what was his business, he hadn't any. According to the story, he brought a small capital to America and has greatly increased it by profitable investments. At any rate, he seemed to have plenty of money. He told me that he was engaged in raising funds for Russian Relief and sending it abroad secretly. The secrecy was necessary because he couldn't support the present Russian government without appearing to betray his old friends."

"That's what I'm afraid of," said Loasby. "International complications."

"Lenkoran told me that he was continually watched and spied upon by Russian government agents. I don't know if that's true. Anyhow, he was bitter about it."

Loasby ran a hand through his hair. At fifty, he still had plenty of it, and was vain of the fact. "Good God, Mr. Mappin, if he was shot by a Russian government agent, look what a position that puts me in! We are allied with that government; we're fighting this war side by side. To arrest one of their agents would be very unpopular!"

Lee shrugged as much as to say that was Loasby's headache.

"What about the dinner tonight?" asked the Inspector.

"There was nothing special about it," said Lee. "Lenkoran asked me to meet some of his Russian friends because I was interested in Russia. There were three Russians present; White Russians like Lenkoran, as I understood. Their names were Scharipov, Goroshovel and Tashla. Scharipov I had met once before, the other two were new to me. Goroshovel, I gathered, lives somewhere near New York; the others were out-of-town men. A number of places were mentioned. They said they traveled around collecting money for Lenkoran."

"What happened during dinner?"

"Nothing out of the way. All the men were devoting themselves to the handsome young lady. You know the kind of chatter."

"I know, but give me some detail."

Lee related everything that had been said at the table so far as he could remember it.

"After the girl left, they all talked Russia until I was sick of the subject. I went home at ten o'clock."

"But the girl hadn't left."

"I thought she had."

"Why didn't she leave the apartment?" demanded Loasby.

"I don't know. You'll have to ask her that."

"I have asked her and I'm not satisfied with her answer. That young woman is no better than she ought to be, if you ask me."

"What has given you that idea?" asked Lee in his mild way.

"She's too handsome, if you know what I mean."

"Don't jump to conclusions," warned Lee. "Remember that women permit themselves more freedom than they used to."

"Mr. Mappin, you're the most acute observer I know of," said Loasby. "You had the opportunity to study those people throughout the whole meal. Something must have happened at the table that would give you some clue as to who shot Lenkoran."

"Nothing whatever," said Lee. "You overrate my powers of observation. This was just the usual polite dinner with everybody on their best behavior. How would I know what was going on beneath the surface."

"Don't you agree with me that it was probably the girl?"

"I am not in possession of the evidence. I have reason for thinking it could not have been the girl."

"What is it?"

"Absence of motive. Her association with Lenkoran was of too recent a date to bring about a situation involving murder. She could have no cause as yet to feel that he had wronged her. Having just been raised to the position of the Prince's number one lady friend, every woman in that set envied her. Why should she upset the applecart?"

"Well, if it wasn't her, perhaps one of Lenkoran's seeming friends was an agent of the Russian government."

"That is more likely," said Lee.

"Or the waiter, Elias, may have been a spy. Perhaps this Prince was plotting against the Russian government. If they have proof of it, that would justify his killing in wartime."

Lee shook his head. "If they had proof, they should have come to you or to the F.B.I."

"Sure! Sure!" agreed Loasby. "But I don't know how the Russian mind works," he added helplessly. "What do you know about this woman?"

"What does one ever know about the attractive women one runs into here and there?" parried Lee. "She says we met for the first time at the World's Fair. Maybe we did, but I have no recollection of it."

Lee took a drink. Loasby, biting his lip in indecision, was anxiously studying his face. Suddenly the Inspector blurted out:

"Mr. Mappin, will you work with me on this case? I certainly would appreciate it!" Fearful that Lee was about to raise objections, he hurried on: "Oh, I know you don't like to work in the field; your place is the study, you always say. But this is your kind of a case. Especially if it involves international intrigue, where you are at home, and I am all at sea."

"Certainly I'll work with you," said Lee.

Loasby looked surprised. His former appeals for help from this quarter had never been granted so promptly.

"This man was my friend," Lee went on, "and I shall do everything I can to avenge his murder. It is nothing to me if it turns out to be the work of an agent of our ally in war. Murder is murder whoever does it."

Loasby's face had cleared. "Gosh! I'll be glad to have your help! We'll have to take care not to stir up an international hornet's nest."

"What are those papers you have?" asked Lee.

"Statements I have taken from the two suspects. Here, read what the girl said." He shoved the papers along the bar. Lee read:

My name is Jocelyn D'Arcy. I was born in Wooster, Ohio, twenty-eight years ago. My parents are dead. I have no near relatives so far as I know. I have no regular occupation. I have independent means. [She went on to describe the circumstances of her marriage, her divorce and the subsequent death of her former husband.] I have lived in Chicago for the greater part of my life. [She named her various addresses in that city.] Three weeks ago I moved to New York. I had no special reason for the move. I am free to do as I please, and I wanted a change, that's all. I took a suite at the Ambassador Hotel, where I now reside.

Shortly after my arrival in New York, I was introduced to Prince Alexis Lenkoran at a ball in aid of refugee children at the Ritz-Carlton Hotel. A Mrs. Basil Donlon introduced us. I don't know her address. I suppose it's in the telephone book. The Prince seemed to be attracted to me, and since that time he has been paying me a good deal of attention. I mean he invited me to accompany him to restaurants, theaters, night clubs and so on. I found him an agreeable companion, that's all. He never volunteered any information about his private life or his personal affairs and I never asked questions. I believed him unmarried.

Tonight he asked me to dinner at his apartment to meet several of his Russian friends and also Mr. Amos Lee Mappin, whom I had met before several years ago. I had been to Prince Lenkoran's apartment on several previous occasions but only when other persons were present. The Prince said this was to be a stag dinner really. He just wanted me to start things off agreeably for the men. So I understood I was to leave as soon as we finished eating. [Here Jocelyn told about the dinner in detail. She described the three Russians. There was nothing in this part that Lee did not know already.]

I got up to leave about half past nine. I was not wearing a watch and I cannot tell you the precise time. Prince Lenkoran escorted me from the room and in the foyer he said that he had changed his mind; that he was tired of these men and for me to wait in the bedroom and as soon as he could get rid of the men we would go out together. So I went into the bedroom at the rear of the apartment and sat there reading.

The door from the foyer into the rear passage was closed, but I left the bedroom door open so I could hear when the men left. In about half an hour I heard voices and went into the passage to listen. That was

Mr. Mappin leaving. Prince Lenkoran showed himself to me at the door of the bedroom for a moment just to say he wouldn't keep me waiting much longer. There was a smile on his face, but I got the impression that something had angered him. I should have mentioned this before, because I was aware of it when I first entered the apartment and all through dinner. He was not angry at me. It was something which happened before I got there.

In spite of what he had said, I had to wait a considerable time longer. I began to get impatient. I felt thirsty and I telephoned down to the restaurant for a highball. As near as I can judge, it was about eleven when I heard the shot. There was only one shot. I can only say that it came from somewhere in front of the building. There must have been several closed doors between because the sound was muffled.

I was terribly frightened. I couldn't do anything but stand there helplessly. The worst thing was the silence that followed the shot. No cries; not a sound. Then I heard a scramble from the front of the apartment. I was too frightened to look out. Doors were banged open and men running. As near as I could judge they all ran down the stairs of the house. Then silence again.

After what seemed like an age but I suppose it was only a minute or two, I heard a dreadful low cry from the foyer. That was Alexis calling me. He could scarcely make himself heard. That frightened me more than ever, coming from a man I had lately seen so strong and full of life. I made myself go out to the foyer. Alexis was leaning against the wall a little to the left of the entrance door. That door was wide open. Elias, the waiter, was standing in the doorway staring. He had the highball on a tray. Prince Lenkoran's face looked deathly. Both hands were

pressed against his breast and blood was oozing between his fingers. "I'm shot!" he whispered, and sank
down to the floor before I could reach him. He never
spoke again. I couldn't lift him. I sat on the floor
beside him, supporting his head on my arm. That's
how I got the blood on my dress.

I have had no experience of death. I could not
tell the exact moment when he passed away. I was
numbed. Elias said: "Shall I telephone for a doctor,
Madame?" At the sound of his voice I realized that
Alexis was dead and everything turned black. When
I came to myself, Elias had placed me in a chair in
the foyer and he was bathing my temples with ice
water. Prince Lenkoran's body was still lying there.
I do not know how long I was unconscious. As soon
as I was able, I went to the telephone to call the police. I wouldn't let Elias do it, because it seemed to
be up to me. And I wouldn't let Elias go downstairs
to give an alarm because I didn't want all those restaurant people to come rushing up. The police arrived within a moment or two. Nothing was moved
or changed except that I closed Prince Lenkoran's
eyes because I couldn't bear to see his fixed stare.

I didn't see anybody in Prince Lenkoran's apartment during the evening except the guests I have
named, Elias the waiter, and Vassily, the Prince's
personal servant. Vassily left the apartment about
nine o'clock. He lives out. I don't know his other
name or his address. No, I didn't actually see Vassily
leave the apartment, but he could hardly have been
hidden in that little place all that time without my
knowing of it.

When Lee put down the sheets, Loasby asked eagerly: "What
do you think of her story?"

"How can I tell?" said Lee. "Sounds true on the face of it. A half-hysterical woman could hardly have invented so circumstantial a story on the spot."

Loasby did not agree. "She wasn't at all hysterical when she dictated it. She was a little too self-possessed, if you ask me. I am convinced that she is lying some where."

"What does the waiter say?"

Loasby handed him another paper and Lee skimmed over it. Elias, so far as he went, corroborated Jocelyn. He and Vassily had been dismissed for the evening about nine o'clock and went downstairs together. He saw Vassily leave the building. His name was Vassily Gorbol and he lived in Fifty-fourth Street somewhere east of Second Avenue.

It was about eleven o'clock when Miss D'Arcy telephoned for a highball; the restaurant was almost empty because people had not yet started to come from the theater. He, Elias, had reached the top of the first flight of stars when he heard the shot. He was startled and he hesitated, not knowing what to do. The sound was muffled. All he could say was, that it seemed to come from somewhere above. Two of the private dining rooms on the second floor were occupied but none of those people were alarmed by the shot. It is true, the doors of the private dining rooms were closed. So far as he knew, all the windows in the house were open, including those of Prince Lenkoran's apartment, both front and back. He didn't like to give an alarm in the restaurant because he wasn't sure; he thought maybe the shot had been fired somewhere outside the building.

Then he heard the door of the apartment overhead bang inward and the three Russians came plunging down the stairs. They looked frightened. As they brushed past him he asked what had happened, but nobody answered him. He looked over the stair rail and saw them run out of the front door of the house. He was very much frightened then and he started down the stairs to give an alarm. But he remembered the young lady upstairs and felt that he ought to go to her. So he turned and went upstairs.

From this point, his story followed that of Jocelyn. He said that she was unconscious for a long time, or so it seemed. Perhaps ten or fifteen minutes. He dared not leave her to give an alarm. When she came to, she would not let him give the alarm in the restaurant but telephoned directly to the police. Neither he nor Miss D'Arcy had left the apartment while waiting for the police. She had made no explanation to him of what had happened. Said she didn't know.

"The man is certainly lying," said Loasby when Lee finished reading. "If he was as frightened as he says, he would never have gone upstairs alone to see what was the matter. Not a man like him. Why, for all he knew he might have come face to face with Lenkoran with a smoking gun."

"I don't know," said Lee. "Even a poor waiter might have an impulse to go to a woman's assistance. She is a beautiful girl."

Loasby snorted in disbelief. "Granting that," he said, "the shot was fired at eleven o'clock . . ."

"No," Lee corrected, "Elias said the order for a highball was received about eleven."

"All right. The police were not notified until eleven twenty-five. What were they doing all that time?"

"He said he was trying to bring the girl to."

"That's not reasonable. He had only to telephone downstairs for help."

"Who knows?" said Lee. "It is possible that Elias was hoping to get her out of the house before the police came, so she wouldn't be implicated."

"And leave him to take the rap?" said Loasby. "That is even less reasonable. Somebody is lying. I can smell it!"

"You have a keen sense of smell," said Lee dryly. "Of course, you will check their stories. Lenkoran once told me that he rented the top floor also. Have you been up there?"

"Sure," said Loasby. "Two little empty flats. The doors were padlocked. We couldn't find any keys and we broke in. Absolutely empty. No indication that they had been visited in years."

"Who was the next to arrive on the scene?" asked Lee.

"Lieutenant O'Malley. He reported finding the girl, the waiter and the body just as they have been described. The lights in every room were turned on. There was no sign of a struggle in the apartment. Nobody on the lower floors of the house was aware of any trouble until the police arrived. The diners were questioned. Nobody had heard a shot. Some of them had heard the men running downstairs; they thought it was some guests skylarking. Upstairs, the girl was perfectly cool when O'Malley arrived. She did the talking. She told her story as you have read it and O'Malley took it down. I was at Headquarters when the report of the shooting came in, and I got here within a quarter hour."

"No gun?" queried Lee.

Loasby shook his head. "If it is true that the girl hasn't been out of the apartment, maybe she handed it to one of the Russians."

Lee smiled. "You are determined that she did it! Why couldn't it have been one of the Russians?"

"Sure! Sure! I have that possibility in mind, too."

"Has the bullet been extracted?"

"It passed clean through him," said Loasby.

"It has been found?"

Another shake of the head. "No trace of it. Nor any mark on walls or ceiling or floor where it could have struck. It is very strange."

"Have you found blood in any of the other rooms or in the hall outside?"

"Only in the foyer. That's another point that casts a doubt on the girl's story."

"If he was still on his feet, his clothes would soak up a lot of blood before it began to drip," Lee pointed out. "I noticed his clothes were drenched with it."

"That's right. Won't you question the two suspects and see if you can't break them down?"

Lee shook his head vigorously. "Not my line at all! I'm no breaker down. You're much better at it. I suggest that we start on the assumption that they are telling the truth. As soon as any discrepancies appear, we can get after them again."

"It would save time to break them down in the beginning," insisted Loasby.

"That's up to you," said Lee. "You should, of course, do everything that you do customarily in such a case, and let me proceed on my own."

Loasby's face fell. "How is that going to help me, Mr. Mappin? I will need your advice at every turn."

"Of course! We must keep in the closest touch in order to avoid duplicating our work. We won't solve this case until we can lay our hands on the three Russians. Why not assign me to the job of rounding them up?"

"Very well, if that's what you want to do. I have already sent out a general alarm. All the railway stations are watched, also the bus terminals, the bridges and the highways out of town."

"Right! But they no doubt separated at once and it would be fairly easy for them to slip away one at a time in different directions."

"If they have left town."

"Right again," said Lee. "I leave it to you to comb the city for them. My opinion is they would not stay in New York because none of them, judging from their talk, seemed to have much familiarity with the town. Their talk at the table gave me several leads that I will follow up. I'll take George Welby to assist me and you can give me a man to make the arrests when we run them down. If I leave town I'll report to you frequently."

"Okay," said Loasby. "Then you don't want to talk to these two?"

"Not tonight. Let me think things over first."

Lee went home. A few minutes later, Welby joined him there.

"Okay?" asked Lee.

"Okay, Mr. Mappin," said Welby.

As a result of their consultation, Welby spent the rest of the night at the telephone organizing his little force of operatives and setting them in motion, in New York, in Brooklyn, in Cleveland, in San Francisco. Scharipov did not return to his room at the Biltmore, nor Tashla to the Roosevelt, nor Goroshovel to his flat in Brooklyn. Welby had been instructed by Lee to engage a couple of additional men who would certainly be needed. He knew where to lay his hands on them. Richardson, they were keeping in New York.

CHAPTER TEN

THE MORNING PAPERS carried only a brief announcement of Prince Lenkoran's death, since the police had not released the whole story until after they went to press. The afternoon papers started coming out at eight o'clock in the morning with the details. Jermyn, according to instructions, brought them to Lee's bedside. In skimming over the stories, Lee found that they contained nothing he did not already know. Lenkoran was presented in his usual character of the wealthy, aristocratic playboy; there was no hint of any sinister activities. It was told how Lee had attended his dinner, but not that Lee had actively interested himself in solving the murder.

Lee sent for Jermyn and told him to telephone the different newspaper offices to say that Mr. Amos Lee Mappin would have a statement to make to the press at his office on Madison Avenue at ten o'clock.

Lee enjoyed matching wits with the bright lads of the press, and to a man they were his admirers and supporters. At their meeting in his office a good time was had by all. The brief statement that Lee gave them was on the streets before noon. It merely set forth Lee's close friendship with Prince Lenkoran and his determination to leave no stone unturned in bringing his dastardly murderer to justice. "He was one of the most delightful companions I have ever known," said Lee; "a citizen of the world in the best sense, which is to say a truly civilized man,"—etc., etc. Lee had refused to discuss the details of the case with the reporters.

"You boys know very well," he had told them, "that I never discuss the evidence in a case before it comes to trial."

When this edition came out, Inspector Loasby lost no time in calling up Lee. He was none too pleased by what he had read. "Was that alleged statement from you authorized?" he demanded.

"Why yes," said Lee. "I thought I had made that clear."

"It was so unlike you I couldn't believe it," said Loasby. "Always before this you have insisted on keeping out of print when you were working on a case. That was why I didn't tell the reporters last night that you were in it."

Lee smiled wickedly into the transmitter. "You can't have all the publicity, Inspector."

"I don't want it! I don't want it!" said Loasby warmly. "I am no publicity hog!" (Lee's smile broadened.) "But I should think it would hamper your work very much to have everybody know what you were up to."

"In this particular case I think it will help," said Lee.

Loasby's voice trailed off. "So unlike you! So unlike you . . . !"

They made an appointment to meet at Headquarters later.

The next edition of the papers carried an item which brought no smile to Lee's face. A new witness had come forward, a young insurance adjuster called Algernon Evans, who occupied a rear apartment on the south side of East Fifty-fourth Street. Mr. Evans stated that as he was preparing for bed the night before, he happened to look out of the window and his attention was attracted by a woman in a white dress who came to a window facing his across the back yards and threw something out. The time was 11:27. He could swear to the time because he had just wound his watch. It had been established that the window was one in the rear of Prince Lenkoran's apartment. The police immediately searched the yard back of the Tsarkoe Selo restaurant and were rewarded by finding a .25 caliber automatic under the shrubbery. Four shots had been fired from it. Mr. Evans, upon being brought to Headquarters, had positively identified Jocelyn D'Arcy as the woman he saw at the window and had described the dress she was wearing.

In the same edition was the story of a waitress at the Tsarkoe Selo who said that it was known around the establishment that Elias had some reason for hating Prince Lenkoran; that he had been heard to make threats against the Prince.

From the moment that these stories appeared, the press, without of course making any charges, tacitly assumed that Jocelyn D'Arcy had shot Prince Lenkoran, with, very likely, the assistance of Elias the waiter. The public went along with them and Jocelyn became a highly romantic figure in the popular imagination. Crowds gathered in the streets wherever it was supposed there was a chance of seeing her.

For the present, Jocelyn was detained at Police Headquarters. Lee had no difficulty in obtaining an interview with her. Inspector Loasby authorized it. When she was brought to him Lee was relieved to see that she had recovered from the shock, and had already made a conquest of the officer who was conducting her. They were both laughing when they entered at some crack of Jocelyn's. The officer remained by the door. He could not overhear what they said to each other.

When Jocelyn faced Lee her smile faded. "Lee, I did *not* do it!" she murmured.

"I have already said that I believed you, my dear. If you had shot the man I wouldn't consider it a crime. He was an enemy and a traitor."

"But I didn't shoot him."

"Okay. Okay."

"What a fool trick it was for me to throw the gun out of the window! I lost my head!"

"Oh, well," said Lee, "if you hadn't thrown it away, the police would presently have found it on you and you would be just as badly off."

"I forgot all about the damn gun until I hung up after calling the police. I had it on me—never mind where. I had noticed the shrubbery in the yard of the restaurant and I ran to the back window in a panic and threw the gun out. I hoped to be able to retrieve it before anybody else found it. It hadn't occurred to me then that I might be arrested."

"What about the four shots that had been fired from it?"

"Oh, I did that one day practicing, when Lenkoran took me to the country—but he can't corroborate that now, can he?"

"I blame myself for this accident," said Lee. "I should have taken the gun from you when I first came, but I was so concerned with other aspects of the case I forgot. The killing of Lenkoran undid all my work up to that moment, and naturally I was upset."

"I suppose the police think they've got a strong case against me now," said Jocelyn.

"Of course they think so. I'm afraid it will take a little longer to get you out. I hope you can stand it."

Jocelyn smiled in her own fashion. "Don't worry about me, duckling. Having the time of my life. It's such a novel experience and the policemen are *so* good-looking it's a pleasure to be jailed by them!"

Lee laughed. "You are game! . . . This is what I'm concerned about," he went on; "now that they are sure you're guilty, they'll give you no rest. They'll be questioning you at all hours in the hope of breaking you down."

"I'm not afraid of a lot of dumb cops," she retorted. "I'll give 'em as good as I get. As for the handsome Inspector, you will presently see him eating out of my hand."

"Is there anything additional you want to tell me?" asked Lee.

She shook her head. "Not much. I've had plenty of time to think things over, too. . . . There's one odd circumstance, but I'm not sure if it has any meaning. After the shot was fired, while I stood in the bedroom listening, it seemed to me that the three men did not rush out of the living room together, but that they came separately from different directions. I seemed to hear three or four doors opening. Could that be so?"

"Perhaps. I'll have it in mind."

"I suppose it was one of the Russians," she went on, "but I have no idea what the motive could have been. These men seemed to me to be Lenkoran's creatures, you know what I mean, stooges, yes-men. Why would Lenkoran's stooges turn on him suddenly?"

"How should I know, my dear?"

"Of course, it *could* have been Elias. I have seen Elias looking at Alexis when he thought he was unobserved with pure hatred in his eyes. Perhaps he had good cause. Alexis could be a brute."

"Time will tell," said Lee rising. "I'll be seeing you often, though I reckon you would rather it was a handsome police officer. One thing you can depend upon; now that they believe you guilty, they'll treat you with the greatest consideration."

"How come?" asked Jocelyn.

"In their minds you are the heroine of a crime of passion!"

"Gee!" said Jocelyn with her boy's grin. "Quit your kidding!"

Lee proceeded to Inspector Loasby's office. Loasby had plenty of "news" for him to which Lee listened as if he didn't know it already. Scharipov was a frequent visitor to New York, Loasby said, and had always stopped at the Biltmore. He was registered there at present, but had not returned to his room since the murder. An inquiry of the San Francisco police had brought the information that he was a well-known coffee importer who moved in the best circles of society. Of Tashla a similar story was told; he was the proprietor of an optical goods store in Cleveland and stayed at the Roosevelt when he came to New York, Only of Goro shovel, the police had no information. The publication of that unusual name had brought no echo from any quarter. Nobody knew such a man. Lee did not offer to supply Loasby with Goroshovel's address or his Brooklyn alias.

"They seem to be solid sort of men," said Loasby.

"On the face of it, yes," said Lee. "But why have they all disappeared?"

"Well, nobody wants to be mixed up in a murder. Perhaps they actually witnessed the shooting, and are reluctant to testify against a beautiful woman."

"I can understand that, but now that their names have been brought in they can't get away with it. Certainly not if they are men of position and means. They can only be looked upon as fugitives from justice."

"Naturally," said Loasby, a little nettled. "I expect them to turn up at any moment. Anyhow we shall relax no effort to find them.

But you must admit that it is not of the same importance now that we *know* we have the murderer."

"Sure," said Lee blandly, "*if* you have the murderer."

Loasby shook his head with an irritated smile. "You are a stubborn fellow, Mr. Mappin. Once you get an idea fixed in your head, nothing can shake it!"

"I might say the same of you," remarked Lee.

Loasby made believe not to hear it. "I am free to admit," he went on, "that I am delighted there is no suggestion of international complications in this crime. It was only the rash act of an infuriated woman."

"What infuriated her?"

"I don't know yet. I'll find out."

Loasby said further that Vassily Gorbol, Prince Lenkoran's servant, had been found and subjected to an exhaustive questioning by the police. He had contributed nothing to the known facts. One thing only was clear; he had been terrified of his master. Apparently it was a kind of psychic terror, for it did not appear that Lenkoran had ever injured him. Unless he was lying, which did not seem likely, Vassily knew nothing whatever about Lenkoran beyond what everybody knew.

"Here's another development in the case," Loasby went on, "but it doesn't seem to be of any particular importance. Roland Armiger, a lawyer with an office at 40 Wall Street, called me up to say that he was Prince Lenkoran's attorney; that he had his will and an inventory of his securities if the police had any object in seeing them."

Lee listened to this very sharply. "He brought them to you?"

"Yes."

"Who is Lenkoran's heir?"

"His cousin," said Loasby, "another jaw-breaking name; I wrote it down; Count Deduchin, now a resident of Philadelphia. The will was very brief; it bequeathed all property that Lenkoran might die possessed of to his cousin without any restriction. The cousin was appointed sole executor and was not to be required to give an accounting."

Lee listened to this with an indifferent air, but the moment he left Loasby's office he called up Welby and transmitted the information to him.

"This is a rare piece of luck," said Lee. "Send a dependable man to Philadelphia at once to learn all he can about this Count Deduchin. The Count very likely will lose no time in claiming his inheritance and our man may pass him on the way. You had better keep a watch on Armiger's office so that we will know when the Count gets here."

LEE REMAINED AT HOME all afternoon to receive the reports of Welby's agents which were coming in at frequent intervals. Among other things he learned that the lawyer Armiger had gone to the Pennsylvania Station where he met Count Deduchin as he descended from the three o'clock train. The Count had brought a secretary and several servants with him. The lawyer and the Count had taxied direct to Police Headquarters, where they had been closeted with Inspector Loasby for half an hour. Loasby himself had then driven them in a police car to East Fifty-third Street, where they visited the Lenkoran apartment. After issuing from the building, Loasby had driven the Count to a fine town house on East Sixty-seventh Street, where he dropped him and returned to Headquarters.

At five Jermyn came to report to Lee that there was a man on the telephone who wouldn't state his business. "Says he is secretary to Count something or other, I couldn't just get the name, sir."

"Let me talk to him," said Lee, eagerly reaching for the phone.

A voice with a slight foreign accent, having made certain that he was speaking to Mr. Mappin himself, said: "This is Count Deduchin's secretary. The Count presents his compliments to Mr. Mappin and begs Mr. Mappin to excuse him for calling in this summary manner. Could Mr. Mappin find it convenient to come and see the Count immediately on a matter of pressing importance in connection with the death of the Count's cousin, Prince Lenkoran?"

"I should be delighted to wait on the Count immediately," said Lee, winking at Jermyn, who was standing by.

"Thank you very much, sir. We are occupying Mr. Winstanley's residence on East Sixty-seventh Street. Are you sure you have the name right—Count Deduchin?" The secretary spelled it out.

"I have it," said Lee.

CHAPTER ELEVEN

THE WINSTANLEY HOUSE occupying a fifty-foot frontage a few doors east of the Avenue, was one of the grand establishments that are being closed up one by one during these difficult times. A manservant in plum-colored livery ushered Lee up a noble stairway. He was a brawny, ill-favored fellow with a furtive, watchful expression. During subsequent visits to the house, Lee saw several others of the same type. These were the servants Deduchin had brought with him. They were supposed to be Russians, but Lee doubted it. Lee was conducted into an immense salon done in maroon and silver. Modern overstuffed furniture was interspersed with tastefully chosen French antiques; a vast Aubusson carpet covered the floor; paintings of the newer French schools were displayed on the walls.

Three men were waiting in the room. The Count was a small man dressed as if for a wedding in a braided cutaway and striped trousers. He had a face like a mummy. There was a touch of rouge on his cheeks. The servant announced Lee at the door, but the Count made believe not to be aware of his entrance until the secretary brought him up for a formal presentation.

"Mr. Amos Lee Mappin . . . Count Deduchin."

Whereupon the mummy stirred and presented two limp fingers. "Ah!" he said in a tired, high-pitched voice. "How good of Mr. Mappin to come so quickly in response to my call!"

Lee, bowing with a grave face, answered: "I felt it an honor to be summoned by Count Deduchin."

There was not much of the natural man to be seen. He wore a beautifully made toupee of an odd yellowish hue and a double set of false teeth; his little shoulders were padded, his chest built out, his waist pinched in with a corset; he had lifters in his shoes that gave him the mincing gait of a woman wearing French heels. Yet he was far from being the fool that all this nonsense suggested. The sharp little eyes in his parchment face missed nothing. The color of his eyes seemed to be changeable, sometimes on the yellow side, sometimes a pale, murky blue. It was evident that he had assumed his grand airs in order to impress us democratic Americans. It seemed to work, for the lawyer was overawed in the Count's presence, the young secretary hushed and deferential. Lee played up to the Count, too, but not too abjectly, for the old man's eye was sharp.

Lee and the Count discussed what a noble fellow the late Prince Lenkoran had been, and how foul the crime that had cut him down in his prime. Compliments were passed back and forth. Lee had heard so much about the Count's beautiful place on the Main Line. The Count expressed the gratification he had felt upon reading that the famous Amos Lee Mappin had interested himself in the tragic death of his cousin. Now he felt assured that justice would be done. The police! He held up his little beringed claws in mute protest. Said the Count:

"It appears as if this unhappy business will necessitate my spending some time in New York. I have therefore taken my friend Mr. Winstanley's house for the time being. Winstanley, as Mr. Mappin undoubtedly knows, is president of the Beaver National Bank. The Winstanleys are at their summer place in Bar Harbor."

"It's a fine house," put in Lee.

"It will do; it will do!" said the Count with a wave of his hand. "I like the privacy of a house; and I prefer to be surrounded with my own servants. I employ only men servants."

When all this, and more, had been duly registered, the Count said to the lawyer and the secretary: "Now, if you will be so good, gentlemen, I should like to have a little private conversation with Mr. Mappin."

They beat it. Lee took note of the Count's sharp glance to make sure the double doors were completely closed. The room had no other doors.

The Count now dropped a part of his toplofty manner and addressed Lee with a kind of royal graciousness that was supposed to afford Lee intense gratification. Lee registered gratification. The plum-colored servant brought the makings of highballs and a box of the most expensive cigars from the Dunhill humidor. Still the Count did not come to the point. For a long time, as they discussed the murder, he was subtly sounding out Lee and feeling his way with him. Lee made it easy for him. When he saw his opportunity, Lee said:

"Prince Lenkoran was a true aristocrat! That's why I admired him so much. His bold and fearless manner of addressing inferior beings delighted me. So refreshing in a society where all men are reduced to a common level! One longs for a return to a regime where the superior few will rule!" At this point Lee looked around him fearfully. "I suppose it is treason to voice such sentiments now!"

The Count grinned with pleasure. At such moments he looked like a monkey. "You are safe with me, Mappin." He now dropped his grand manner altogether and spoke to the point. "Mappin, what is the nature of your arrangement with the New York police?"

"I have no 'arrangement' with them, Count. I simply volunteered to do everything I could to solve the murder of my friend."

"Then you will not be paid by the police for your services?"

"No, sir! It would require a special act of the Legislature to authorize them to pay my fee."

"Do you feel free to consider a private commission from me in connection with this case?"

"Certainly, sir," said Lee, looking as pleased as a man ought to look when a fat fee is dangled before him. "That's how I earn my living."

"If you are successful in this case you will never have to work for your living again."

"What!" exclaimed Lee, affecting astonishment.

"I speak advisedly, Mr. Mappin. There is a very large sum of money involved."

"Oh, my God, Count!" said Lee agitatedly. "Enough to keep me in comfort for the rest of my life?"

"More than comfort, Mappin, in luxury." He waved his hand to indicate their surroundings. "Like this!"

"What must I do to earn it?" asked Lee.

"Nothing crooked, I assure you," said the Count with a thin smile.

Lee waved this away as much as to say he wouldn't dream of suspecting the Count of anything off-color.

"It need not conflict with your agreement with the police," the Count went on; "for God knows I'm as anxious as anybody to see my cousin's murderers caught and electrocuted, but there are certain private aspects of the case that must not be revealed publicly. That is why I am consulting you."

"I quite understand, sir. Please go on."

"The woman in the case is unimportant," said the Count. "There was always a woman in Lenkoran's life. With him such relationships were entirely superficial."

"I know that," said Lee.

Count Deduchin raised his fist. "It was the three men!" he said, viciously champing his teeth together.

"That's what I have said from the beginning," put in Lee.

"Your handsome police inspector is a dunderhead!" exclaimed the Count. He smiled evilly and gave Lee a sidelong glance. "Perhaps for our purposes it is just as well that he is."

"Sure," said Lee, smiling back.

"Fill your glass," said the Count. "Note that I say it was the three men," he went on. "No one of them could have got away with it without the connivance of the others. It was a plot!"

"What was their motive?" asked Lee.

"The simplest and the basest of motives: robbery!"

Lee rubbed his upper lip. "His own men!" he said with a shocked air.

"Exactly! Robbers, murderers and traitors! . . . Did Prince Lenkoran ever tell you how he occupied himself privately?"

"Yes," said Lee. "He said he was engaged in collecting money for Russian Relief and forwarding it."

"Ah, I see he admitted you to his confidence. That's right. It was contributed by Russians of the old regime, who are scattered all over the Americas, many of them living under assumed names in order to escape the attentions of the present government of Russia. Owing to the difficulties of getting the money into Russia, it can only be sent twice a year. The time had come to send it and all the arrangements were made. Consequently the Prince had a very large sum in cash in his possession. The three men knew that."

"In what form was it?"

"As it was received, the Prince changed it here and there to treasury notes of high denominations so it wouldn't bulk so large."

"Where did he keep it?"

"Did you ever happen to notice an antique carved and painted chest in his apartment?"

"My God, yes!" exclaimed Lee. "The last place one would have expected."

"That was how Lenkoran figured. A safe, he said, would only have attracted the attention of a spy."

"How much was in the chest?"

The Count turned cautious. "At this moment I cannot tell you. I will check the amount. It will run well into seven figures."

"My God!" murmured Lee.

The Count raised his shoulders. "A vast sum to you or to me, Mappin, but in war a mere fleabite!" The Count pulled out the tremolo stop. "Ah! but the sick, the hungry Russians are so terribly in want of it! Their need is desperate and immediate!" He flexed his skinny fingers. "I should like to kill the robbers with my bare hands!"

"A despicable crime!" agreed Lee warmly. "You are certain they got away with it?"

"Absolutely! The terrified waiter who met them running down the stairs was not asked if they were carrying anything. I don't know whether they were or not. In any case, three men could have concealed a lot under their clothes. I suppose they had a car waiting.

Only yesterday I was assured that the money was ready in Len-koran's chest. Today the chest is empty."

"How do you know?"

"I have a duplicate key. Long ago it had been arranged that if anything happened to Lenkoran, I was to take up his work. When the Inspector was showing me the apartment this afternoon, he was called out of the living room for a moment. I looked in the chest and it was empty! . . . You must recover that money for my sick and starving people, Mappin!"

While the Count's tongue was dripping with such humanitarian sentiments, his eyes as hard and bright as polished agate were trying to probe Lee's soul. Lee made his eyes hard, too.

"What am I to get out of it, Count?"

It was the right note to strike. The Count showed his monkey grin. "I like your bluntness, Mappin. You and I are going to understand each other, I see. You are to have one-third of all money that may be recovered through your assistance."

Lee gave a representation of a man overcome by the magnitude of such a prospect. He gaped at the Count and repeatedly wiped his face. "Okay . . . Okay," he stammered. ". . . There will be difficulties!"

"Naturally," said the Count. "That's why I came to you. Absolute secrecy is necessary. If the fact of the existence of this money were to get out, the needy Russians would never see a penny of it. The present government of Russia would seize it on the pretext that it was intended to be used for subversive purposes."

"My whole life has been spent in keeping secrets," said Lee.

"What difficulties do you foresee?"

"When these men are arrested for the murder, how can we keep the secret of the money?"

"As you find each man," said the Count, showing his perfectly fitting teeth, "you must give me an hour alone with him, before turning him over to the police."

"But I have no authority to make arrests. I have to take a policeman along with me for that purpose."

"Well, any common policeman can be bribed, can't he? Or, better still, fooled. No policeman would dare question your orders."

"Perhaps you're right," said Lee. "But suppose we run down our men in distant towns. How could I convey them to you without the knowledge of the police?"

"I will come to you," said the Count. "Whenever the chase grows warm, I will be at your side."

"How can I provide a proper place for you to interview the men secretly?"

The Count turned a ring on his finger. "Really, Mappin, I'm surprised at your lack of resources. In every large town there are furnished houses to be had when expense is no object. In a house of one's own, one has entire freedom of action."

"I get you," said Lee dryly.

"That's all for now," said the Count. "From Russian sources I'll see what information I can get about the men that may help you."

"I'll be expecting to hear from you," said Lee.

As soon as he got home Lee sent for Welby to come to his apartment. "This is too good for the telephone," he said.

Seated opposite the smooth-faced, matter-of-fact Welby, Lee said: "I have just had a protracted interview with the ineffable Count Deduchin. I've got to tell somebody and you're the only person in the world I can tell."

When he had finished the story, the two men looked at each other, clapped their knees and laughed until the tears stood in their eyes.

"He has hired you to find the money you yourself lifted!" said Welby.

"One of the most piquant situations in my whole career!" said Lee.

"Completely cock-eyed!"

They started laughing again.

"Amongst all his camouflage the truth appeared just once," said Lee. "Deduchin said: 'It had been arranged that if anything happened to Lenkoran, I was to take up his work.' Welby, that means that our work is not broken off by the death of Lenkoran. It goes on. How fortunate for us that Lenkoran was such a secretive man. He failed to warn Deduchin against me. Consequently the antique Count has fallen into my trap! . . . We must have a drink on the strength of it!"

CHAPTER TWELVE

LEE MAPPIN VISITED POLICE HEADQUARTERS every day to confer with Inspector Loasby and thereby assure himself that the police were not finding out more about the Lenkoran case than he wished them to know. There seemed to be little danger of that happening, because the police were convinced they had the murderess and her accomplice, and their chief efforts were directed toward obtaining confessions. So far as police channels went, nothing came in respecting the whereabouts of Messrs. Scharipov, Goroshovel and Tashla. It was evident that Count Deduchin was keeping tab on the police, also; in a drawer of Loasby's desk Lee saw a box of the scandalously expensive cigars favored by the Count. Daily Loasby would ask Lee:

"When are you taking to the road to look for your Russians?"

"My agents are on the job," Lee would reply. "I'm only waiting for a lead."

Jocelyn D'Arcy continued to be held at Headquarters for the convenience of the police. At all times a little crowd stood in the street outside the rear door on the chance of seeing her transferred. Lee made a point of visiting Jocelyn frequently. Her morale gave no sign of failing, but he did not know how much strain and distress might be concealed under her gay and derisive manner. Loasby encouraged Lee's visits, fondly supposing that Lee was doing his bit to persuade the girl to confess.

Said Jocelyn: "I'm leading the life of Reilly, duckling. They have put me into one of the elegant little chambers reserved for distinguished guests, and all day I have a stream of visitors."

"Visitors?" said Lee, surprised.

"Oh, of course the public is not admitted to view the animals, but dozens of officers find an excuse to stop by and pass the time of day. They bring me all sorts of delicacies and other gifts, the darlings! Home was never like this!"

"What about the questioning?"

"That's a bore sometimes, but they haven't really turned on the heat yet. You see, I'm so nice to them they can't get very tough with me. It's fun, rather."

"Fun?"

"Playing the innocent kid, I mean, and making my big questioners look foolish. The bigger they are, the more foolish."

"Don't they ask you some pretty awkward questions?"

"No. They haven't come within a mile of guessing what you told me I must not tell them." She yawned.

"You're not getting enough sleep?" suggested Lee.

"I don't mind a little lost sleep," she said; "I'll be dead such a long, long time. They like to send for me at night just when I'm dropping off. I have too many visitors in the daytime to make up sleep."

"I had it in mind to tell you," said Lee, "that if it gets too bad, if they wear you out, you must let me know at once and I'll take measures to relieve the strain."

"What measures, duckling?"

He shook his head, smiling. "You must leave that to me. . . . I want to let the situation ride as long as I can. I'm playing for time now. The killing of Lenkoran has thrown the enemy into confusion just the same as it has our side. As soon as they get the cars running over the bridge again, I'll be able to see my way."

"Oh, I can hold out for a long time yet."

"Thanks, Joss. I'm playing a ticklish game, my dear, trying to fool the lawful police on the one hand and the enemy on the other."

"I'm backing you, duckling."

LEE WAS SPENDING the greater part of the time at his office or at home telephoning and receiving reports; the office was for his public activities, home for more private matters. On the third day after the murder, Welby came to the apartment to give him the latest news. He said:

"Nick Tashla is the proprietor of a long-established store in Cleveland doing business under the name of Merriman Brothers. It sells optical goods, cameras, chronometers, etc. Tashla purchased the business nine years ago . . ."

"Odd," interrupted Lee, "how often that nine years comes up. This conspiracy was organized while our country was dreaming of perpetual peace."

"That's right, Mr. Mappin! . . . Tashla has an efficient manager and sales force and takes very little part in directing the business. His purpose in buying it was merely to give him standing in the community.

"As you already know, he turned up in Cleveland at nine o'clock on the night following the murder. How he got there, I can't tell you. He was picked up when he visited a woman whose apartment we were watching. He remained there two hours. Apparently he made no effort to communicate with any employee of the store. I might say that the store people, so far as we can learn, are good patriotic Americans.

"Tashla issued out of the woman's apartment dressed as a workingman. He took a night train to Detroit and in the morning he applied for work at Ford's big Willow Run plant. Here he posed as an American machinist called William Brown. He was provided with letters of introduction, a birth certificate, a union card, a social security card, all presumably forged, and he was hired. My man could not get close enough to hear the story he told. No doubt it was a good one. He was given a job on the assembly line. He has had experience as a machinist. The woman turned up in Detroit yesterday afternoon. She now poses as his wife. They have taken a modest flat of two rooms and have apparently settled down for a stay.

"So much for Tashla," Welby concluded. "Any instructions?"

"Let him stay where he is for the time being," said Lee. "I will see that the management of the plant is notified through the proper channels and instructed to watch him without arousing his suspicions. I do not believe, however, that he has any designs against the plant. He needs it as a hide-out and will therefore conduct himself very prudently while there."

"That's how I saw it," said Welby.

"None of these men must be alarmed," said Lee, "until my case is complete. Otherwise the big boss may slip through my fingers."

"Next about Goroshovel," Welby continued, "or Estevan, as he is known in Brooklyn. After waiting for twenty-four hours he was satisfied that the police had no line on his apartment, and he returned there as cool as you please. He has no suspicion as yet that we are on his tail. No photograph of him has been published—the police have no way of getting one; consequently he feels safe. He evidently intends going on with his work in spite of the death of Lenkoran, because last night he was drinking in the bars along Sands Street and keeping his ears open just the same as before."

"Goroshovel is a cleverer and more dangerous enemy than Tashla," said Lee. "I suggest that you see the Commandant of the Navy Yard. Explain the situation to him and ask for his co-operation."

"Wouldn't the Federal Police arrest Goroshovel at once?"

"My friends in Washington will take care of that. . . . What about friend Scharipov? He's the most dangerous. It is essential to learn whether the loss of the money has stopped him or whether he is still carrying on."

"There's not much about him that is new," said Welby. "He's a cool one! As you know, he telegraphed to his clerk in San Francisco an hour after the murder. This was before the news got out. I have now seen a copy of the telegram. It reads: 'Tragic accident has occurred. See papers tomorrow for details. Necessary for me to keep under cover in order to secure evidence which will clear me. Carry on. Regards. Scharipov!"

Lee smiled. "That was a plant. He expected it to fall into the hands of the police."

"Exactly," said Welby. "His clerk, according to my reports, is a young man of the highest character."

"He would be," said Lee. "It is the settled policy of this gang to surround themselves with honest men."

"The only thing new I have had direct from San Francisco," Welby went on, "is this. Yesterday afternoon, just as Scharipov's clerk was about to close his office, he was visited by a woman in black who attracted our man's attention because of her nervous and agitated manner. She remained twenty minutes and when she came out she looked as if she had been crying."

"Did he describe her?"

"Yes; age 45, weight 150, dark hair and eyes. A former beauty. Expensively dressed, but in a plain style as if anxious not to attract attention."

"Good! Go on!"

"Our man attempted to follow her, but she caught a taxi at the corner and when he succeeded in getting another she was gone!"

"Bad luck!" said Lee. "The telephone in Scharipov's office should be tapped."

"That has been covered," said Welby.

LATER LEE HAD A CALL from East Sixty-seventh Street. The young voice of the secretary, who always spoke of his master with a touch of awe, said: "Count Deduchin's compliments to Mr. Mappin, and could Mr. Mappin make it convenient to wait on the Count this morning? The Count has received information that he doesn't care to entrust to the telephone."

"Mr. Mappin will come at once," said Lee dryly. "Confound the little monkey!" he added to Jermyn after he had hung up. "I'm tired of being at his beck and call!"

Jermyn smiled with discreet sympathy.

"However," Lee went on, "some day he shall dance to the tune I call!"

In the grand house on 67th Street, another little comedy had to be played through before the Count got down to business. Lee was announced by the manservant, announced again by the secretary and given two languid fingers to shake.

"The heat is very trying," drawled the Count. "New York is so humid! if I am obliged to remain here on account of this sad business, I really must have a house in an airier situation. They tell me the town of Riverdale stands high and cool. Do you suppose it would be possible to obtain a furnished house there suitable for a gentleman's establishment?"

"I don't know Riverdale," said Lee, "but I shall be happy to inquire."

"I should be infinitely obliged to you."

"I understand that Prince Lenkoran has left you a charming little place near Tuckahoe," said Lee.

"Too small! Too small!" said the Count, waving it away.

After the secretary had tiptoed out of the room, closing the door behind him, the Count's manner changed. His little pale eyes glittered. "What have you got to report?" he demanded.

Lee spread out his hands. "Not much as yet, Count. I have organized a search, that's all."

"I expected quick results from a man of your reputation," said the Count sourly. "Tell me exactly what you have done."

To convince him that he was doing all a man could do to earn his million dollars, Lee launched into a detailed account of activities which had not got anywhere in particular. The Count was not completely satisfied.

"Any ordinary detective could do as much," he grumbled.

Lee took it humbly. "You said you had some information for me," he suggested.

"I have. From Russian sources I can learn nothing about Goroshovel except a hint that he is living somewhere in Brooklyn."

"That will help," said Lee.

"Of Tashla I have learned that he has a set of papers in his possession identifying him as William Brown, a machinist. It appears that he actually has had experience as a machinist. He is therefore likely to seek employment in some large factory as a means of cover."

"Splendid!" said Lee, with business of making a note in his little book.

"As for Scharipov, his San Francisco friends have been led to believe that his wife is in Russia; that is not so. She is living under the name of Mrs. Crispin in the village of Sebastopol in Sonoma County, north of San Francisco. I assume that he visits her."

"Have you a description of this woman?" asked Lee eagerly.

"I have seen her," said the Count. "She was a beautiful girl. She must be forty-five now; dark hair, dark eyes, a quiet manner; always dresses in black."

"If he visits her again we'll have him!" cried Lee, in seeming glee.

"Shouldn't we fly out to San Francisco?" suggested the Count.

"Wait until we get a line on which way he's going to jump. He may tell the woman to join him elsewhere. If he does, she will lead us to him."

UPON REACHING HOME, Lee got Welby on the wire. "Here's your woman in black who visited Scharipov's office. She's his wife. She lives very quietly in the village of Sebastopol in Sonoma County. Is known there as Mrs. Crispin."

"Linder is to call me up at noon," said Welby. "I'll tell him."

EARLY ON THE FOLLOWING MORNING Welby relayed a message from San Francisco to Lee. "This came in at two o'clock this morning," said Welby, "or 11 p.m. San Francisco time. As it was not urgent I didn't wake you."

> Proceeded to Sebastopol this morning on receipt of your message. No difficulty in locating Mrs. C. For several years past she has boarded with the family of a well-to-do storekeeper of the village. Passes as a widow with no living children. Has the name of a very reserved woman, but pleasant-spoken. Has joined the village church and takes part in church affairs. Has never been visited by anybody from outside the village, but frequently goes to San Francisco for a day or a night to visit her "sister." This afternoon she proceeded in her own car to Berkeley (a

much larger place than Sebastopol) where she engaged a small furnished flat that has a telephone.
Her first act was to give her name to the Central
Office, saying that she was expecting a long-distance
call. She did not give up her room in Sebastopol but
told her friends there that she would be back "in a
few days." In Sebastopol I learned that she had had
a long distance call from New York four nights ago.
It made some talk in the village because the conversation was in a foreign tongue. I suppose the operator let this out. That, I am sure, is why Mrs. C. went
to Berkeley. Her calls would not be noticed in the
bigger place.

As I reported earlier, I got in touch with the Russian Consulate when I first arrived in San Francisco.
The people there are all Russian patriots, and they
have never had any relations with Scharipov. This
afternoon I borrowed a clerk from the Consulate and
installed him in the Bayview Hotel, Berkeley. He
is a linguist who knows all the dialects of Central
Europe. The side windows of this hotel overlook the
building where Mrs. Crispin has taken an apartment.
The Russian clerk will remain in his room day and
night until Mrs. C. receives her long-distance call.
With the help of the local police, I have arranged
with the telephone company that the Russian is to
be plugged in on her conversation.

                                             Linder.

CHAPTER THIRTEEN

LEE SOON LEARNED a good deal about Count Deduchin's antecedents. He was said to come of an ancient family of a province in Central Russia. Unlike most of the émigrés, he had succeeded in bringing a great part of his fortune to America. Perhaps he had foreseen the coming of the Russian revolution in time. About fifteen years ago he had purchased a handsome estate near Ardmore, Pennsylvania, and he had been living there ever since. He was said to be a widower with one son who, however, had never visited him in America.

His wealth and his title had assured him admittance to the best society of that exclusive neighborhood—to a certain extent. That is to say, he was invited to belong to the fashionable clubs and was included in all the formal entertainments. In return he gave magnificent parties several times a year. But he was such an ugly and peculiar little man that he never gained any real intimacy with his American neighbors. He didn't seem to want it. After so many years, he was looked on as a feature of the community, but he had no close friends. When his American associates were questioned, they were surprised to realize how little they knew about him.

Some of his ways were regarded as strange, such as his always keeping five or six male servants about the house, but a good deal of latitude was permitted him as a foreigner. He had always been an ardent Czarist and was much visited by other Russians of the same persuasion. Since the war had broken out, however, he had become very quiet on this subject. His Russian friends dropped away and he now posed as a good American who came to the fore in all patriotic movements and drives to raise funds.

IN HIS NEXT REPORT, Welby communicated to Lee that the Admiral commanding Brooklyn Navy Yard had promised full co-operation in the case of Goroshovel or Estevan. Within forty-eight hours, Lee received a telephone message from the Admiral's secretary asking if it would be convenient for Mr. Mappin to come to see his chief.

Lee duly had himself taxied across the river. As soon as the two men faced each other, it appeared that the Admiral had received advices from Washington which smoothed Lee's way. Consequently, it was not necessary to explain himself, and after a brief exchange of amenities the Admiral came directly to the point.

"A draughtsman here in the Yard reported to me this morning that he had been approached by the enemy agent Estevan of whom you informed me. I would rather not tell you the draughtsman's name unless it is necessary to you."

"Not in the least necessary, at this juncture," said Lee.

"Well," continued the Admiral, "the draughtsman led the man on in order to find out what he was up to, and after several meetings accompanied by a good deal of drinking, Estevan told him that he wanted to buy the blueprints for the new landing device for planes that is to be installed on the carrier we are building."

"That tallies with my information," said Lee.

"This is a dangerous situation!" said the Admiral with considerable heat. "Why don't you arrest the man at once? You have the evidence now."

"This Estevan is only an agent," said Lee in his mild voice. "If he is arrested, another agent will immediately take his place. I am hoping that if we give Estevan rope enough, he will lead me to his principal so that I can destroy the conspiracy root and branch."

The Admiral was mollified. "Fair enough!" he said. "Of course I'll do everything I can to assist you, short of letting Estevan see the blueprints for the landing device. Our draughtsman has a date to meet him again tonight. What do you suggest he should say to Estevan?"

Said Lee: "Let him describe the difficulties of getting hold of the blueprints for the landing device, but hold out hope for the future. While they are waiting for an opportunity, let the draughtsman try to sell Estevan something else."

"That's an idea," said the Admiral.

"What could you offer him that he would fall for? The deal must be carried through, you understand. Estevan is a smart fellow; he can read a blueprint; he will not be easy to fool."

After thinking it over for a moment or two, the Admiral broke into a grim laugh. "How would this do, Mr. Mappin? The Navy Department has sent us blueprints for a new and secret device for directing antiaircraft guns on shipboard. These were acquired from the enemy, I needn't say how. If I had copies made, there would be nothing on them to show where the prints had originated. We might sell those back to Estevan."

Lee joined in the Admiral's laugh. "An excellent idea!"

"I'll have copies made immediately," said the Admiral, "and the draughtsman can carry them to Estevan tonight."

Lee shook his head. "Don't let us appear to be in too much of a hurry, or Estevan will certainly smell a rat. Let your draughtsman tell him about the new aiming device tonight, and if he falls for it, your man can carry the blueprints to him at their next meeting."

"Very well," said the Admiral. "It shall be done that way. I'll keep you informed of what happens."

"Please communicate with me through my assistant, Mr. Welby," said Lee. "You see, I have gone to a good deal of trouble to get myself suspected of disloyalty at this juncture, and it would spoil my game if I were caught having relations with our Navy."

"I will see to it."

They parted.

This interview took place on a Tuesday. On Tuesday night the Navy draughtsman met Estevan-Goroshovel in a saloon on Sands Street according to agreement. A report of their meeting was in Lee's hands before he went to bed Tuesday night. The draughtsman made his proposition and Estevan offered him a thousand dollars for the blueprints of the aiming device if they were as represented.

The two arranged to meet again on Wednesday night in Court Square, Brooklyn. The draughtsman was then to bring Estevan the blueprints and receive the money.

On Wednesday at midnight Lee was waiting in his apartment in the expectation of getting a report of this meeting. As his clock struck the first quarter, a bell rang, not from the telephone as he expected, but at the door of the apartment. Jermyn had been sent to bed and Lee hastened to the door. It was Welby, and his bland face was wearing the widest of grins.

"Everything is going all right, I take it," said Lee, when he had closed the door.

"Sure!" said Welby. "There has been a most odd and unexpected development!"

In a situation so critical, Lee didn't relish the suggestion of a surprise. "What's that?" he asked sharply.

"You would never guess where Goroshovel is at this moment!" said Welby laughing.

"I shan't try to guess," said Lee. "Where is he?"

"Ten minutes ago he entered Count Deduchin's fine house on Sixty-seventh Street."

Lee became painfully agitated. "What are you telling me? Why wasn't I warned? Goroshovel will be put to torture there. The Count told me as much."

"I can't break my heart over that," said Welby, "when I think of our boys who have been killed."

"You don't understand!" cried Lee. "If I thought Deduchin would shoot the man down, I wouldn't raise a finger to save him. It would be the best thing that could happen. But to think of Goroshovel being tortured, slowly, for something you and I did, Welby, that I cannot bear!"

Welby shook his head. "I don't get it, sir. Isn't it always good strategy to get your enemies fighting among themselves?"

Lee flung up his hands. "I can't argue it with you. Every man has his weaknesses. The thought of torture sickens me! I can't allow it to go on!" He started shouting for Jermyn. To Welby he said: "I've got to get the man out of that house!"

"How can you get him out now he's in," protested Welby, "without giving away your whole game?"

"I don't know," said Lee. "I'll think of something. We must go up there quick!"

"You can't enter the house now," said Welby in distress. "It's a den of thugs! If the Count saw that you were wise to him, you'd never be allowed to leave it. You must have a force of police with you!"

"I don't want the police in this," said Lee. He slowed down and became thoughtful. "Perhaps I won't have to enter the house . . . if I can create a diversion in the street."

Jermyn entered from the rear, gaunt and disheveled in an old terry-cloth bathrobe that was too short for him. Lee's visible agitation astonished and alarmed him. "You wanted me, sir?"

"Wait a minute!" said Lee. He stood for a moment or two in intense concentration. "Jermyn, have we anything inflammable in the apartment?"

"How do you mean, sir?" asked the wondering Jermyn. "I have about a pint of benzine in a Mason jar that I use for removing grease spots."

"That will do," said Lee. "Fetch it quickly! . . . and some newspapers; about four will be enough."

Jermyn ran out.

Welby, perceiving Lee's purpose, gasped: "Mr. Mappin, it's too risky, too risky!"

Lee was recovering his usual calmness. "Every house in that block except the Count's is closed for the summer," he said smiling. "At this hour it will be as solitary as a graveyard."

Welby continued to shake his head.

Jermyn came back with what was wanted. Lee thrust the jar of benzine under his coat, handed the newspapers to Welby and snatched up his hat. "Come on! . . . Jermyn, you'd better stay up until you hear from me."

"Yes, sir." It reassured Jermyn to see that Lee was himself again.

Lee and Welby hastened out of the building. In First Avenue they hailed a taxi and ordered the driver to let them down at Sixty-seventh

Street and Madison. On the way Welby reported to Lee what had led up to the present situation.

"The Navy draughtsman met Goroshovel in Court Square, Brooklyn, at nine o'clock, according to their agreement. Goroshovel took him for a hell of a long walk through the streets. This was to make certain they were not followed. I was not trying to follow them. The draughtsman told me about it afterwards. During the walk Goroshovel stopped by a lighted show window and examined the blueprints to make sure that they were *bona fide*. When he was satisfied that the Navy man was on the level, he took him to his apartment on Montague Street, where he paid him a thousand dollars and received the blueprints. Afterwards they drank together.

"Richardson and I were watching the house. When the draughtsman came out, I followed him away according to our understanding, leaving Richardson on watch. After the draughtsman had described to me what had taken place, I returned to Montague Street. Richardson had gone, and I knew by that that Goroshovel must have gone out. It had been arranged that if that happened, I was to go home and wait for a message from Richardson. Later Richardson telephoned me that Goroshovel had come out a few minutes after the draughtsman left. He stopped in a drugstore to telephone and then taxied over the bridge and up to Count Deduchin's house. So I hustled over to tell you.

"What happened is clear enough. Goroshovel doesn't know that the Count suspects him of murder and robbery. Therefore, when he received the blueprints his first thought was to recommend himself to his new chief by turning them over. Goroshovel had read in the papers that the Count had come to New York and had rented the Winstanley house. So he telephoned him, and of course the Count said: 'Come right up!'"

"I can see him grinning like an obscene monkey," muttered Lee, "and rubbing his little crooked paws together!"

They got out at the designated corner and Lee paid off the driver. As they crossed the street Lee pointed to a fire-alarm box on the south corner.

"That would be the nearest," he said.

"Mr. Mappin, I don't like this!" complained Welby. "It's too wild a scheme! Something is sure to go wrong."

"You can go home if you don't want to be mixed up in it," said Lee equably.

"You know I'm not going to do that!" said Welby in a reproachful voice.

They proceeded west through Sixty-seventh Street. As Lee had foreseen, it was like a street of the dead. Not even a cat stirred on the asphalt.

"We'll find Richardson somewhere close by," said Welby.

As they passed by on the other side of the street, the great bulk of the Winstanley house was as dark and blank as its neighbors. At the Fifth Avenue corner just beyond, they ran into young Richardson. On this hot summer night there were still people promenading on the Avenue, and Richardson could mix among them without attracting attention to himself, while he still kept a sharp eye on the Winstanley house near by.

"He's inside," said Richardson. "Nobody has come out of the house since I telephoned."

"The windows are all dark," said Welby.

"It was lighted up like a Christmas tree until after Goroshovel went in," said Richardson. "Then all the lights went out."

"They are holding their rites in a back room," said Lee grimly.

The three men started back through Sixty-seventh Street. As they came abreast of the Winstanley house, Richardson said:

"The windows have all been closed. They were open when I came."

"Closed to prevent a man's screams from being heard," muttered Lee.

The big house was designed in the bastard French Renaissance style so popular with the rich forty years ago. At the street level there was an ornate carved stone entrance in the middle. The front door was a formidable steel grill lined inside with plate glass. At either side was a pair of windows, protected by wrought-iron bars, bulging out below and ending in a row of spikes at the top.

"I am hoping," said Lee, "that with the protection of those bars, they don't bother to lock the windows."

Welby was keeping a sharp watch up and down the street. Shoving his arm between the bars, Lee tried the first window. It was immovable. The second sash, however, went up easily. The room inside, as far as they could tell, was a small reception room, opening off the great central hall.

"It will do," said Lee. "Hand me the newspapers."

The sight of the famous Mr. Mappin preparing to enact the role of an incendiary, appealed to young Richardson's sense of humor, and he chuckled softly. The nervous Welby silenced him.

"Richardson," said Lee calmly, "walk at a moderate pace to Madison Avenue. You will find a fire-alarm box on the southwest corner. Turn in an alarm as soon as you get there. The benzine won't burn long and I shan't start it until I hear the alarm go off. After you have pulled the hook, you should quietly lose yourself. When the engines arrive, you can come back to see the fun."

Richardson started away. While Welby kept watch, Lee was quietly crumpling up the newspapers and dropping them through the open window until there must have been a good pile inside. He then waited until he heard the whir of the fire alarm from Madison Avenue. It sounded loud in the stillness. Lee deliberately unscrewed the top of the Mason jar and, thrusting his arm between the bars, emptied the contents on the newspapers. He struck a match, dropped it inside, pulled down the window. Instantly the room became lurid with flame. Lee and Welby started without hurry toward Fifth Avenue.

The New York fire department is one of the most efficient in the world. In those blocks which lie immediately east of Central Park live some of the richest of the city's inhabitants, and the department is therefore especially on the *qui vive* for an alarm from that quarter. Already, as the two men were turning the corner of Fifth Avenue, they heard the first distant hoots as the apparatus charged out of its stations. They walked a little way up the Avenue and returned. When they reached the corner again, the first pumper was roaring through Sixty-seventh Street from the east; others could be heard approaching from uptown and down. People arrived running with the fire trucks; another stream poured in from

Fifth Avenue. Almost instantly, the quiet street was a bedlam of panting engines and pushing, loud talking people.

Policemen came with the firemen and the people were thrust back. Lee and Welby in the first rank were interested spectators. A battalion chief leaped out of his red car and, when he saw the barred windows and the steel door, starting cursing furiously.

"God damn! that's a hell of a place to get into! Is there anybody inside?"

A policeman answered him. "It's occupied for the summer."

A name ran like wildfire among the spectators. "Count Deduchin . . . Count Deduchin." The Count had been well publicized in the newspapers.

A policeman stood at the entrance keeping his thumb pressed on the bell. Firemen were dragging a hose. As soon as it was connected, they thrust the nozzle between the bars and through the glass into the blazing room. Meanwhile the chief was yelling for a short ladder. Planted on the doorstep, it reached to the windows of the salon above. A fireman ran up with an axe. As the glass crashed in, Lee remarked to Welby:

"That ought to break up the Count's party."

The chief and others of his men ran up the ladder and disappeared into the salon. A moment later the lights in the entrance hall came on, the steel grill swung in, and the firemen could be seen in the hall; also some of Count Deduchin's servants running around crazily. More firemen pushed in from the street. As soon as the water was turned on the blazing room was blacked out.

Suddenly the gaunt, wild-looking figure of Goroshovel came out of the house. He had no hat and his thin hair was sticking out in all directions. Hot as it was, his coat collar was turned up. At the door a policeman asked him a question. Apparently his answer was satisfactory; his wildness appeared natural during an alarm. He was allowed to pass out. He turned east on the sidewalk.

"It worked!" said Lee laconically to Welby.

"You're a wonder!" said Welby admiringly.

"You stay here," said Lee, "and report to me later what happens."

Lee followed Goroshovel on the other side of the street. When he got beyond the crowd and the confusion he crossed over and, coming up behind the Russian, touched his elbow.

"Why, Mr. Goroshovel!" he said in a voice of surprise.

At Lee's touch the man gasped and broke into a frantic run without even a glance behind. Lee pursued him, saying:

"Wait, Mr. Goroshovel, wait! It's me, Lee Mappin."

As they passed under a light, Goroshovel turned a ghastly face, recognized Lee, and stopped running. He was gasping for breath, unable to speak.

"What has happened?" asked Lee.

"I don't know," said Goroshovel hoarsely. "A lot of firemen broke in. I escaped." He suddenly clasped his hands to his head. "Oh God! Oh God!" he groaned. "What is to become of me!"

"You are ill," said Lee. "Come and have a drink."

Goroshovel shook his head. "I can't be seen anywhere. I have no shirt!"

"No shirt?"

"They tore it off me," he moaned. "When the firemen broke in all I could find was my jacket."

"Then you shall come home with me," said Lee soothingly. "I have a servant about your size who will lend you whatever you need."

Goroshovel seemed scarcely to hear him. "I'm lost! I'm lost!" he was moaning.

Lee glanced over his shoulder to make sure that none of Deduchin's men were following them. Everybody in the street was still moving the other way. At the Madison Avenue corner Lee hailed a taxi and bundled Goroshovel in ahead of him. Goroshovel fell back in his corner, moaning inarticulately and shivering. Lee made no attempt to question him.

CHAPTER FOURTEEN

HALF AN HOUR LATER, the two were facing each other across Lee's dining table. Goroshovel, thanks to Jermyn, was completely dressed; his thin hair was combed and he had stopped shaking. A bottle of whisky stood before him. At short intervals he filled a jigger and downed it neat. He had already drunk more than half a pint, but it had had no effect beyond steadying him. As he regained his grip, he became tight-lipped and refused to answer questions.

"You have been kind to me, Mr. Mappin," he said defiantly, "but of course that was only because it suited your purpose. What happened tonight is my business and I shall not tell you—nor anybody else. Nobody can make me tell."

"You don't have to tell me what happened tonight," said Lee. "It was written in your face when you came out of that house."

Goroshovel shivered at the recollection and poured himself another drink.

"What are you going to do when you leave here?" asked Lee.

"I'm not talking," said Goroshovel. "I suppose I'm in your power and you can turn me over to the police if you want. But I shan't talk."

"I don't want any hand in turning you over to the police," said Lee.

Goroshovel, after studying him searchingly, turned away his puzzled eyes. "I don't understand what your game is," he said. "But that's your affair."

Lee smiled. "At the moment I am merely a psychologist and you are an interesting subject. I cannot understand how it is that a misbegotten wretch like Deduchin can still command your loyalty."

Goroshovel said quickly: "It is not for the Count that I risk my life."

"Okay," said Lee. "We won't go into that. When you leave here you can't go home because Deduchin has your address and his men will be waiting for you. I assume that the first thing they did to-night was to search you and take everything of value. What are you going to do, then?"

Goroshovel lowered his head to hide the despair in his eyes. "Perhaps you would lend me a few dollars for the sake of human-ity," he muttered.

"No," said Lee coolly. "As you have pointed out, you have your purpose and I have mine. If I did give you money it wouldn't do you any good. Your occupation is gone. Deduchin is certain to run you down."

"He must be mad!" Goroshovel broke out, forgetting himself. "I have not been a traitor. I went there tonight to . . ." He suddenly shut up.

"You went there tonight to prove your loyalty," Lee put in quietly.

Goroshovel looked at him in surprise. "I guess you know a lot more than you let on," he said.

Lee disregarded this. "I won't give you money," he said, "but I can direct you to a safe hiding-place."

A crazy eagerness sprang up in the supposed Russian's eyes.

"You are accused of the murder of Lenkoran," said Lee.

"I had no hand in it," Goroshovel said quickly.

"If that is true, then you have nothing to fear from the police. I recommend that you surrender yourself to them. You'd be safe there from Deduchin."

Goroshovel, grasping his chin, stared ahead of him, considering.

"So far as I can see, you have no choice in the matter," Lee went on carelessly. "Nobody can make you talk, you say; you won't be-tray any secrets. And when the truth comes out about Lenkoran's death, Deduchin will see that he has misjudged you."

"But if I was cleared of Lenkoran's murder I wouldn't go free," muttered Goroshovel. "The Federal dicks would be waiting for me at the door of the city prison."

"Sure they would," said Lee coolly. "But you wouldn't die with the name of a traitor. You'd be a hero and a martyr to your own people."

After a while Goroshovel said heavily: "All right. I don't know what your game is. I do this, not because you advise it, but because I don't see anything else I can do."

They left the apartment.

First Avenue was empty at the moment, all the upstairs windows open and dark. As they stood on the corner waiting for a cab, Goroshovel, with a sidelong look at Lee, said:

"You've got money on you. What's to prevent me from throttling you and dragging your body into the doorway behind us."

"I also have a gun in my side pocket," said Lee, "and my hand is on it now."

Goroshovel said no more.

A taxicab came along. They entered it and Lee asked to be driven to the corner of Astor Place and Lafayette Street.

As they sped downtown, Lee said: "Are you willing to tell me what happened the night Lenkoran was killed? That, I take it, would not be betraying any of your friends."

"No," said Goroshovel, "because I don't know who killed him. That's the truth, believe it or not. . . . After you left the Prince's apartment that night, he got restless and absent-minded. He seemed to be listening for something. He was drinking heavily, but it didn't affect him. In the end he left the room without a word of explanation. He closed the door after him. That is the way he always was; abrupt and secretive."

"What happened then?"

"After a little, five or ten minutes maybe, Scharipov and I went out of the living room together. We left Tashla sitting in a chair by a window smoking a cigar."

"The window was open?"

"Sure, all the windows were open."

"Go on."

"I turned into the dressing room and toilet, just outside the living room door. You may have noticed it."

"I have noticed it."

"Scharipov went on to get a drink in the bar."

"Can you swear that he went into the bar?"

"No, I couldn't swear to it. He said he was going to the bar. I was already in the dressing room before he opened the door into the foyer."

"Go on."

"I was in the dressing room when I heard the shot."

"From what direction?"

"That I cannot tell you. It was muffled, but my instinct told me it had been fired close by. I was badly scared. I ran out and collided with Tashla in the passage. In the foyer we met Scharipov. All scared, all asking each other what had happened and nobody could answer. We all had the one thought, to get out of the place, and we beat it; that's all I know."

"Your rush to get out of the house without even waiting to see what had happened doesn't sound reasonable to me," commented Lee.

Goroshovel shrugged indifferently. "We all had things to hide. We were in no position to be questioned by the police. You know that quite well, so I'm not telling you anything."

"Well, if you're telling me the truth," said Lee, "it seems as if it couldn't have been Tashla; because you left him in the living room and after the shot you met him coming out of there . . . But wait a minute! Suppose Lenkoran had quietly returned to the living room?"

Goroshovel would not commit himself. He merely shrugged.

"Or it could have been Scharipov," said Lee, studying his face. "You said you came on him in the foyer."

"That's right. But Prince Lenkoran wasn't there."

"The shot might have been fired in the bar."

"It could have been."

"Let's go into this in more detail. How long had you been in the dressing room when you heard the shot?"

"Long enough to do what I went there for."

"Say two minutes."

"About that."

"You ran out and collided with Tashla in the passage. Which of you was the first to enter the foyer?"

"I was."

"And Scharipov was where?"

"On my right, just coming out of the bar. He had his hand on the door.

"How did he look?"

"Scared. We were all scared."

"Could you see into the bar?"

"No. He was pulling the door to."

"Looks like Scharipov," said Lee cheerfully. "Or perhaps your whole story is a tissue of lies and you did it yourself."

"Perhaps I did," said Goroshovel sullenly.

"On the level, who did shoot him?" asked Lee. "You must have a theory."

"The girl," said Goroshovel. "Everybody connected with the case is satisfied of that but you."

As THEY APPROACHED Astor Place, Lee said: "You will get more credit from the police if you represent that you are giving yourself up of your own free will."

"It is of my own free will," said Goroshovel quickly. "Don't alarm yourself, Mr. Mappin. I have good reasons of my own for not saying anything about you."

"Excellent," said Lee. "In that case we should not be seen approaching Police Headquarters together. Do you know how to get there?"

"I do."

"When we get out of the cab, you walk on ahead and I'll follow."

"Aren't you afraid I'll make a break for freedom?" suggested Goroshovel grimly. "My legs are longer than yours."

"Obviously," said Lee, "but where would you go?"

"I don't know. I'm desperate enough to rob the first man I see."

"Go ahead and make a break," said Lee. "I'm an excellent shot."

Goroshovel did not try it. The cab was dismissed at Astor Place. They waited on the corner until it had turned around and set off uptown, then Goroshovel started down Lafayette Street with long strides, Lee toddling along to keep his distance a dozen paces in the rear. At Houston Street they struck through to Mulberry, and Goroshovel ran up the steps to Police Headquarters. From a doorway across the street Lee watched for a while, then returned to Lafayette Street and hailed a cab bound north.

Before he went to bed he put through a long-distance call to Washington.

AT AN EARLY HOUR next morning Inspector Loasby called Lee on the telephone. "Goroshovel dropped in at Headquarters at three o'clock this morning and gave himself up," he announced in a voice full of glee.

"Really!" said Lee.

"Yes, sir. My men were pushing him so close, he saw that it was hopeless and surrendered. . . . In this case," the Inspector added with sly satisfaction, "we were able to pull the trick without your valuable assistance."

"I congratulate you," said Lee blandly. "But surely, if you had the man under surveillance, it would have been only fair to let me know."

"Right," said Loasby; "but things happened so quickly I didn't have an opportunity."

Lee smiled into the transmitter.

Loasby went on: "You must come down and question him at your earliest opportunity, Mr. Mappin. He tells a detailed story of what happened in the Lenkoran flat which strengthens the case against the girl. However, as he seemed to want to be locked up, I obliged him."

"Naturally," said Lee.

A slight note of unsureness crept into the Inspector's gleeful voice. "Here's a funny thing, Mr. Mappin. I have already had a memo from the Commissioner instructing me that Goroshovel must be held and held absolutely incommunicado. This order came from the Mayor who had received it, I'm told, from a very high personage in Washington. What do you suppose that indicates?"

"How should I know?" said Lee innocently. "I suppose it is one of those annoying international complications you spoke of."

"That's what I'm afraid of," said Loasby. "Meanwhile I'm keeping Goroshovel here at Headquarters. There are too many underground channels in the City Prison. I'd like to discuss this with you at your convenience."

"I'll give you a call as soon as I see an opening ahead."

LATER IN THE MORNING Lee made a date to call on Count Deduchin. He found the little man in a frame of mind the reverse of gleeful. The Count wasted no time on comedy today; the secretary was not present, and the moment the door of the salon closed, he opened up on Lee.

"There was hell to pay here last night!"

"What happened?" asked Lee, full of pretended concern.

"I had Goroshovel here . . ."

"Goroshovel!" echoed Lee in an amazed voice. "How did you get him here?"

"He came," said the Count evasively.

"How would he dare present himself to you with such crimes on his conscience?"

"Never mind that now," said the Count impatiently. "He came. It was a bluff, of course. He wanted to recommend himself to me. I suppose he thought that I didn't know what had happened. Well, before I was able to get what I wanted out of him, there was an alarm of fire!" The Count champed his teeth in a paroxysm of rage and brandished his little fists. "Was there ever such a damned unlucky accident! Just at that moment!"

"An alarm of fire!" repeated Lee, registering wonder.

"Just so! Without the slightest warning the firemen came smashing their way into the house like an attacking army. In the confusion that followed, Goroshovel escaped!"

"What a damned unlucky chance, as you said, Count."

"And what's more," continued the Count viciously, "the swine went and gave himself up to the police! He knew that was the only place where he would be safe from my vengeance!"

Lee shook his head sympathetically. "Was there a fire?" he asked.

"Yes. An insignificant blaze in a reception room downstairs. Some passer-by saw it and turned in an alarm. The Fire Marshal said he found partly burned newspapers in the room. It was evidently the work of an insane firebug, he said, who had opened one of the front windows and shoved the papers through the bars. God! just a meaningless accident and it wrecked all my plans!"

"I can't tell you how I feel for you!" said Lee.

"The hell with your sympathy," snarled the Count. "The man is confined at Headquarters, where, I am told, he is held incommunicado. Well, you are hand in glove with the police. You will be admitted to see him. It is up to you to discover where he has hidden his share of the loot."

"I'll do my best," said Lee.

"Do your best? What kind of a way is that to talk? Do your job if you want your fee!"

The Count rose to signify that the interview was at an end. Lee made haste to open the door for him and humbly followed him out. The Count started up the stairs without a look behind him, and Lee went down.

In the entrance hall below, one of the liveried men servants was always in attendance. When Lee appeared on the stairs he started forward to open the street door for him. Toward the front of the hall the handsome, blonde young secretary was standing with his hat in one hand, brief case in the other, gazing all amazed through an open door into the wrecked reception room. As Lee approached, he said:

"What a dreadful thing to happen, sir! They tell me it was the work of a crazy man. Nobody is safe, it seems. And to think it should have happened when I wasn't here!"

This simple remark arrested Lee's attention. He stopped and smiled at the polite young foreigner; his eyeglasses glittered. "So you weren't here?"

"No. Just a little while before it happened, Count Deduchin had sent me on a hurried trip to Philadelphia to obtain some papers that he required. I took the sleeper down and I have just got back."

The servant was standing behind them. Lee stole a look at him out of the corner of his eye. The man's too-indifferent look suggested that he was listening with stretched ears.

"Luckily the fire didn't spread," said Lee.

"I believe the house is fireproof."

"Insured, I suppose?"

"I assume so, but I don't know yet."

By a stroke of good luck, the bell rang at that moment and the servant went to open the door.

"I have never been told your name," said Lee pleasantly.

"Raoul Duplessis."

"French?"

"My father was French."

"I might have known it by your accent."

"I don't have to speak with an accent," said Raoul, smiling. "My mother was an American. The Count prefers it. He thinks it gives style to the establishment."

"I agree," said Lee, smiling back.

Meanwhile the servant was admitting a man at the door. He had come to see about the insurance. The servant in his broken English requested him to be seated in the hall while he sent word to the Count. The servant then disappeared at the back.

"How long have you been working for the Count," asked Lee.

"Three months."

"You are attached to him?"

The young man's face showed no enthusiasm. "He is very liberal," he said earnestly. "This position was a Godsend to me. It's a little lonely, of course, because they always speak their own language among themselves. I offered to learn it, but the Count forbade it. He prefers to speak English with me for practice."

"You have been in this country long?"

"Nearly two years. I escaped from France after the fall of Paris. Very soon I shall be able to take out my first papers."

"Good! Do you ever have any time off?"

"Oh, yes! My hours are uncertain, naturally, because I have to be on hand whenever the Count needs me."

Lee glanced toward the rear of the hall. The servant had not reappeared. "I wish you'd come to see me," he said. "I loved Paris. I should like to have you talk to me about Paris."

The young man flushed with pleasure. "When may I come?" he asked.

"As soon as you like. Today, if you get an hour to yourself; or tomorrow. Have a meal with me if you are free." Lee gave him the address and made him repeat it. "Don't forget that."

"I could never forget such kindness!" said Raoul warmly.

"I would recommend," said Lee with quiet emphasis, "that you do not tell anybody in this house where you are going."

Raoul looked at him in astonishment. Lee let himself out.

CHAPTER FIFTEEN

DURING THE AFTERNOON Welby brought Lee a further report from San Francisco.

AT ELEVEN O'CLOCK this morning San Francisco time, a long-distance call from Cincinnati, O., for Mrs. Crispin was received in Berkeley and my Russian friend was plugged in on it. The conversation was not in Russian, but in Latvian, a language he knows. Here is the translation:

"Hello, Clara?"

"Oh, Sergei! Oh Sergei! Are you well?"

"Perfectly well, I assure you. The only thing that troubles me is that my plans have been upset by this accident and I am prevented from attending to my business."

"Oh, Sergei! how terrible that you should be accused of such a crime!"

"Please don't waste the time in being emotional, Clara."

"Can't I join you, Sergei?"

"Certainly not! It would double the risk!"

"It is so terrible to be alone at such a time!"

"Please, Clara, this call is expensive. Listen carefully. You must remain where you are, to provide me with a means of communicating with my office. I

dare not call Henry [his clerk] direct, for I have reason to believe that the office phone is tapped by the
police. You must bear that in mind and take care
never to say anything to Henry over the phone that
would help the police. Go into San Francisco at once.
Keep away from my office. If the police discover who
you are, we are lost. Go to a hotel and send a note to
Henry by a messenger boy to come to you. Ask him
if he has had any word from the steamship *Arcturus*. If he says no, you are to go into San Francisco
every day to ask him the same question until the ship
is heard from. Each day you should arrange to meet
Henry in a different hotel. Under no circumstances
is Henry to call you up in Berkeley. Let him suppose
that you are still in Sebastopol. I will call you up at
midnight your time tonight from wherever I may be,
to hear what he says. Are you getting all this?"

"Yes, Sergei, yes! I am making notes on the back
of an envelope."

"Attend! When the *Arcturus* arrives. Henry
knows everything that has to be done in relation to
clearing our coffee and so on. You don't have to
trouble yourself about that. But Captain Miller of the
ship will be looking for a private communication
from me of which Henry knows nothing. Mark this
well; Henry is not to be told anything about my private business with Captain Miller. I am writing to
the Captain now and will send it by air mail tomorrow to Mrs. A. B. A. Munson, c/o General Delivery,
San Francisco. Write that name down: Mrs. A. B. A.
Munson."

"I have it, Sergei."

"Call for the letter at the General Post Office day
after tomorrow and hold it until you are able to put
it in the Captain's own hands."

"Will there be any answer, Sergei?"

"Certainly. The Captain will write an answer and deliver it to you sealed."

"What am I to do with it?"

"I will instruct you later. Naturally, I have to keep moving from place to place."

"Couldn't I help you more intelligently if I knew what was in these letters, Sergei?"

"You must be content with my instructions, Clara."

"It is so terrible when you are in danger not to know . . ."

"Please, Clara. This is not the first time I have been in danger."

"But we are growing old now. I no longer have the same courage . . ."

"If your courage fails you, then I will be in danger."

"I'll be brave! I'll be brave! But Sergei, just one little word . . ."

"The three minutes is up, Clara. Expect another call from me at midnight, your time."

So much for the telephone conversation [Linder added.] At the Maritime Exchange I learned that the steamship *Arcturus* from La Guaira, Venezuela, is expected any day now. Her cargo consists mostly of coffee, of which 600 bags are consigned to S. Scharipov. The *Arcturus* belongs to the California-Brazil Line and is regularly employed in the coffee trade. On account of the submarine menace in the Atlantic, she no longer trades to Sao Paulo, her former port, but now picks up a cargo of mountain coffee at La Guaira. Her owners are Finch, Doughty and Co., long-established San Francisco merchants. The present partners, Wilson Finch, John E. Doughty III, and Finch Doughty, are all wealthy men of the highest standing; leaders in all patriotic and

civic affairs, men absolutely above suspicion. Of
Captain Miller, not so much is known, but he is
highly spoken of in maritime circles; has been coming into San Francisco on the *Arcturus* for some
years past. ["Probably nine years," Lee remarked
dryly to Welby.] He is said to be a Norwegian.

Unless something important transpires between
Scharipov and his wife in their talk tonight, I won't
call you again until tomorrow.

Linder.

"Is any action to be taken in regard to this?" asked Welby.

Lee shook his head. "Not at present. Let us wait until we see
Scharipov's letter to the Captain of the ship."

"Our case seems to be coming to a head, Mr. Mappin."

"It better had," said Lee dryly. "Our position is precarious. Next
time you have Linder on the wire, congratulate him from me on a
good piece of work."

ON THAT SAME EVENING, young Raoul Duplessis presented himself at
Lee's apartment with a beaming face. "I hope I have not come too
soon," he said deprecatingly.

"You could not have come at a better time," said Lee. "Tonight
I am eating alone."

"The Count is entertaining ladies at dinner," said Raoul, "and
he said my presence would not be required."

"Obviously," said Lee smiling, "the contrast between him and
you in the company of ladies would be too painful."

Raoul blushed modestly.

There was nothing of the sophisticated, worldly-wise young
Frenchman about this specimen. His fresh color and candid
blue eyes gave him the look of a boy, but he told Lee he was twenty-
three years old. His story was a commonplace one. He was an only
child. His American mother had been dead for some years; his
father, an officer in the French Army, had been killed during the

first onslaught of the Germans. He had been welcomed by his mother's relatives in America, but he was of an independent character and could not rest until he had found a job.

With dinner, Lee gave him some of the wines of his beloved France. Of their talk together, it need only be said that after Lee had satisfied himself that the boy was really as simple and honest as he had appeared, he told him the truth about his job.

Raoul turned pale. "My God! I'll leave at once!"

Lee shook his head. "By staying there now you can serve your adopted country. This man, like others of his gang, is a naturalized American. He has sworn to up hold our flag. Help me to get the evidence that will hang him."

"Hang the Count!" said Raoul in a shocked voice.

"Just the same as any common traitor!" said Lee sternly.

The boy's dismayed face hardened. "Very well," he said. "I'm your man. But as you have seen, I am not allowed to know anything that is going on. I am simply used as a front."

"I know. But your eyes are opened now, and everything that happens will have a new meaning for you . . . This is a post of great danger, Raoul."

"So much the better, Mr. Mappin."

"All right. Don't let your enthusiasm carry you too far, or your usefulness will come to a sudden end. Don't try to pry into the Count's affairs. Continue to do exactly as you have been doing, until you get specific instructions from me."

"I will obey you in everything, sir."

Lee now instructed Welby to remove the watch on the Sixty-seventh Street house. It was much more satisfactory to have an agent within.

Twenty-four hours later, Raoul called Lee at his apartment. "I am speaking from a booth in Grand Central Station," he said. "The Count sent me here to purchase tickets and sleeping accommodations for a party of five to Detroit on the eleven-thirty train tonight."

Lee was taken by surprise. "Detroit!"

"I don't know what his business is, or why it requires so large a party. I can only tell you that he received a letter from Detroit to-day, written in his own language. It excited him very much."

"I can guess what his business is," said Lee, "and I will take pleasure in spiking it."

"What must I do, Mr. Mappin?"

"Go along with him as if nothing was the matter. Like the famous three monkeys, you should make believe to hear no evil, see no evil, speak no evil. Call me up when you get back."

Lee summoned Welby to the apartment and told him what had happened. "Evidently Tashla has already tired of the assembly-line," he said. "He has written to Count Deduchin asking for another assignment."

"How do you want me to handle this?"

"I want to have Tashla or William Brown, as he is known at present, warned."

"But after two of these men have applied to him, Deduchin may begin to doubt that they were treacherous."

"It doesn't matter. Deduchin and Tashla must not be allowed to meet. Can you lay your hands on a Latvian?"

"I could borrow one from the local office of the F.B.I."

"Good! Send him out to Detroit. Let him fly out and he can beat the train by several hours. Let him look up Tashla before he leaves home in the morning. Your man makes out to be a conspirator of Tashla's own variety. He tells Tashla what happened when Goroshovel went to Count Deduchin's house. Let him make out to be the Navy Yard draughtsman. He sold Goroshovel the blueprints. Goroshovel took them to Deduchin, etc., etc. He escaped from the house by an accident. Before giving himself up to the police, he came to the draughtsman's home and asked him to go to Detroit and warn Tashla for God's sake to keep out of Count Deduchin's way; that Deduchin has apparently lost his mind, etc., etc."

"Okay," said Welby. "But how would Goroshovel have learned of Tashla's alias and his address in Detroit?"

"That will have to go by default," said Lee. "Your Latvian can simply say he doesn't know. It doesn't matter particularly, since we are warning Tashla, not setting a trap for him. God help him if he disregards our warning . . . If he decides to beat it away from Detroit, take care that he doesn't slip through your fingers."

"No danger of that," said Welby grinning. "Tashla-Brown and the man who works next to him on the assembly line are now just like that." Welby crossed two fingers. "The Browns have taken him in as a boarder."

Welby went away to start things in motion.

Count Deduchin, accompanied by his secretary, flew back to New York on the following afternoon, leaving the rest of his entourage to follow by train. Raoul Duplessis found an opportunity to advise Lee over the telephone of their arrival.

"I still can't tell you what took him out there, Mr. Mappin. All I know is that the journey was all for nothing. He has come back in a savage rage."

"Well, I won't break my heart over that," said Lee.

"Me, neither," said Raoul chuckling.

Hard on the heels of this message, Lee received another, this in the secretary's official voice. "Would Mr. Mappin be good enough to come to Count Deduchin's house immediately?"

Mr. Mappin would.

"Here's where I have to do some more heavy lying," said Lee when Jermyn brought his hat and gloves.

Jermyn's seamed and leathery countenance was full of concern. "Mr. Mappin, if you'll pardon the liberty, sir, you shouldn't go to that house, sir, you should not! It's too dangerous!"

"I know it," said Lee smiling. "That's why I get such a kick out of it."

"Ah, I am not funning, sir! You should not take such an appalling risk. Mr. Welby thinks the same as I do. What's to be gained by it?"

"I must keep up relations with the Count as long as I can."

"It seems like flying in the face of Providence, sir."

"Anyhow, nothing will happen to me today," said Lee, "because the greater part of the gang is out of town."

At the Deduchin house, Lee was admitted by one of the plum-colored menservants. This accounted for four of these thugs in the Count's employ; perhaps there were more. The little Count was alone in the salon. He had doffed his formal costume, including the high-heeled shoes, corsets, toupee, etc., and was wearing a dazzling cerise dressing gown that Lee eyed admiringly and a silk handkerchief twisted like a turban to hide his baldness. His ugly little face was distorted with rage. The hell with old-world courtesy now.

"What have you got to report?" he demanded as soon as the door closed.

"No good news, sir," said Lee silkily.

"In God's name, what am I paying you for?" cried the Count, glaring.

Lee might have retorted that he hadn't received any pay so far, but he didn't; he merely looked grieved.

"Day after day you bring me the same story!" the Count went on, waving his hands. "No news! No news! Is that how you earned your reputation. To me it's a sham!"

There was a good deal more of this. When he had a chance, Lee said in gentle protest: "I would be more successful if I enjoyed your confidence, sir. How can I produce results when I am kept in the dark?"

"What do you mean?" demanded the Count.

"When Goroshovel came to see you I was told nothing."

"I suppose you could have prevented the fire," sneered the Count.

Lee rubbed his lip. "Hardly that, sir. But I could have suggested a much safer place than your own house for interviewing Goroshovel."

The Count, having no answer for this, walked away to the window, cursing in impotent rage.

"And today," Lee continued dryly, "you made a trip to Detroit without telling me. I suppose you were on the track of Tashla."

The Count whirled around. "How do you know I went to Detroit?"

"One of my men happened to be on the same plane."

"How did you know Tashla was in Detroit? And why didn't you tell me?"

"I was only waiting until I had made sure. There are so many William Browns! One of my agents traced Tashla from Cleveland to Detroit. There he lost him for a while. Only this morning he learned that there was a William Brown employed at the Willow Run plant. When he got there, he learned that Brown or Tashla had not come to work today. When he proceeded to the home address they gave him, the bird had flown for parts unknown."

The Count broke into further lurid cursing.

"How did you learn that he was in Detroit?" Lee asked politely.

"He wrote to me. Tried to pull the same stuff as Goroshovel. Wanted to resume his work for Russian relief and so on. Thought I didn't know how he had betrayed us!"

"After writing to you like that, what do you suppose led him to beat it so suddenly?"

"How the hell do I know—unless your agent tipped him off?"

"That's impossible," said Lee calmly. "By the time my agent located him he was gone! . . . Isn't it possible," Lee went on wickedly, "that Goroshovel might have found the means of warning Tashla of the treatment he might expect at your hands?"

The Count looked at Lee, livid and speechless with rage. Lee bore it with an expression of innocent bewilderment behind his gleaming glasses. The Count started pacing back and forth across the big room. When he was able to speak, he barked:

"What have you done about Goroshovel?"

"I have not been permitted to see him, sir. It appears that he is being held strictly incommunicado upon orders from Washington."

This touched the Count in a vulnerable spot. He stopped pacing. "Did they tell you why?"

"Washington gave no reason for it."

The Count waved his hand in an attempt to recover himself. "This is the work of the Russian Government, do doubt!"

"No doubt," agreed Lee.

After chewing on this unpalatable piece of information for a while, the Count said: "Are you doing anything about Scharipov?"

"Yes, sir. Acting on the tip you gave me, I have kept his wife under surveillance for several days. She has had several conversations with her husband by long-distance."

"Then why haven't you nabbed him?" cried the Count excitedly.

"He is keeping on the move. Each call originates in a different city."

"Can't you arrange to listen in on their conversations?"

"No, sir. Not without calling on the aid of the police, and that, I understood, was not your wish . . . Their talks apparently have to do with Scharipov's coffee business. Each day after she has talked with her husband, Mrs. Crispin or Scharipov goes in to San Francisco to meet his clerk."

"Well, what *are* you planning to do?"

"Just as soon as Mrs. Scharipov goes to meet her husband, we'll have him!"

After mulling this over for a moment, Count Deduchin said rudely: "That's all now. You can go."

Lee bowed and went out softly. When he got the door closed, he turned and sent an eloquent look through it.

Five minutes later, as he entered his own place, he said: "Quick, Jermyn! a double Scotch and soda to take a foul taste out of my mouth!"

"Yes, sir! Directly, sir! Mr. Welby is waiting in the living room."

SCHARIPOV'S LETTER addressed to the mythical Mrs. Munson arrived in the San Francisco post office at noon that day, and was handed to Lee's man Linder. Inside the envelope was another sealed envelope addressed to Captain Miller. Linder unstuck both envelopes, copied the contents of the letter and sealed all up again. The letter was then sent to the General Delivery division, and Linder called up Welby in New York. The letter was in English.

Lee, while he sipped his highball, read and reread the contents, weighing every word in the effort to decide if Scharipov was lying to his associate, and if so, where he was lying.

The letter:

> Dear Captain:
> I have to report a terrible disaster. While you were
> at sea, our great Director was shot and killed in his

New York apartment. A woman who calls herself Jocelyn D'Arcy is charged with the crime. I know nothing about her antecedents. She appears to be just another of the pretty women that the P. was continually taking up with and dropping again. Nothing has come out that suggests she was in the pay of our enemies. It seems to be just a common crime of passion that has robbed us of this great man.

I was in the apartment at the time, along with two of our associates, Goroshovel and Tashla, having been honored with an invitation to dinner by our Director. The shooting took place in another room and I did not see it. We three had to get out of the place in a hurry to avoid the police; consequently, all of us are now suspected of having had a hand in the murder. As far as it concerns me, the suspicion is ridiculous. While I did not have a personal affection for the P., I recognized his great services to our Cause. I am very reluctant to believe that either of our associates could be guilty, but the truth must be faced; *either one of them could have done it.* The P. as you know was a hard and overbearing man. I, myself, have had to submit to his rages, but I bore myself at such times with quiet dignity. It is possible that something the P. said in anger may have rankled in the breast of one of our associates, and that he struck blindly to avenge a fancied insult. It is all very sad.

I and the other two are in hiding and all our affairs are interrupted. But it may turn out that the suspicion of murder directed against us is not so great a misfortune as at first appears. It has blinded the New York police to our real activities. In all the columns of sensational stuff published in connection with the P.'s murder, there has not been a word to suggest our undercover work. We are still in a position to carry on our operations—as well as we can operate without the guidance of our great Director.

We have nothing to fear from the New York City police, but there is an individual, Amos Lee Mappin by name, who the P. felt was dangerous to us. I have met this Mappin. He is an insignificant little fellow who affects to look as mild as milk, as innocent as a three-year-old child. [Lee laughed heartily at this point.] He is a writer and a so-called authority on crime. Something that happened gave the P. reason to believe that Mappin has been employed by the Federal Government to watch us. The P. was confident of his ability to outwit him, but we who remain have not the same bold and astute character, and we should beware of this little man as of the devil. Mappin is now talking a lot in the newspapers of his love for our dead Director, and his determination to avenge his murder. Such talk does not deceive me.

The P. is succeeded as Director of our work in America by Count Deduchin of Philadelphia. I do not know if you are acquainted with this Count. I am, and I am sorry to tell you (in strict confidence) that he is far from being the man his predecessor was. I am terrified that all our work may come to ruin through his folly, particularly the complicated and delicate operation in which you and I are engaged. This is no work for a fool. I have not tried to communicate with Count D. The fact that I am in hiding gives me a good excuse to keep away from him. I do not know how he stands as regards our project. Our late Leader, I am pretty certain, told him nothing about it. Nor do I know if the Count is in communication with Overseas. The Prince has had his method of communication for some years. He wouldn't confide it in the Count unless he was forced to. *I am the only other person who knows the secret!* It would be extremely difficult to establish a new means of communication now that the Americans are fully aroused. What I am hoping is that you and I may accomplish this heroic feat without bringing the Count into it, so that all the credit may be ours.

It is true that the Count now holds the money bags; however, a large part of the bribes has already been paid, and after it is all over we can laugh at those who expect further pay. They are traitors to their own; they have no come back. The sale of the coffee you are bringing me will furnish the balance of the money we need. Everything else is ready. Diehl will be on his feet when you return to La Guaira. The radio transmitter is operating, and you have the code with which to signal the U-boat. You have only to act boldly, Captain. Remember the maxim of our great Director: There is safety in boldness! When the truth of this exploit is published to the world, you will go down in history forever! And in the day of victory a grateful government will lavishly reward you.

The shortage of shipping increases and you will not be allowed to remain long in San Francisco. We ought to have a talk, but it would be extremely dangerous to show myself in the city where I am so well known. Somewhere near by, perhaps. I will advise you. Should I not be able to see you while your ship is in port, my clerk, who holds a power of attorney from me, will sell the coffee and hand you the cash "to buy more coffee in Venezuela." I will then join you by plane in La Guaira. I have the necessary papers for such a journey. Since Goroshovel has got himself into jail and Tashla is in hiding, they will have to save themselves as best they can. Nothing must be allowed to stand in the way of the Cause!

Destroy this as soon as you have digested the contents. Hand your answer to my wife, who will see that it reaches me. She knows nothing about our affairs, but is loyal to me personally, of course. I must know when you are to sail.

With warmest personal regards,

Sincerely yours,

S. Scharipov.

"With warmest personal regards," Lee murmured aloud. "What creatures of habit men are! He writes exhibiting the blackest treachery and ends it with the phrase, 'With warmest personal regards. Yours sincerely!'"

"Odd the letter should be written in English," suggested Welby.

"Evidently Captain Miller does not speak Latvian."

"He doesn't give us much information about their plans," grumbled Welby.

"On the contrary, I would call his letter illuminating," said Lee. "Notice how well it bears out the first conversation between Lenkoran and Scharipov that you transcribed for me. No wonder we couldn't find Diehl, the purser, in San Francisco. It was in La Guaira that he was taken sick. This letter confirms the fact that it is on the *Arcturus'* next voyage north that the 'project' is to be pulled off. This new information demands a change of strategy from us, Welby."

"Shall you proceed to San Francisco, Mr. Mappin?"

"Yes. We'll take the plane tomorrow afternoon. That will give us time to hear again from Linder tomorrow."

"What will you tell the Count?"

"Nothing," said Lee coolly. "He's already suspicious of me."

"I reckon he's sorry now that he hired you," said Welby.

"Undoubtedly. And he can't fire me because now I know too much."

Welby said gravely: "Other ways of getting rid of you will occur to him, Mr. Mappin."

"I have it in mind . . . Meanwhile, Tashla is to be arrested and turned over to the New York police. I believe, too, that Scharipov should be taken just as soon as we can come up with him. There is too much risk in letting these saboteurs perfect their plans."

CHAPTER SIXTEEN

DURING THE NIGHT and the following morning Welby received additional messages which he immediately transmitted to Lee.

The agent who was posing as a mechanic, and who had become Brown-Tashla's side-kick, told how the Latvian from New York had arrived at their flat in Detroit before they were up in the morning. The agent had not been allowed to overhear the story the Latvian told Tashla, but he could report how effective it was. Tashla, who had an appointment to meet Count Deduchin a few hours later, was thrown into a panic. He and the woman threw their clothes into their bags and prepared to leave town instantly. His "pal" offered to share their lot and the three of them left on a morning train for Baltimore by way of Pittsburgh and Harrisburg. They reached Baltimore in the evening and found beds in a rooming house on North Calvert Street.

Tashla and his friend decided that since they could not satisfactorily explain why they had chucked their jobs at Willow Run so suddenly, it would not be prudent to seek work in any other war plant. A later report described how they had been taken on in one of the big repair garages in Baltimore that was starving for mechanics.

At four o'clock in the morning, Linder had called up from San Francisco to say that the steamship *Arcturus* had been reported and was due to dock in San Francisco at noon, thirty-six hours later. At midnight, Pacific time, Scharipov had called up his wife in Berkeley as usual. This call was from Tucson, Arizona. When she told him of the expected arrival of the *Arcturus*, he said he would proceed further westward at once, and would call her up from some point in the vicinity of San Francisco at three o'clock on the following afternoon.

She was to go into San Francisco in the morning, see his clerk and instruct him to sell the coffee immediately (if he had not already done so), turn the proceeds into cash and hand the cash to Captain Miller with instructions to buy all the coffee he could in Colombia or Venezuela, as he, Scharipov, was expecting a sharp rise in price. She was to remain in the city until the ship docked and hand Captain Miller her husband's letter. As soon as the Captain gave her his answer, she was to return to Berkeley and await further instructions.

"If the ship is delayed," Scharipov had told her, "and I get no answer when I call you at three, I will keep calling at intervals from different points until you get home.

"And shall I see you, Sergei? Shall I see you?" the poor woman kept repeating. "Will you take me with you now?"

"Just as soon as I can arrange it, my girl," he had replied smoothly.

"All goes well," said Lee to Welby upon hearing this.

As Lee was eating his lunch that day, he received a call on the telephone from a police officer who declined to give his name. The officer explained that he was speaking for Miss Jocelyn D'Arcy, who would like to see Mr. Mappin whenever it was convenient. Lee promised to be at Headquarters within an hour.

He telephoned to Inspector Loasby to say that he was starting downtown and that he would like to see the Inspector after he had talked to the prisoner.

Jocelyn, when she was brought to him, greeted him with her usual gay and wicked smile. Somehow she still contrived to look as crisp and smart as if she had dressed for the Colony, instead of a cell at Police Headquarters. There was, however, a strained look about her brilliant eyes and a touch of rouge in her cheeks. As it was not her custom to wear rouge, it looked as if it had been put on to conceal too telltale a pallor.

"How nice of you to come so quickly, duckling!"

"I was coming anyhow this afternoon," said Lee.

"Were you? Then I'm sorry I sent a message. Makes it look too important."

"You are feeling the strain?"

"A little," she said carelessly. There was a tremor in her voice. "I have, as they think, resisted them so long they're turning ugly now. They have changed their tactics. They no longer have me up before the brass buttons every few hours to be questioned. I am not allowed to have any visitors. They have given me two wardresses, one of whom stays in my room all the time—*all the time, duckling!* Ah, how I would enjoy murdering *them!*"

"Damnable!" said Lee.

"They follow different lines," Jocelyn went on; "the day woman makes believe to be my friend. She is always trying to lead me on to talk about the murder in the hope of trapping me. The other woman stays awake all night watching me. Every time I fall asleep she wakes me and asks me if I'm ready to confess."

Lee pressed her hand. "You're a stout girl, Joss!"

She snatched her hand away. "Oh, for God's sake, don't sympathize with me, or you'll have me bellowing like a heifer calf! Nobody can make me cry when they try, but a kind word unlooses the floodgates!" She jumped up and went to the window to hide the rising tears. "I'm that kind of a fool!" she muttered.

"Very well, I'll be stern," said Lee. "Buck up and show me your quality!"

"I'm not at the end of my string!" she said crossly. "And I didn't call you down here to listen to my griping. I have an idea."

"What is it?"

"Lee, if I confessed and had done with it, they'd leave me in peace."

Lee's eyebrows made two little round arches above his glasses. "Confessed!" he exclaimed.

"After all, if Lenkoran was an enemy and a traitor to our country, it wouldn't be such a bad crime."

"Certainly not, but confess to a murder you never committed!"

"After you have brought out the real truth, people would praise me because I lied for my country!"

"Of course, they would, but . . ."

She turned around, showing the old, naughty schoolboy smile. "And oh, Lee! I have thought up a peach of a story to tell them! So romantic and detailed. It provides for everything."

"I'm sure it does but . . ."

"It's the only thing that has kept me going the last few days. Let me tell it to you . . ."

"Some other time when we can relax," said Lee.

Her face fell absurdly. "Ah, you don't approve of my plan!"

"Under other circumstances it would be a brilliant idea, but . . ."

"What's the matter with it?"

"It's not necessary. I aim to get you out of here within the next few days, and a pretended confession would spike it."

"Get me out!" she breathed, with an eagerness that betrayed what she had been through. "How, Lee, how? How can you persuade them to release me?"

"By producing the real criminal."

"You have found him? Who was it?"

"Don't ask me to tell you that. Give me three days, four at the outside, and I will have him here."

"Oh, Lee!"

"Can you stand it for four days more?"

"Four days? Four weeks, if I know that rescue is on the way."

"I'm going away this afternoon," said Lee. "When I come again I hope to bring the order for your release!"

Jocelyn embraced him like a sister. "When I get out you shall take me to lunch at Larue's, duckling! We'll have crême Vichyssoise sunk in a bowl of ice and caviar—or can only Russians eat caviar in wartime?"

"Americans can eat it, too, if they have the price," said Lee.

Upstairs Inspector Loasby greeted Lee with a smile of dubious welcome. Like Count Deduchin, but for quite other reasons, he seemed sorry that he had called in Lee on the Lenkoran case.

"Well, Inspector," said Lee, rubbing his hands in pretended gleefulness, "our troubles are almost at an end!"

"Has she confessed?" demanded Loasby eagerly.

"No, I can't say that."

Loasby pulled a long face. "What did you get out of her?"

"Nothing pertaining to the murder. I might register a protest against the means that have been used to force a confession from her, but I'll omit that if you'll agree to let up on her until I get back."

"It was the District Attorney, not me," said Loasby sullenly. "What's on your mind?"

"I have completed the job you gave me."

"How do you mean?"

"First take down two addresses, said Lee. "You will find Nick Tashla living under the name of William Brown at — North Calvert Street, Baltimore. He is working at the Wallin Motor Company's garage on the Fallsway."

"Is that all? There's no evidence against Tashla."

"Nevertheless, he must be arrested immediately," said Lee in a tone that caused Loasby to look up quickly.

"All right," he said. "What about Scharipov?"

"I have a sure line on him, too. I am flying to San Francisco this afternoon, and I shall need a man from you, according to our agreement, to make the arrest."

Loasby pushed out his lips. "I don't know that I would be justified in going to all that expense just to arrest a witness."

"I'll make you a sporting offer," said Lee. "I'll pay the expenses of your man to San Francisco and return, and the cost of bringing Scharipov East, and I will not ask you to reimburse me unless one of these three, Goroshovel, Tashla or Scharipov, is convicted of the murder of Prince Lenkoran."

"Still harping on the Russians!" grumbled Loasby.

"It is evident," said Lee in a mild voice, that nevertheless conveyed a warning, "that there is more in this case than appears on the surface. I'm sure you don't want to appear to be going against the Federal authorities."

"All right, said Loasby. "I'll assign Detective-Sergeant Boker to accompany you. You know Boker. He worked with you on the Letty Ammon case."

"Surely!" said Lee. "I couldn't ask for a better man. . . . We had better not travel together. Welby and I are taking the direct plane at six o'clock. If Boker goes by way of Washington he'll arrive a couple of hours later. I'll be at the St. Francis under the name of Cephas Watson."

"I have it."

"One thing more, Inspector. You agree to remove the two wardresses from Miss D'Arcy's room, and to leave the girl alone until we see what is in this other line?"

"Ah, you're hipped on that girl," grumbled Loasby. "I still feel that she's as guilty as hell. However, if you insist."

"I do insist."

"Very well. I agree."

On his way uptown, Lee stopped off to view the Lenkoran apartment again. The police were still in charge. They made no objections, of course, to Mr. Mappin's studying the scene of the crime.

DURING THE AFTERNOON, no further message was received from San Francisco except the usual report that "Mrs. Crispin" had met Scharipov's clerk in the lounge of a hotel. In New York, Welby's wife was instructed where and how to relay any additional messages that might come.

Lee's last act before starting for the airport was to call up Count Deduchin's house. He hoped that Raoul Duplessis might answer and thus give him a chance to warn the boy that he was leaving New York. He got a report of no answer, which caused him a certain disquiet. It seemed odd, in the case of a house full of servants. From the airport he tried again with no better success. Young Richardson was instructed to investigate and report.

CHAPTER SEVENTEEN

Toward noon of the following day, Lee and Welby arrived in San Francisco and proceeded to the St. Francis Hotel. Here they were joined in their suite by their agent, Linder, a well-setup young man, blonde as a Viking, with an absolutely dead pan when he was on duty. He said:

"The *Arcturus* has been passed at Quarantine and will dock within an hour. The owners, who are men of influence, have expedited the formalities. There's a big gang of stevedores waiting; they hope to have her ready for sea again by this time tomorrow."

Said Lee: "That suits us very well, eh Welby? We don't want to hang around."

"As I have previously reported," Linder went on, "the owners, Finch, Doughty and Company, are one of the leading shipping houses. They have no suspicion of what their Captain is up to. It's a good setup for the plotters, because the *Arcturus*, as an American ship, arouses no suspicion with the authorities."

"What about Scharipov's coffee?"

"I learned on the Exchange that it has been sold. The money is to be paid to Scharipov's clerk as soon as the coffee is unloaded on the pier."

"Have you learned anything further about Captain Miller?"

"No, sir. He is well thought of, but appears to have no close friends in San Francisco. No family. I judge that he is a very different sort of character from Scharipov; a high-minded man who happens to be on the wrong side in this war."

"All the more dangerous to us on that account," murmured Lee. "What about the crew?"

"Said to be mostly Norwegian, sir. Brought into this service by Captain Miller."

"I doubt if any of them ever saw Norway," said Lee. "I expect you're right. Are you going to see the Captain?"

"Not until after I learn this afternoon how he reacts to Scharipov's letter. . . . What about Mrs. Scharipov or Crispin?"

"Her husband did not call her up last night."

"He was on a westbound train," put in Lee.

"She came into the city this morning and saw Scharipov's clerk at one of the hotels. He gave her a pass from the owners admitting her to the *Arcturus*. I let her go then, as I knew she would be simply killing time until she could get on the pier."

"The pier is well guarded, I take it?"

"Yes, sir. The whole Embarcadero is patrolled by the coast guard as a provision against sabotage. There are two men on fixed post at the entrance to each pier to keep out unauthorized persons. They issue a badge to every person who enters and collect it when he leaves."

"Difficult for Scharipov to board the ship if he wanted to?"

"Almost impossible, I'd say . . . I'll pick up Mrs. Crispin again when she leaves the pier."

"Hardly necessary," said Lee. "She'll go home then and wait for her husband's call . . . How are your relations with the police of San Francisco and Berkeley?"

"Excellent, sir. My credentials smoothed the way everywhere."

"I hope it has not been necessary to take them into your confidence."

"Oh, no, sir. The local police have a wholesome respect for Federal matters."

"And your friend from the Russian consulate?"

"He will be on hand in our room at the hotel in Berkeley at half past two, sir."

"Good! Then we're all set and we'd better separate and meet in Berkeley."

"I have installed a man in my room at the Whitcomb Hotel," said Linder. "He is there at all times and I keep in close touch with him. If you want me, call the Whitcomb extension 5420."

"You have thought of everything," said Lee.

LEE WAS LOOKING OUT of the window of their sitting room. "This is one of my favorite cities," he said to Welby. "It has style! The sun has burned up the fog. Let's relax and take a stroll."

They sauntered around the square and south on Powell to Market, looking at the flower stalls and the show windows, taking note of the characteristics of the passers-by. Lee was delighted with the color in the cheeks of the San Franciscans and the brisk manner in which they stepped out on a cool summer's morning. On Market Street, approaching the Palace Hotel, scene of so many of San Francisco's historic gaieties, Lee said:

"Let's drop in for a snifter."

Turning in at the door of the bar, they had a shock. Count Deduchin and Raoul Duplessis were coming out. Lee had an impression that there were two hulking men with them, who at sight of Lee quietly turned around and faded. Both couple stopped dead in their tracks. But Deduchin was more surprised than Lee. His apelike expression of stupefaction brought a smile to Lee's face.

"Well, here's a surprise!" said Lee.

Deduchin instantly arranged his face in a glad smile. "It's mutual!" said he.

Young Raoul, who was slightly in the rear of his master, turned pink with pleasure and satisfaction.

"What brought you here?" asked Deduchin.

"A tip that Scharipov was on his way."

"Why didn't you let me know?" asked the count reproachfully.

"I had to leave New York in a hurry," said Lee. "I called you up before I left home, and again from the airport, but could get no answer."

"My experience exactly," said the Count laughing. "I called you up twice myself. . . Come, we are blocking the doorway. Let us have a little drink together."

"It must be a brief one," said Lee. "We are due back at our hotel in fifteen minutes."

They turned into the bar, the Count and Raoul in advance. Lee murmured to Welby:

"Here goes for another bout of lying."

Inside, the Count commanded a table in his most royal manner. The two thugs were nowhere visible. The Count, complete with false teeth, corsets and elevated heels, attracted every eye. Some were impressed by his lofty air; others smiled. When they sat down he made Raoul sit opposite Lee, the latter noted. Did he suspect that they might be in secret communication? At the table, Raoul was the subservient secretary, with eyes for none but his master.

"Well, anyhow, our meeting was a stroke of good fortune," the Count said affably. "Now we can work together."

"My good fortune," said Lee.

"What was the nature of the tip you received?" asked the Count.

Lee had to talk fast. "My agent reported that Mrs. Scharipov or Crispin, as she is called, was obviously expecting a visit from her husband."

"What made him think so?"

"Oh, she was purchasing various aids to feminine charm. You know how women are."

"That doesn't seem like very conclusive evidence. Hardly sufficient to bring you across the continent." The Count laughed in his silent, ugly fashion. "Maybe it was for another man."

Said Lee: "My information is that Mrs. Scharipov is a true wife to her worthless husband."

"Ha!" said the Count. "I have yet to find such a woman. . . . Where is she now?"

"She came into San Francisco this morning. My agent is tailing her. He will report on her doings later and I will transmit it to you."

"Good! where are you stopping?"

"At the St. Francis. Under the name of Cephas Watson."

The Count wrote it down. "I'm at the Mark Hopkins. No need, of course, for me to adopt an alias."

When the drinks came, they toasted each other with elaborate courtesy.

"What brought you to the Coast at such short notice?" asked Lee politely.

The Count raised his padded shoulders. He had a trick of holding a shrug in the Continental fashion. "No special reason. I knew I should have to come sooner or later, and I thought I had better make it sooner.

"Of course," said Lee. Presently, after glancing at his watch, he tossed off the balance of his drink. "This is very pleasant, but Welby and I have to beat it."

They rose. "You and Mr. Welby must dine with me tonight at my hotel," said the Count with royal graciousness.

"You are very kind. Unfortunately, I have already accepted an invitation from an old San Francisco friend."

"Ah! too bad! Call me up at the Mark Hopkins as soon as you have news."

"I'll do that, sir." They made their way to the street.

"Couldn't stand it any longer," muttered Lee. "The desire to punch his nasty little face was too strong!"

"Same here," growled Welby.

"Nobody on either side was deceived by the lying," said Lee.

"Sure. You might as well have told him to his face to go to hell, Mr. Mappin."

"I can't do that until I am ready to order his arrest."

"He has changed his tune. Butter wouldn't melt in his mouth today."

"A sure sign he is planning mischief."

"Why did you tell him the name you were registered under?"

"What difference does it make? I like to garnish my lies with bits of the truth when I can safely do so."

After a moment Welby said: "We are being followed, Mr. Mappin."

"I expected as much. We will lead him straight back to our hotel, because that's the easiest place to shake him off. When we are ready to go out again, there are half a dozen exits."

Lee's quiet voice continued as if he were communing with himself: "I wish I knew if Deduchin had succeeded in establishing communications with his headquarters overseas. I believe that he has done so. He has been told about the *Arcturus*. That is the only thing that could have brought him to San Francisco in such haste."

"Scharipov will be disappointed," said Welby.

"If my plans work out, Scharipov will never know that he came," said Lee. "It is important to keep them from meeting . . . If Deduchin comes up with Mrs. Scharipov, it will gum everything. The woman has not been warned against him, you see, and she would naturally greet him as an old friend and fellow-countryman. Luckily, I never told Deduchin that she was living in Berkeley, and she was ordered not to tell Scharipov's clerk where she was. We can only hope for the best." They returned to their suite at the St. Francis. At one o'clock, Detective-Sergeant Boker of the New York police telephoned from the airport to announce his arrival. He was instructed to proceed to Police Headquarters, identify himself, and show his warrant. Later he might have to call on the police for assistance. He was then to go to Berkeley for the same purpose. He was to wait in the main police office at Berkeley until he heard from Lee.

"He's a good fellow," Lee said to Welby when he hung up, "but he mustn't be allowed to learn too much either.

They lunched in their suite. During the meal the telephone rang again and Welby looked at Lee. "Expecting another call?"

Lee shook his head. Welby picked up the instrument with care and listened. He heard an arrogant voice demanding to know if it was Mr. Mappin. Welby softly replaced the instrument.

"Deduchin," he said.

"The hell with him," said Lee.

ARRIVING AT THE HOTEL in Berkeley a few minutes before three, they were taken to the room upstairs where Linder and the young man from the Russian consulate were waiting. The Russian was a stringy, dark-haired fellow with a snub nose and an expression of great good humor. He regarded the proceedings as a lark. Linder said:

"As far as we know, Mrs. Crispin has not come home yet. That is her car standing by the curb across the street. She does not use it for her trips into San Francisco."

The Russian, producing a pack of cards, suggested a game of "biritch" while they waited. It turned out to be of the same family as bridge. The table was arranged in such a fashion that Linder commanded the entrance to the apartment house across the street while they played.

After several hands had been dealt, Linder said suddenly, "Here she is!" And immediately afterwards: "Somebody is bringing her home."

Welby glanced out of the window and cried out: "Look, Mr. Mappin!"

A black Packard limousine of an old model, evidently a hired car, had drawn up in front of the apartment house opposite. A handsome, matronly woman in black was crossing from car to entrance door, followed by the dandified figure of Count Deduchin. Both were smiling. Deduchin's devilish grin promised no good.

"Damnation!" muttered Lee.

Through the window of the car they glimpsed the arm of another man inside. The roof hid his face from them. The car waited.

"Welby," said Lee, "go downstairs and take a gander without showing yourself. If the young Frenchman is in the car we must find a means of warning him."

Welby went out. In five minutes he returned, saying:

"Raoul is not with them, but only two of Deduchin's plug-uglies."

"Find a telephone," said Lee. "Call up Deduchin's suite at the Mark Hopkins. If Raoul answers, tell him he is in danger. Tell him to go to Linder's room at the Whitcomb and wait there for us."

They waited in suspense for a summons from the telephone in the room.

Welby returned the second time with a shake of his head. "The Mark Hopkins Hotel reports no answer from Count Deduchin's suite."

Again they settled themselves to wait for Mrs. Scharipov's telephone call.

"It's half past three now," said the young man from the consulate; "Scharipov must have called before she got home. It may be an hour before he calls again. Let's continue our game."

They seated themselves at the table and the cards were dealt around. But only the Russian could give full attention to his hand. The others kept glancing at their watches and looking out of the window to see if the car was still waiting. The minutes passed with leaden slowness. When, finally, the telephone sounded a shrill peal, all four jumped up and flung down their hands.

The Russian picked up the instrument and, after listening for a moment, smiled widely and nodded to the others as much as to say: This is it! He held the instrument by the transmitting end, covering it with his fingers, and drawing pencil and paper toward him, started to write rapidly in shorthand.

Linder stood looking out of the window; Welby shuffled the cards idly; Lee paced back and forth with his hands clasped behind him. The telephone conversation ran to some length, and it did not make the suspense any easier to bear to see how the Russian's expressive face was registering keen interest, excitement and amusement as he listened. When he hung up, he let out a shout of laughter and cried: "Hot stuff!" They bombarded him with questions.

"Does it give us a line on Scharipov?"

"Surely! It's perfect!"

"Where are they going to meet?"

"At Walnut Creek. There is no hurry."

"But if we know where they're going, we ought to get there first."

"We are not going."

"What the hell . . ."

"Scharipov is going to fool Deduchin! What a comedy!"

"How do you mean, fool him?"

"Boys! Boys!" protested Lee, waving his hands. "Give him time to translate it all in order."

While the Russian was still writing, Linder at the window said anxiously: "They're coming out. Are you sure it's okay to let them go?"

"Absolutely okay!" said the Russian. "They will never come up with Scharipov, but we will!"

CHAPTER EIGHTEEN

Translation from the Latvian:

"Clara, are you there?"

"Yes, Sergei, yes! And who do you think is here beside me?"

"There beside you? For God's sake, what are you talking about?"

"It's Count Deduchin!"

[Long pause, the translator wrote here.]

"Sergei, are you there? Are you there?"

"I'm here."

"Oh! I thought you had been cut off."

"What is Count Deduchin doing in San Francisco?"

"He came on our account, Sergei. Such kindness! Such great friendliness! He read in the paper about the terrible trouble you were in and he flew all the way across the continent to see if he could help. He was sure I would know where you were. At first he went to Sebastopol, but of course they told him there that I was away visiting. He then went to your office to ask for me. Henry told him he didn't know where I was stopping but that we met sometimes to talk business and that he could give me a message. So the Count told Henry his name and his hotel and

Henry told me. And was I delighted! It was like a little miracle to have an old friend and a fellow-countryman turning up at such a moment! I went to his hotel immediately. We lunched together. What a happy meeting! I told him that I expected you to call me at three, so he brought me over to Berkeley in his car and here he is!"

[Another pause, the translator wrote.]

"Are you there, Sergei?"

"I'm here."

"Isn't it wonderful, Sergei?"

"Perfectly wonderful!" [This sounded pretty sour: Translator.]

"He wants to speak to you, Sergei."

"Just a moment. Have you got my letter from the Captain?"

"Yes, Sergei."

"Did you tell him anything about that?"

"No, Sergei."

"Good! *Don't tell him!* . . . Put him on the wire now. I will want to speak to you again afterwards."

"Yes, Sergei."

"Hello, Sergei?" [A new voice: Translator.]

"Count Deduchin! What a surprise and what a pleasure."

"I say the same, Sergei."

"How good it is to hear your voice again!"

"My poor fellow! I couldn't rest until I learned how it was with you!"

"How extraordinarily kind of Your Honor to take so much trouble on account of me!"

"You are my friend, Sergei. And not only that. You are extremely valuable to the cause we are both fighting for. How is it with you?"

"Not too good, Your Honor. It is humiliating to be hunted like an animal. It makes me burn with indignation that I should be suspected of the murder of one of my best friends. You know better than anybody, how attached I was to our late Director."

"I know, Sergei! I know!"

"There is not a shred of evidence against me. Yet what could I do but hide? I dared not let myself be arrested. For even though I was triumphantly cleared of the charge of murder, the risk was too great that our undercover work would be exposed to the enemy. Our work, of course, comes first always!"

"You did exactly right, Sergei. But what are you going to do now? What are your plans? We must have a meeting in order to discuss these matters."

"Certainly, we must have a meeting, Your Honor. My pursuers are following me close and there is a considerable risk in it for me, but I cannot deny myself that pleasure."

"What do you propose, Sergei? Where are you now?"

"I am speaking from the town of Martinez, about an hour's drive from Berkeley. I dare not wait for you here, but I will proceed cross-country to Walnut Creek, which is about the same distance from you. Meet me there at the Colonial Inn in an hour's time."

"We'll be there, Sergei."

"You understand, Your Honor, if I find I am followed, I shall have to take the time to shake off my pursuers. I may have to keep you waiting a while."

"Naturally, Sergei. We'll wait at the hotel until we see you, or get a message from you appointing another meeting place."

"I thank Your Honor. Let me speak to my wife, please, before the connection is broken. I want to give her directions how to reach Walnut Creek."

"We have road maps, Sergei."

"Surely. But there are certain precautions against discovery that must be taken."

"Here she is."

"Hello, Sergei?" [The woman's voice: Translator.]

"Listen carefully, Clara. Hold the receiver tight against your ear. Betray no surprise. Speak guardedly. There are reasons why I do not wish to see the Count. I will explain to you when we meet."

"Yes, Sergei."

"I shall not come to Walnut Creek. Keep him waiting there as long as you can."

"Yes, Sergei."

"Put the Captain's letter to me under the pillow of your bed."

"Yes, Sergei."

"Is the street door of your apartment house open at all times?"

"Yes, Sergei."

"Is there a mat outside the door of your apartment?"

"Yes, Sergei."

"Very well. Let the Count precede you downstairs when you leave and slip the key under the mat unseen by him."

"Yes, Sergei."

"I'll call you again late tonight. Should the Count still be with you, when you answer the phone make out that it is a wrong number call and hang up again."

"Yes, Sergei."

"Now repeat after me: Very well, in an hour then. Good-bye Sergei; and hang up."

"Very well, in an hour then. Good-bye, Sergei."

When this was read aloud, the four men in the room laughed and looked at each other in some wonder.

"What a cinch!" murmured Welby. "Providence is working on our side today!"

"Good comedy!" said Lee, "with a grim edge to it. I venture to say that little Count Deduchin is already choking on his own bile. They don't trust each other, and the Count is smart enough to suspect he is being led on a wild-goose chase."

"Let him choke!" said Welby.

Linder, at the window, said: "The coast is clear. Shall we go across the road and retrieve the letter?"

"Welby and I will go," said Lee. "Too many of us would attract attention."

"You will need me to translate the letter," said the Russian.

"This letter will be in English."

"Shouldn't we all go over, one at a time," the young man suggested eagerly, "and wait in the apartment until Scharipov pops in on us? It would be such fun to see his face!"

"Sorry I can't give you that treat," said Lee. "Scharipov is not to know that he is being apprehended for treason. Murder is the charge. The police will take care of him and I shall not appear in it at all."

Lee and Welby went downstairs, stopped in the corner drugstore to buy a tube of library paste, and proceeded to the apartment house. It was a small, walk-up house with four apartments to a floor. At the top of the first flight, under the mat of the right-hand door, they found the key as they expected and walked in. The rooms exhibited the deadly sameness of the typical furnished suite: living room, bedroom, bath and kitchenette. Everything was perfectly clean and tidy; there were no personal belongings on view.

Lee walked into the bedroom, pulled down the peach-colored bedspread, and slipped his hand under the pillow. He drew it forth with the letter.

"Light one of the burners and put on the kettle with a little water. I want to steam this open."

"Why don't we take it with us?" asked Welby.

"For the same reason that I gave before. Nobody is to know as yet that we possess evidence of treason." When the letter was opened, Lee read:

Dear Mr. Scharipov,

I have carefully read your letter. I hope we will be
able to meet while my ship is in port, but should that
be impossible, make your mind easy. If the money
is put in my hands before sailing, I swear to you that
I will carry through our great enterprise on my next
northward voyage. I have received a message that
purser Diehl is recovering.

At the same time it would be well for us to talk
things over. You are a cleverer man than I am. I must
sail as soon as my cargo is stowed. That will be about
noon tomorrow. There is no possibility of postponing
it. As you would have difficulty in getting aboard the
ship on account of the pier guards, tonight I shall take
a room at the Stewart Hotel in the city, in the hope that
you may be able to come to me there. I will register
under my own name and be waiting for you in the lobby
until very late. Come to me at any time, or, if you feel
that it is too dangerous, telephone. But if I do not hear
from you I will expect to see you in La Guaira.

Mr. Scharipov, in case I do not see you here, there
is something I want to say to you, and I hope you
will not take it amiss, because it is offered in friendship. I think you wrong yourself in going against
Count Deduchin. I do not know the man, but whatever
his personal character, he has been set over us by those
whose will we dare not question. We must serve him
or risk the imputation of disloyalty to the cause
which is dearer to us than life itself. What is fame to
me, when the chances of my surviving are about one
to a thousand? So I beg of you, Mr. Scharipov, that
you establish relations with Count Deduchin during
the few days that remain, that we may be all working in harmony when the great moment arrives.

                              Sincerely yours,
                              Arnaud Miller.

When he heard this, Welby exclaimed: "It's like taking candy from a child! All we have to do is to go into the Stewart tonight and nab him!"

Lee slowly shook his head.

"What! you're going to let him sail?"

"I must."

"You have evidence enough to hang him!"

"Perhaps. But the conversations we have overheard and the letters we have intercepted are not sufficiently explicit. We don't yet know what they're planning to do. We know it's dangerous, that's all. Unless we expose their plot completely we run the risk of having other traitors carry it through when the first lot is arrested."

"You are right," said Welby.

Lee copied the letter on a page of his notebook and Welby attested it. The original was then returned to the envelope, sealed and replaced under its pillow. Lee looked around to make sure that everything in the place was left exactly as they had found it. They closed the door behind them, slipped the key under the mat, and departed.

The Central Police Station was not far away, and they went there to get in touch with Detective-Sergeant Boker. Boker was waiting. He was a large, quiet man in whom everybody felt confidence at sight. Satisfactory relations had been established with the Berkeley police, and two local officers were detailed to help him make the arrest.

Lee explained that Scharipov would turn up between quarter to five and five.

"I've never seen him," said Boker.

"I'm going to leave Welby with you. Welby has seen him, but Scharipov has never seen Welby, so that won't tell him anything."

Lee went on to explain that he was anxious not to create a local sensation. He suggested that they have a car without any police markings waiting at the door of the apartment house, and that they should conceal themselves in the hall out of sight of the street. Scharipov could then be hustled into the car without attracting too much attention.

It was explained to Lee that the prisoner must be taken to the police station to be booked. He could not be removed from the state unless he was willing to waive extradition.

"There won't be any difficulty about that," said Lee. "He has his own good reasons for wanting to put San Francisco behind him at this moment. He may, however, want his arrest to be known. Can we keep it out of the papers?"

"Certainly," said the local chief, "if it's in the interest of justice."

"He is not to be allowed to see anybody," said Lee; "nor to telephone or send out any messages. If he waives extradition, get him aboard the first plane for New York. You can't make the six o'clock. There's another at nine and one at midnight."

Lee returned to the Hotel alone. He said to the Russian: "Everything has been done now that can be done. You don't have to wait any longer unless you want to."

Naturally the young man wanted to witness the last scene of the afternoon's comedy-drama.

They stationed themselves at the windows to watch. A car drove up across the street; Detective-Sergeant Boker, Welby and two local plain-clothesmen got out and disappeared within the apartment house. On the very spot of 4:45, as if he were keeping an appointment with them, Scharipov appeared on foot across the street. Lee smiled at his notion of a disguise. He had shaved his mustache and, putting off the attire of a conservative banker, had come out á la Hollywood in a loud checked jacket, white pants and saddle shoes. On his head he was sporting a brown straw hat with a snap brim and a white puggree wound around the crown. The neat pince-nez had given place to horn-rimmed spectacles.

"Motion picture director," murmured Lee to his companions.

"And how!" said the young Russian.

Scharipov was nervous. He kept glancing from side to side and continually looked behind him. There was nothing in the quiet side street to alarm him. The standing car was empty. Paying little attention to it, he disappeared within the apartment house.

"Wham!" said the Russian. "What a painful surprise!"

They could hear nothing. In about two minutes, the two plain clothes men appeared, thrusting the pseudo-movie director between them. Scharipov was holding back and vigorously protesting. Welby and Boker followed, Boker carrying the fancy hat. Scharipov was thrust into the waiting car and the others piled after him. A plain-clothes man slid under the wheel, and the car was driven rapidly away. The arrest had attracted no attention whatever.

"Well, that's that," said Lee. "I'm going back to the city. Linder, I'm afraid I'll have to give you the tedious job of watching for the return of Mrs. Scharipov and Deduchin."

"I'm accustomed to watching and waiting, Mr. Mappin."

CHAPTER NINETEEN

Lee's first act upon returning to San Francisco was to proceed to the towering Mark Hopkins Hotel on Nob Hill and inquire at the desk for Count Deduchin. A report came back that there was no answer from the Count's suite. All the members of his party were out. Lee was told that the party consisted of a man secretary and four servants. They occupied a four-bedroom suite on the twentieth floor.

From a doorman at the main entrance, he got a little additional information. After lunch the Count, with a lady and two servants, had gone out in a limousine hired through the hotel. The doorman supplied Lee with the address of the driver. He owned the old Packard, and it was his sole means of support. A little earlier the young French secretary and the other two servants had left the hotel in a private car driven by a chauffeur. This car had called for them; the doorman, naturally, had taken no note of its license number. None of the party had since returned.

Lee then got in touch with the local office of the Federal police and set in motion a quiet search for Raoul Duplessis. With the assistance of the local police, they were to discover if the Count had rented a house, according to his custom. There was to be no publicity. They were asked to pay especial attention to any persons masquerading as White Russians. Such persons might have Americanized their names.

At eight o'clock, as Lee was eating his solitary dinner, Linder called up from Berkeley to report that the Count with Mrs. Crispin and the two servants had just returned to Mrs. Crispin's apartment. The woman was in obvious distress. The car had been dismissed, and they all went in the house and remained there. An order had been received in the hotel for dinner for four to be sent across the street.

As soon as he had finished eating, Lee proceeded to the address of the driver of the black limousine. He lived in the crowded Mission district or, as they say in San Francisco, "south of the slot." In his plain little flat the young man was eating his dinner. His name was Macklin. He appeared to be a decent, honest fellow, but he was reluctant to testify against the Count, and Lee guessed that he had been liberally paid for his afternoon's work, and expected further employment from the same source. That was what Lee wanted to know. Macklin could tell nothing new about the afternoon. He had driven his party to Walnut Creek and waited two hours; he had then driven them back to Berkeley. He couldn't hear anything that his passengers said. When he was paid off, the old guy told him to stay at home until he was summoned by telephone.

"Okay," said Lee. "Take the work he offers you and keep your eyes and your ears open. In the meantime, there is no reason why you should not accept a little tip from me, is there?"

The young man hesitated. "I don't like to give away my customers' business, Mister."

"Let me put it this way. If he's on the square, he has nothing to fear from anybody in this world, has he?"

"Well . . . no."

"And if he's crooked, it's up to every square man to bring him to book."

"I guess that's right, Mister."

Lee held out a ten-dollar bill.

"Okay," said Macklin, pocketing it.

Lee took down his telephone number.

He returned to his hotel. Welby came to him about nine-thirty with a long face. He said:

"Scharipov kicked up a little rumpus at the airport. I'm afraid it will make publicity."

"What sort of a rumpus?" asked Lee.

"He had been demanding permission to write or to telephone his wife and it was refused. Driving to the airport, he was perfectly quiet, but waiting at the gates there, when he got a number of people around him, he suddenly began to shout: "My name is Scharipov! I'm well-known here! I'm being railroaded! I demand my rights as a citizen!" And so on like that. Sergeant Boker showed his badge and hustled him aboard the plane. But there were a hundred people there who will bring the story back to town. There's been a lot in the local papers about the hunt for Scharipov. Luckily it's early yet. I suppose you can keep it out of the morning papers if you want."

Lee shook his head. "If it's out, it's out," he said. "It's just one of those things. Better not try to tamper with the newspapers. This was Scharipov's way of getting a warning to his friend, Captain Miller."

Sure enough, the next morning's newspapers carried the story of Scharipov's arrest. It was an incomplete story, because no one who was connected with the case would talk. As the reporters got it, the New York police had received a tip that Scharipov, the well-known coffee importer, wanted in connection with the death of Prince Lenkoran, was in the habit of visiting a woman in Berkeley named Mrs. Crispin. A detective had been dispatched from New York to effect his arrest, and Scharipov was taken when he tried to sneak into the woman's apartment. All that the Berkeley police had to give out was that the New York detective's warrant was okay and they had helped him make the arrest. Scharipov had signed a waiver of extradition and had been put on the first plane for New York.

Mrs. Crispin was a newcomer in Berkeley, the story continued, and nothing was known about her antecedents. She was called up on the telephone, and a man's voice answered, angrily refusing all information. When reporters were sent to her apartment, they were refused admission. The Berkeley police said there was no charge against the woman. Lee's name was not brought into the story.

"Not that it makes much difference," he said to Welby, "because I cannot hope to play the game with Count Deduchin much longer. However, as long as my name has not been printed, we can continue to lie to each other."

Linder reported from Berkeley that Deduchin and his two servants had remained in Mrs. Crispin's place all night, presumably in the hope that Scharipov would call her up again. Early in the morning, one of the servants had been sent out to buy a newspaper.

Half an hour later, Linder called up again to say that the same black limousine had driven up to the door of the apartment house and that Count Deduchin and his two servants had departed in it.

Lee sent his young friend from the Russian consulate over to Berkeley on an errand of mercy. "That unfortunate woman may be in need of medical assistance," he said. "See that she is taken care of. You will find that she won't talk. Bear in mind that she is guilty of no crime except that of being loyal to her husband. She knows nothing about his plots, consequently there is no object in tormenting her with questions. Her great desire will be to go to New York where she can be near him. If she lacks the money, give it to her, but do not tell her that it comes from me."

Men placed at the Mark Hopkins Hotel to watch for Deduchin presently reported that he and his two servants had returned in the black limousine and disappeared within their suite. Presumably they needed sleep, because nothing further was seen of them. A watch was kept on the telephone, of course. Deduchin made no calls nor received any.

Meanwhile Lee was waiting in vain for news of Raoul's whereabouts. The members of the FBI, always so miraculously efficient and successful, were obliged in this instance to report that there were no clues. A general alarm for Raoul, which had been sent throughout California and the neighboring states, had produced no results. The French boy and Deduchin's other two servants appeared to have disappeared into thin air. The local chief of the FBI wanted to arrest Count Deduchin.

"I am opposed to it," said Lee. "There is nothing to be gained. We have no evidence. He's not going to tell you what he has done with the young man, and unless you find Raoul by your own efforts, you will only have to release the Count again."

The guards were doubled at the pier where the *Arcturus* was discharging and loading freight, and a couple of coastguardmen were placed aboard the ship. When she was ready to sail, she was held up until a final search could be made from stem to stern, and every member of the crew checked. She finally cast off at two o'clock. Lee was assured that no person or persons could possibly have been spirited aboard her. Deduchin had made no attempt to visit the ship but the Captain had come ashore as soon as she docked, and there was a possibility that Deduchin had made contact with him then.

After the ship had sailed out of the Golden Gate, Lee called up the Deduchin suite at the Mark Hopkins. The Count himself answered. Lee said:

"I suppose you have read the newspapers, Count. I seem to have fallen down completely on my job. I'd like to come and express my regrets in person if it's convenient to you."

The Count's voice was overfriendly. "Why, of course, Mr. Mappin! Come right up to my hotel!"

When Lee hung up, Welby said: "Suppose he's carried away by rage and shoots you on sight!"

"Not likely," said Lee. "He's too careful of his own neck. And anyhow I am armed myself."

"Take me with you," pleaded Welby. "Two guns are better than one."

"Very well," said Lee.

They taxied to the Mark Hopkins, standing so boldly on its hill. Since the Count was occupying one of the most expensive suites in that swanky hotel, anybody who asked for him was treated with great respect by the servants. One of Deduchin's so-called Russian servants admitted them to the suite. He said in his broken English:

"Count Deduchin is expecting Mr. Mappin."

They were shown into a big living room with windows commanding glorious prospects of the city, the bay, and the distant mountains. The little Count, formally dressed, was waiting for them. While his pale eyes glittered with rage, his face was wreathed in smiles and his cracked voice was honeysweet. He said, laughing pleasantly:

"Mr. Mappin, I really feel for you; a man of your reputation having to come and confess failure."

Lee lied like a man. "Yes, I do feel badly, Count. The arrest of Scharipov was pulled off without my knowledge. I'm afraid my friend, Inspector Loasby, suspects me of holding back on him. At any rate, he sent this Sergeant Boker out here without telling me. One of the best men on his staff. I seem to have got myself in wrong with everybody."

"Well, forget it! forget it!" said the Count, waving his hand.

Lee affected to be overcome by his generosity. "Really, Count, I never expected you to take it like this. It makes me feel worse than ever!"

"There's no use crying over spilt milk," said the Count. "That's what I always say. After all, I understand the New York police have very little evidence that Scharipov was concerned in the murder. They want him for a witness. They may have to release him soon, and then it will be my turn."

"And will you want me to act for you then?"

The Count smiled oddly. "That will depend on circumstances. As it stands today, I think we had better cry quits. If I want you later, I'll send for you."

"Always at your service, sir."

Nothing was said by either side about recompensing Lee for the time and money he was supposed to have spent in the Count's service.

"When will you be returning to New York?" asked the Count politely.

"Very soon. Tomorrow night, perhaps. As long as I am here I want to take the opportunity to look up a couple of old friends."

"It is the same with me," said the Count. "I, too, shall probably be flying back to New York tomorrow. It would be nice if we could travel together. I would enjoy a long talk with you."

"That would please me very much," said Lee.

"Very well, keep me informed about your arrangements." The Count stood up to let Lee know that the interview was at an end. "Do you know," he said, "this is a very good hotel. I am really surprised by the excellence of the service."

"This room is charming!" said Lee.

"Should you like to see the rest of the suite?"

"I should indeed."

The Count proceeded to lead Lee through. There was a small paneled dining room and four bedrooms, all the windows revealing magnificent views. In one of the bedrooms sat the two hulking servants doing nothing. They sprang to attention at the entrance of their master. The Count went to the trouble of opening every door.

"Each bedroom has its own bath, you see, and such a wealth of closet space! Really admirably arranged."

The Count's object patently was to show Lee that Raoul, living or dead, was not hidden anywhere in the suite. An ugly, apelike smile clung about his lips. Welby, who had not uttered a word since they entered, was inwardly fuming. Lee matched the Count, smile for smile.

They left amidst almost affectionate farewells.

According to reports which reached them later, the Count then sent for his car and spent the rest of the afternoon driving around town. He would know, of course, that he was followed. He was trying to persuade his watchers that he had nothing more important on his mind than sight-seeing. He visited the usual places of interest and stopped here and there to buy souvenirs. It seemed odd that he should carry his two servants around with him.

There is always a hazard in following a car through traffic, and at five-thirty, in the press of the home-going crowd, the Count gave his trailers the slip. An alarm was immediately sent out for the car, but it was not reported. Lee was disappointed; still he supposed that Macklin, the chauffeur, must return home sooner or later and he expected to learn from him where he had driven the

Count. Linder was sent down to Macklin's place in the mission district to wait for the chauffeur.

One hour, two hours, three hours passed. Macklin had not come home and Lee's anxiety continued to grow.

CHAPTER TWENTY

AFTER IT HAD GROWN DARK, a letter bearing a special delivery stamp was brought to the hotel for Lee. It had been posted at the general post-office an hour before. It was addressed in pencil in a round, boyish hand, and Lee's face became grim as he read it.

Dear Mr. Mappin:

Yesterday before lunch Count Deduchin told me that a San Francisco gentleman had lent him his residence and that we would move out there for the rest of our stay here. I was to go on ahead with two of the servants and he would follow later in the day with the others. I suspected nothing. A car supposed to be sent by the gentleman whose house we were to occupy came to the hotel for us. As I am a stranger to this city, I cannot tell you where it took us. It was driven too fast for me to read the street signs. We drove first to the west, then to the south, about five miles I should say, part of the way through an extensive public park. It is a district of very fine houses standing in their own grounds. We drove through a gateway and stopped before a big house of rough gray stone in a florid style of architecture. It is not a new house, but well kept up.

The door was opened by an elderly woman servant. As soon as it closed behind me, I was somehow warned of danger, and I turned to escape, whereupon the two Russians jumped on me and beat me down. The woman stood looking on. I shouted for help but they told me that it was useless. I had heard the car driving away. After I had exhausted myself, they carried me upstairs to a bedroom and handcuffed me by my left wrist to a steampipe running from floor to ceiling. This permits me to sit on a chair or to lie down on the floor and sleep.

The woman brings me my meals. As she seemed less brutal than the men, I have been trying to make friends with her. Yesterday she would not speak to me, but today she softened a little and at last she said she would carry a letter out of the house and post it for me if I would give her my ring. She brought me pencil, paper and envelope with which I am writing this. I have tried to persuade her to take the letter to you, but she says she wouldn't dare remain away so long; that she can only drop the letter in the nearest mailbox. I will give her the money for a special delivery stamp. She tells me that this is the house of Wilmer Warren; it is called Warrenton, and it is on the Argonne Drive.

Help me quickly, Mr. Mappin! I am convinced they mean to kill me! The suspense unnerves me. To die fighting would be glorious. But like this, like a rat in a hole, seems to be more than I can bear.

Raoul.

Welby was reading over Lee's shoulder. "It's a trap!" he said instantly.

"No doubt," said Lee. "The woman told him she'd drop it in the nearest box. As a matter of fact, it was brought into the city and posted. That was to make sure it reached me tonight."

"A trap!" repeated Welby.

"Sure! But you must admit it has odd features. Of course the boy is not a party to it. He writes bravely and breaks out at the end in a cry of pure despair."

"They are using him to entrap you!"

"So it would seem. But I still don't get it. They must know that I'm not going out there without taking an adequate force. How do they expect to deal with that?"

Welby shook his head.

Lee bestirred himself. "Anyhow, such an appeal calls for instant action."

They went to the local FBI headquarters. In this situation, Lee chose to call on them rather than on the city police, because the FBI men were in a position to enforce secrecy, while the city police were pretty closely dogged by the press. In a quarter hour, a force of ten keen and stalwart young men was assembled, including the chief. Some of them were San Franciscans, who knew all about Mr. Wilmer Warren, a highly-respected manufacturer. He was accustomed to close his house for part of every summer and take his family and servants up to Lake Tahoe. They doubted if he was a "friend" of Count Deduchin. More likely that the Count, perhaps with the assistance of San Francisco confederates, had simply commandeered the empty house.

When they were ready to start, Welby made a last plea. "Mr. Mappin, you should not come with us. This is a trap for you. If the young Frenchman is in that house, we can get him out just as well without you."

The chief Federal officer added his voice to Welby's. "Really, sir, there is nothing you can do to help us. You are only exposing yourself unnecessarily to danger."

Lee turned obstinate. "Useless to try to stop me. I got the boy into this trouble."

"Very well," said Welby. "Then my job tonight will be to watch over you."

They set out in two cars. After pursuing separate routes, they came together ten minutes later in a handsome, tree-shaded avenue in the suburbs. The houses that lined it were invisible.

"This is the Argonne Drive," said the Chief.

Drawing up alongside the curb, they left a man in each car, and proceeded on foot. Entering one by one through a pair of handsome gates, they separated in side, taking advantage of every bit of cover. The sky was heavily overclouded, and the reflection of the lights of the city filled the air with a faint, pinkish radiance. Welby, gun in hand, stuck to Lee closer than a brother.

"Your figure would betray you to them even at night," he grumbled.

"It's not my fault if God made me short and tubby," said Lee mildly.

After entering the grounds, they neither saw nor heard more of the FBI men. Stealing around the edge of an open space, they moved cautiously from tree to tree, Welby continually glancing from side to side and behind them. Nothing stirred.

"So nice to have a bodyguard," murmured Lee. "Saves me the trouble of keeping on the alert."

Welby grunted softly.

They came to a stand in the shadow of a clump of bushes at the edge of another open space. Across a stretch of grass rose the mansion. It was a tall house in the old style, imposing in its bulk and making a romantic and forbidding silhouette against the pinkish clouds. Every window was black.

They waited. In the soft glow that pervaded the air, they could see pretty well. They saw the chief mount the front steps with two of his men and pause to ring the bell. So absolute was the stillness, there could even be heard the distant flutter of the bell. Time passed. The bell sounded again. Finally, at a sign from the chief, one of the men raised his arms and they heard the crash of an axe on the wooden door. After half a dozen blows, the door went in. The men disappeared inside. After a moment within the house, lights began to go on.

"Shall we follow them?" suggested Lee.

"Better not," growled Welby. "Inside a house with all its corners and doors, how could I protect you."

"Anybody who tried to shoot me in the middle of the FBI would be courting a speedy end," said Lee.

The words were scarcely off his lips when Welby yelled: "Look out!"

Lee whirled around and saw a man in the act of aiming a gun at him. He had come around the other side of the bushes. At the same instant, his gun flashed and spoke. Welby fired simultaneously. Lee, still in the act of turning around, caught the bullet along the edge of his arm. The man who fired it dropped like a stone in the grass and never moved again.

"Drop!" said Welby. "There may be others!"

Lee, however, drawing his own gun, continued to stand. Welby cautiously explored around the bush. There was nobody else.

The shots brought the FBI men running.

"Are you hurt?" demanded the chief.

"A mere scratch," said Lee.

"There was only one of them," said Welby. "I got him!"

The chief issued crisp orders to his men, who then spread in every direction to intercept possible fugitives. Soon afterward in the distance they heard the cars start their engines.

When a light was thrown in the face of the fallen man, they saw the hole that Welby's bullet had bored in the exact middle of his forehead. He was not a pretty sight. It was one of Deduchin's pretended Russians. There was some money in his pockets but nothing to identify him. As a matter of fact, he never was identified.

Lee was holding his burning arm. The chief, who had a first-aid kit in his pocket, made Lee remove his coat, and after cutting away his shirtsleeves applied a temporary dressing.

"Was there anybody in the house?" asked Lee.

"Not so far as we have gone, sir. There are only two ways out and I left a man at each. If there was anybody inside, he is still inside."

The body was eventually carried into the house. To make a long story short, the house was searched from cellar to garret and there was nobody in it. The gang had taken no care to clean up before leaving, and there were plenty of evidences of their stay and of Raoul's confinement in an upstairs room.

"Poor lad!" murmured Lee. "He will be thinking that his cry for help only got me into trouble!"

One by one, the men came back to report. Nobody had been found inside the grounds, and no suspicious person anywhere in the vicinity. A telephone message had been sent back to town to broadcast a new alarm for the black limousine bearing license plates with such and such a number. The FBI cars had returned.

"If the limousine couldn't be found in the daytime, it won't be found now," grumbled the chief. "They may have a couple of hours start."

Lee stood looking down at the dead man. "Is it possible," he said, "that they sent this man to get me and then deliberately abandoned him to his fate?"

"No doubt they promised to pick him up afterwards," said the chief. "But who knows if they intended to wait for him?"

As they were preparing to leave the house, Lee said: "When this death is reported, it would be of the greatest assistance to me if one of you men would take the responsibility for it. I cannot afford to have Welby detained for an investigation at this juncture."

"I'll take care of that, Mr. Mappin," said the chief. "Neither your name nor Mr. Welby's shall be brought into it."

"Thank you. In a few days it will all be over, and Welby will be glad to come forward."

"Hardly necessary," said the chief. "We are thankful that Mr. Welby was so handy with his gun."

"So am I," said Lee dryly.

It was a glum group of men who returned to the city in the small hours. The FBI's were not accustomed to be balked in this manner. At Headquarters there was no news. The surgeon who served the FBI redressed Lee's wound and lent him a topcoat to hide his bloody sleeve.

As Lee and Welby parted in their suite, Lee said: "Poor lad! Poor lad! I cannot put his vivid young face out of my mind, Welby. There is a single chance . . ."

"What is that, Mr. Mappin?"

Lee shook his head. "Time will tell. I don't want to raise any false hopes."

CHAPTER TWENTY-ONE

LEE SPENT AN UNHAPPY DAY in San Francisco waiting for news of the black limousine and its passengers. The entire resources of the Federal police on the Coast were devoted to the search for the car, and there was nothing that Lee or Welby could do to help. There was no news. Macklin, who drove the car, did not return to his home.

"I'm convinced he was an honest man," said Lee. "I expect they got him."

At the end of the day, feeling that it was useless to wait longer, Lee and Welby took a sleeper plane for New York.

Driving into the city from La Guardia airport next day, Lee said to Welby: "I shan't need you here for the next few days. This would be a good time to search Count Deduchin's fine house on the Main Line."

"I would rather not leave you," said Welby, scowling.

"Ordinarily you wouldn't find anything incriminating," Lee went on; "the Count is much too smart. But as he was called away from home very unexpectedly, and as he has not been able to get back since, there might be something lying around. Take a good man with you, and of course you can obtain what additional help you may need in Philadelphia."

"Okay," said Welby. "Orders are orders. But just the same you shouldn't go around alone. Deduchin may have other thugs on your trail."

"He's no superman," said Lee. "At this moment, I take it, he's fully occupied in saving his own skin. However, just to please you, I'll appoint young Richardson to be my bodyguard until you get back."

In the city, Welby went to look up his man while Lee proceeded to Police Headquarters.

Loasby received him with a deprecating grin. "Well, Mr. Mappin," he said, "seems as if there might be something in your theory about the Lenkoran case after all."

"Yes?" said Lee mildly.

"When Scharipov was arrested in Berkeley, Welby frisked him. He found a gun which he handed to my man. I suppose you know that."

"Yes. I heard it from Welby."

"What you don't know is, that on the day after you left town I made a second search of the Lenkoran apartment, paying special attention to the bar. This time I directed the search myself. In the fancy woodwork behind the bar I found a depression made by a spent bullet, and just underneath, I found the bullet itself inside a pewter beer mug. I can't understand how the first searchers could have been so careless."

"Well?" said Lee.

Loasby shrugged. "Our ballistics expert is prepared to swear that that bullet was fired from the gun taken from Scharipov."

"Good! Then it could not have been fired from Jocelyn D'Arcy's gun."

"Seems not. Judging from the position, looks as if Scharipov had turned in to the bar and found Lenkoran there. And as Lenkoran turned around, he let him have it."

"You can release the girl, then."

"Eventually," said Loasby cautiously.

"Why not now? The evidence against Scharipov is conclusive."

"I don't want to be too hasty, Mr. Mappin."

"Who's in charge of the case at the D. A.'s office?"

"Whittemore."

"A keen young fellow. What does he say?"

"He says the same as me. Don't be in too much of a rush to let the girl go."

"I take it you have Tashla here?"

"Sure. He was brought up from Baltimore the day after you went away."

"Well, why don't we have Tashla and Scharipov up here separately and question them? Ask Assistant District Attorney Whittemore to be present."

"Very well, if you want it that way."

THEY FORMED A TRIUMVIRATE behind Loasby's desk; Lee, the Inspector, and the young Assistant District Attorney. Nick Tashla was brought in between two officers. The meager little dandy, with eyes too large for his face, that still burned with a carnal fire, was full of assurance.

"Hi-ya, Mr. Mappin," he said to Lee.

"You may sit down," said the Inspector.

"Hell! I got nothing to do but sit twenty-four hours a day."

He was invited to tell his story. "Again?" he said.

"Mr. Mappin hasn't heard it."

"What's he got to do with it?" said Tashla impudently. "Is he a cop, too? I thought he was just a gentleman."

Lee rubbed his lip.

"Never mind about that," said the Inspector, frowning. "Keep a civil tongue in your head and let us ask the questions."

"Okay," said Tashla. "You want to know what happened the night Prince Lenkoran was shot. Well, after Mr. Mappin went home, the rest of us sat on. We understood Prince Lenkoran wanted to talk to us . . ."

"About what?" put in Lee.

"Collecting money for Russian relief," said the grinning Tashla.

"Go on."

"But the Prince didn't open the subject. Seemed to have something else on his mind. We didn't like to ask him questions, and we couldn't leave neither. So we just sat there talking about one thing and another. The Prince said if we wanted a drink, go help ourselves at the bar, but nobody went. In the end, he got up and left the room. He didn't say anything and we didn't know exactly what to do. After a bit Scharipov said: 'Well, I'm for a drink' . . ."

"Wait a minute," said Whittemore. "This is important. How long was it after the Prince went out that Scharipov followed him?"

"That's hard to say," answered Tashla. "Seemed a long time to us, just sitting there twiddling our thumbs . . . maybe ten, fifteen minutes."

"Go on."

"Well, Goroshovel, he said he didn't want a drink, but he went out with Scharipov. He only went as far as the dressing room that opened off the passage. Me, I didn't want a drink neither. I thought maybe the Prince wouldn't like us making so free with his liquor, though he had suggested it himself. He was acting strangely."

"How strangely?"

"Well, as I said, he seemed to have something on his mind . . . Well, there I was left alone in the sitting room, smoking a cigar and looking out of the window; then, like a crack of thunder from the blue, the shot!"

"From what direction?"

"You asked me that before and I can't tell you. It seemed to fill the air. Somewhere close by, that's all I can say."

"How long was it since Scharipov had left the room?"

"A minute or two. Time enough for him to get to the bar but not to pour a drink. . . . I ran out of the room. I met Goroshovel coming out of the dressing room. In the foyer we ran into Scharipov. We asked him what happened and he asked us what happened. Nobody could answer. We beat it out of there."

"Where were your hats?"

"Lying there on a table in the foyer. We snatched them up and beat it!"

"Could you see into the bar?"

"I didn't look at nothing, Mister. I was the first on the stairs!"

"Here's a question I didn't ask you before," said Whittemore. "Was Prince Lenkoran armed?"

"I didn't see his gun that night," said Tashla, "but he always went armed. He told me so. Come to think of it, when he left us in the sitting room, I saw him touch his hip pocket as a man does, to make sure that his gun is there."

"He was expecting trouble, then?"

"Maybe."

Whittemore turned to Loasby. "If he was armed, what became of his gun afterwards?"

"Obviously the killer took it with him," said Loasby.

"That's another point in favor of the girl," Lee pointed out. "She never left the place. She threw only one gun out of the window and it was her own."

"Were you armed?" Loasby asked Tashla.

"I was not."

"Do you possess a gun?"

"Yes, I do. I have a license for it, too. But I don't carry it when I'm invited out to dinner."

"When do you carry it?"

"When I'm collecting for Russian relief. Contributions are usually handed to me in cash."

Loasby looked at Lee. "Any more questions, Mr. Mappin?"

Lee shook his head.

"Take him away," said Loasby.

Tashla was led out, still wearing the impudent grin. He felt that he had come off pretty well from this examination.

"His story tallies closely with Goroshovel's," said Lee. "Is there any possibility they could have met to compare notes since their arrest?"

"No, sir! I have taken care of that!" said Loasby.

He went on, while they were waiting for Scharipov to be brought in: "A woman turned up yesterday who claims to be Scharipov's wife. Has been pestering me to be allowed to see him."

"Why not?" said Lee.

"I was warned from very high quarters not to let Goroshovel see anybody."

"That was to prevent him from communicating with Scharipov. You've got them all under lock and key now."

Scharipov entered. Having recovered his baggage from the Biltmore, he was once more dressed like a conservative, old-fashioned banker. The prince-nez was placed just so on his nose; the neat, dark mustache was sprouting again. He was nonplussed at the sight of Lee. Recovering himself, he cried out:

"Mr. Mappin, I'm being railroaded . . . railroaded, I say! The police are making believe they found a gun on me! It's a lie! The police planted it on me! I had no gun! I never had a gun! I wouldn't know what to do with a gun!"

"Keep your shirt on, Scharipov," said Loasby. "I've been a detective for twenty-five years, and I've heard that yarn nine hundred and ninety-nine times! The police planted it on me! And never once a word of truth in it!"

"It's true! It's true!" wailed Scharipov, wringing his hands. "I never had a gun! I'm being railroaded!"

"Cool off," said Loasby, "and tell us your story of what happened on the night Prince Lenkoran was killed."

"What has Mr. Mappin got to do with it?" asked the prisoner suspiciously.

"He is merely a friend of the deceased," said Loasby. "It was Mr. Mappin who ran you down in San Francisco."

"How did he run me down?"

"Ask me another," said Loasby laughing. "Come on, tell him your story."

The prisoner studied Lee with a look of anxiety which Lee could understand, but which meant nothing to the other two. He began slowly to tell his story. In the beginning it was the same story told by Goroshovel and afterwards by Tashla.

"I went into the bar," he continued. "The Prince's strange manner had made me a little anxious, but not greatly so, because he was a peculiar man and often silent. I went behind the bar to look for the brand of Scotch whisky that I preferred. There were many bottles. Before I found the one I was looking for, I heard the shot . . ."

"From what direction?"

Scharipov considered before answering. "From the rear of the apartment."

"He's lying now," said Lee.

"Well, I can't say! I can't say!" said Scharipov. "It startled me so!"

"What passed through your mind when you heard the shot?" asked Whittemore.

"I thought Prince Lenkoran was having trouble with the woman."

"Lie number two," said Lee quietly. "At that time Scharipov didn't know the woman was in the apartment."

"Well . . . well," stammered Scharipov, "I knew he was surrounded by spies. I thought maybe he had surprised a spy in his apartment."

"Did you know he was armed?" asked Whittemore.

"I knew he usually carried a gun."

"Did you see him touch his hip pocket when he left the living room?"

Scharipov snatched at this. "Yes, I did! And that proves that he was expecting trouble somewhere in back. It had nothing to do with me!"

"Why didn't you say so before?"

"I didn't think of it. . . . It's foolish to accuse me of killing Prince Lenkoran. What possible motive could I have had?"

"Ambition," said Lee. "You wanted to run the organization yourself."

Scharipov, hearing his most secret thought exposed, looked at Lee strickenly. "What reason have you for saying that?" he asked hoarsely.

"Mr. Mappin is not here to answer your questions," said Loasby.

"What organization?" asked Whittemore.

"Russian relief," said Lee with a very dry smile.

"It's not true! It's not true!" cried Scharipov. "I never thought of such a thing!"

Loasby leveled a forefinger at him. "When you went into the bar, you found Lenkoran there and you shot him!"

"It's not true!" wailed Scharipov. "How could I have hoped to get away with that?"

"Don't ask me. Maybe Lenkoran said something that put you in a passion."

"I am not a passionate man!"

"Or perhaps you had fixed it up in advance with Goroshovel and Tashla."

"I had no gun, I tell you. I never had a gun!"

"So *you* say!"

"Have you engaged counsel?" asked Whittemore.

Scharipov shook his head. "I have no money."

"What a pity!" said Lee. "You should not have been so quick to donate the proceeds of your coffee to Russian Relief."

This apparently innocent remark caused Scharipov to turn pale. He looked at Lee with terror and a new respect.

Nothing further was elicited by his questioners. When Scharipov was finally taken away, Whittemore said:

"The preponderance of evidence is certainly against Scharipov. I can proceed to ask for an indictment now."

"And release the girl?" put in Lee. "Also Elias, the waiter, and Vassily Gorbol, Lenkoran's servant, who are held as witnesses?"

"Not yet."

"Are you going to ask for an indictment against Jocelyn D'Arcy?"

"I can't prosecute two persons for the same crime unless I have evidence of collusion."

"I recommend that the girl be released," said Lee firmly.

"I'm not prepared to proceed against her at this time," said Whittemore. "The question of holding her is entirely up to the police."

"Sorry to be disobliging," said Loasby obstinately, "but I won't let her or the witnesses go, at least not until Scharipov is indicted."

Lee bestirred himself. "Well, gentlemen, I haven't been home yet. Let me know when anything new turns up."

"Don't you want to see the girl while you're here?" asked Loasby.

Lee shook his head. "No. I promised her that the next time I came I would bring an order for her release. She's no more guilty of this crime, Inspector, than you are."

"Perhaps not. Perhaps not," said Loasby, nettled. "But I have to proceed in proper order."

Lee left them. Out of the tail of his eye he saw the prosecutor looking inquiringly at the Inspector, as much as to say: What's biting him? It was not hard to guess that as soon as the door closed, Loasby would answer disgustedly: He's hipped on the girl. Lee chuckled to himself.

He drove home. His own place looked good to him. The lean and leathery Jermyn, usually so inexpressive, was profoundly moved at the sight of his master all in one piece and apparently undamaged. Ever since the incident of the poisoned wine, Jermyn had been in terror for Lee whenever he was out of his sight.

"And will you be at home for a while, sir?" he asked anxiously.

Lee shook his head. "One more trip, Jermyn, and then I hope, for better or for worse, that this ugly case will be ended."

"I suppose you couldn't take me with you, sir," Jermyn said wistfully.

"I'm afraid it isn't possible, this time."

Lee telephoned to Washington.

In about an hour's time Inspector Loasby called him up. Over the wire his voice sounded like that of a hurt schoolboy. "Mr. Mappin," he said stiffly, "I have received instructions originating in the same high-up quarter as before, that Miss D'Arcy is to be released."

"Good!" said Lee. "Don't think too badly of me, Loasby. I'll be right down."

Upon Lee's return to Headquarters, Loasby's face expressed, like his voice on the telephone, a sense of deep injury. "Mr. Mappin, you and I have been friends for years," he said. "We have worked together on many a case and I have backed you to the limit. In this matter you have not treated me right. Why couldn't you tell me right out what was in your mind, instead of going over my head?"

"Loasby, you're a good fellow," said Lee warmly. "Believe me, I am not working against you. Withhold judgment on your old friend for a while, and everything will be cleared up."

"But what *is* behind it all?"

"International complications," said Lee with a wicked smile.

Loasby frowned and said no more. He signed an order for Jocelyn D'Arcy's release and handed it over.

"How about Elias and Vassily?"

"They will be set free immediately."

When Lee presented himself at the door of the room where Jocelyn was confined, she sprang up and her pale, dull face suddenly became luminous like an alabaster vase with a light inside. It was worth something to see Jocelyn at such a moment.

"Lee!" she cried breathlessly. "You're smiling! Have you . . . is it . . . is it all right?"

"You look like sunrise," said Lee dreamily.

"Damn it, don't keep me in suspense!"

"Pack your bag and put on your things," he said briskly. "We're going up town."

She could hardly take it in. Her face paled, then turned rosy again. "Duckling," she said impressively, "you're a magician, that's what you are!"

"Well, I got you in quod," he said; "it was up to me to get you out, wasn't it?"

She was already flying around to gather her things together.

A few minutes later they were on their way uptown in a cab. Jocelyn said, delicately sniffing:

"Is there anything sweeter than the faint stink of an old street, duckling; gasoline fumes, sewer gas, and the breath that comes out of grimy hallways?"

"I don't know," said Lee. "I never was locked up myself."

"I told you you had to take me out and feed me. It'll soon be dinnertime. I have a dress at my hotel that I've never worn; midnight blue and silver. Where shall we go?"

"Dinner, by all means, darling, and the dress that has never been worn! But let it be at my place. I may have to ask you to double in our show, and we shouldn't be seen in public together."

"Okay by me, duckling." She shivered slightly. "I hope nobody else is going to be murdered."

"I hope not. Anyhow, tonight will be a gala, even if there is nobody present but us and Jermyn!"

CHAPTER TWENTY-TWO

EACH DAY LEE RECEIVED A MESSAGE from Linden in San Francisco which was always the same: No news! Young Richardson said disgustedly: "Have Latvians got wings?

"Even if they have," said Lee," a black limousine can't fly!"

In Philadelphia Lee had better success. At the end of the third day, Welby returned with, as he said: "Enough evidence, added to what we have, to hang Count Deduchin twice over."

"First catch your Count," said Lee ruefully.

Welby had found the Count's attorney in charge of his fine place near Ardmore on the Main Line, attended by the Count's remaining two men servants. There was an extensive farm in connection with the place. The attorney was an unsuspecting American, who instantly put himself and the Count's house at Welby's service. Such, he said, were the Count's instructions. Welby searched the house from cellar to garret. Naturally, he found nothing of interest to him.

The attorney even opened the Count's safe for his inspection. It contained a goodly sum in cash, and a list of the Count's securities which were kept in the vault of a Philadelphia bank. His wealth was invested in gilt-edged American stocks and bonds. The attorney had pointed with pride to the great sum he had put into United States war bonds.

"Can you beat it?" said Welby in reporting this to Lee.

"It serves the double purpose," said Lee smiling, "of allaying suspicion, and of hedging on the Count's bets on the outcome of the war."

Deduchin's will was in the safe and Welby read it. After making various bequests to distant relatives, "if they can be found," the fortune was left to Deduchin's son, who, the attorney explained, was fighting for "the Allied Nations" somewhere in Europe; he didn't know where. The will contained an affectionate message to this son, giving him explicit directions where to find his mother's unmarked grave on the family estate in Russia, "if he was ever permitted to return."

In this paragraph, the quick-witted Welby had immediately smelled a rat. In the first place, Deduchin overplayed the note of paternal affection. Men of this character usually hate their eldest sons. In the second place, the lady must have been dead nearly a quarter of a century. Why had the young man not been told before where his mother lay buried? In the third place, why did Deduchin choose to convey this information to his son in the will?

Without appearing to pay any special attention to the paragraph, Welby memorized it. As soon as he was out of the house he wrote it down and studied it. As a result, he returned to the Count's farm that night, accompanied by his assistant and an FBI man. Following the directions in the will with the substitution of "America" for "Russia," he was led to a cement-lined cache buried at the edge of one of the Count's fields. In it was a tin box containing the Count's most precious family records and mementos. This was Welby's "evidence." Every man has his weakness, and there was an all-revealing letter from the greatest one that the Count had not been able to bring himself to destroy.

With all this, Welby felt that he had failed because he had not been able to discover any clue to the means whereby Prince Lenkoran had communicated with his masters overseas, a service that Count Deduchin presumably had inherited from his predecessor.

Lee sent Welby to Westchester County to see if he could turn up anything at Lenkoran's luxurious little country house north of Tuckahoe. This mission resulted in failure. Lenkoran's servants, an elderly American pair, were still living in the house. They now looked to Count Deduchin as their master. Deduchin had visited the house.

Meanwhile, Lee had paid a couple of visits to the office of Assistant District Attorney Whittemore to urge speed in having Scharipov indicted for murder and brought to trial. Lee seemingly was filled with a desire to avenge the death of his "friend," Prince Lenkoran. When Whittemore doubted if he had enough evidence to take into court, Lee uncovered an additional witness.

This man, an old friend of Lee's, was the president of a big sporting-goods concern in New York. He went to Headquarters and asked to be confronted with Scharipov. Having looked the man over, he identified him as the one who, under another name, had purchased a pistol from him a few days before the murder. The customer had shown a license to carry it, doubtless forged. When the merchant handed the serial number of the pistol to the police, it was found to correspond with that on the gun taken from Scharipov.

"Do you mean to say that you go on the floor and sell goods?" Loasby asked the merchant somewhat incredulously.

"Occasionally, occasionally," was the answer; "when business is heavy. That's the way I keep myself in touch with the customers."

Active preparations were then set on foot to have Scharipov indicted and tried.

Jocelyn D'Arcy, having been outfitted with several extremely becoming nurses' uniforms and caps, furnished with medical certificates that were phony and secret credentials that were *bona fide*, departed for La Guaira, Venezuela, by commercial plane via Miami. Her instructions were to find Purser Diehl of S.S. *Arcturus*, who had been hospitalized on account of fever either in La Guaira or in the neighboring city of Caracas. She was to make friends with Diehl and learn what she could from him.

Lee and Welby had themselves measured for Army uniforms. They took a day off to go to Washington where, in the course of an exceedingly busy afternoon, they were sworn into the United States Army and commissioned as Major Halperin and Captain Talbot.

Back in New York, on the seventh day after their departure from San Francisco, the mystery of the disappearance of the black

limousine was finally cleared up. Linder telephoned that the car
had been found smashed on the rocks at the base of formidable
cliffs on the coast below Pescadoro, fifty miles south of San Francisco. It was the loneliest spot that could be found. Here the main
coastal highway struck inland from the sea for a space; a little-
used dirt road meandered out to the cliffs and the car had been
driven over. Near the wreck lay the crushed and bound body of
Macklin, the driver.

"Poor fellow!" said Lee. "At any rate, the ropes around his body
have cleared his name. He was no traitor."

"But what has become of the Latvians?" said Richardson.

"Obviously, they used their wings," said Lee dryly.

"Seriously, what can you do now, sir?"

Lee took a pinch of snuff. His spectacles glittered. Well,
Deduchin has taken some tricks, but I am not yet set. I still hold
the ace of trumps!"

"How do you mean, sir?"

"Deduchin does not suspect that I am aware of his treasonable
activities. Only Messieurs Scharipov, Goroshovel and Tashla know
that, and they are safely locked up."

At evening of the same day, "Major Halperin" and "Captain
Talbot," complete with despatch boxes, boarded the night plane
for Miami. The Major was hardly a military figure. In the morning
they transshipped to a flying boat, and after calling at Havana and
Kingston, Jamaica, were flown across the blue Caribbean to
Maracaibo, Venezuela. Here they spent the night ashore, and in
the morning flew on to La Guaira. The approach to the latter town,
tucked in on a narrow shelf between soaring mountains and the
sea, was very imposing.

In the small crowd attracted to the landing port by the arrival
of the clipper, stood an extremely pretty young woman, bright-
eyed, dark-haired, wearing a long blue cape over a nurse's uniform. She was attended by several good-looking young Venezuelan
officers, and the two Americans marched past the group eyes front.
When they were out of hearing, the Major murmured to the Captain:

"Joss is on the job, I see."

Venezuela being strong for the Allied cause, the passage of the American officers through the customs was expedited. They hired a motor car for the dizzy drive to Caracas, which is only seven miles away in an air line, but some thousands of feet nearer Heaven. In less than an hour, they were driving through the streets of that gay and rococo little capital. They presented their credentials at the American Embassy, and later went into conference with the naval attaché, who had been advised of their coming.

After lunching with the Ambassador and part of his staff, the two officers were conducted to an upper room "to rest." To them was brought the pretty American nurse with the exceptionally bright eyes.

"Gosh, duckling," she cried, "was I glad to see you get off the clipper this morning. The *Arcturus* is due tomorrow . . . Hi, Welby!"

"I have not lost sight of the *Arcturus*," said Lee, smiling.

"How hard it was not to fall on your blessed necks at the landing port!"

"There were handsomer necks there asking to be fallen on!"

"I didn't know who else might be looking on," she continued. "It's safe for me to come here because everybody in town knows I'm an American."

"You have lost no time," said Lee.

Jocelyn smiled dazzlingly. "I've enjoyed myself while working. I suppose I always enjoy myself, but a touch of conspiracy lends a special zip to it. It's a small place and already I seem to know half the Venezuelan Army."

"Only half?"

"There's something about American girls that gets them. I haven't a word of Spanish and their English is only so-so, but we get along. We get along."

"I could see that."

"The pretty officers are my camouflage. Nobody would ever suspect that I had any serious business in hand." She walked all around Lee. "Bless you, duckling, how cute you look in uniform!"

"*Please*," said Lee ruefully, "don't rub it in. I know how my bottom sticks out in these drill pants!"

"It's all right," said Jocelyn, "somehow one feels that it's right for a major to be round and bottomy! A Colonel, on the other hand, should be hard-bitten."

"Then I shall never win promotion!"

Getting down to serious business, Lee asked: "Have you found Diehl?"

"Sure! No trouble at all. He was a patient in Bon Secours Hospital here in Caracas. I got a job there. They are short of nurses. I didn't kill anybody during my three days duty, duckling. I only had the convalescents."

"Okay, but stick to Diehl."

"He was recovering from a bout of fever. I didn't try to approach him directly, because I learned from the hospital gossip that he was gone on another nurse. She's Venezuelan, pretty as a picture, simple as a lamb, and completely locoed by Purser Diehl. I palled up with Teresa, as they call her, and she told me the story of her love. She speaks English. It doesn't amount to much, but at that it was more than I could have got out of the man. He's suspicious of Americans."

"Is he still in hospital?"

"No. Though he is still weak, he insisted on leaving this morning. If he didn't join his ship on this trip he'd be fired, he told her. He and his sweetheart have gone down to the Hotel Miramar on the coast. As soon as he left the hospital, I fired myself."

"What about Diehl's background?"

"He's a German. He became an American citizen some years ago, but he is still German to the core."

"Has he told the girl anything about his secret designs?"

"Not a word. Their relationship is purely romantic. Like all Germans, he is very sentimental, and he did tell her this; that he had a presentiment of death; that this would be his last voyage and when he sailed away it would be an eternal farewell. She wept gallons when she told me that. Poor silly little fool!"

"What's the gossip around town about the *Arcturus?*"

"The *Arcturus* is a very popular ship. She has opened an American market for Venezuelan coffee. We didn't buy much before. By means of the *Arcturus*, coffee money is pouring into the country. Nobody has any suspicion that the ship has other business besides carrying coffee."

"And the secret wireless station?"

"I haven't had time to locate that, Major. None of the Venezuelan officers is aware of its existence. Venezuela has cracked down on Axis sympathizers, but of course it's not such a vital matter to them as it is to us, and the pro-Axis gang could have a wireless."

"Vital messages will be exchanged tomorrow, and I am still working in the dark!" said Lee.

"I've got good men working on it," said Jocelyn.

"When is the *Arcturus* expected to sail?" asked Lee.

"Her coffee is waiting at the dock. They're going to load all night. She will get away some time during the second night."

"Good! It is not too soon," said Lee.

Jocelyn asked: "What are your plans, Major?"

"I have finished my business in Caracas. The Captain and I will go down and stop at the Hotel Miramar on the sea. They tell me it's good."

"Good! It's sumptuous," said Jocelyn. "One of Dictator Gomez' playthings. You'll see Diehl there."

"What does he look like?"

"Thirty years old. A typical German with a square head and no neck to speak of. Considerably pulled down by fever. A German with malaria! Ugh! Could anything be less appetizing!" She shuddered.

"You had better get out of Caracas, too," suggested Lee.

"Surely! But I can't go to El Miramar. Too grand for a free-lance nurse. I'll take a room at a modest little place in La Guaira. Believe it or not, it's called the Waldorf-Astoria. I can work just as well from there. My officer friends will come to see me. They are the best repositories of gossip in Venezuela."

"Sorry I can't ask you to dinner with us," said Lee, "but Diehl might smell a rat."

"You're right. . . . Any instructions, Major?"

"Not at the moment. I'll keep in touch with you."

ON THE FOLLOWING MORNING the two seeming officers were breakfasting in generous American fashion at the Hotel Miramar. They occupied a table on a terrace looking out to sea. There was a delicious morning freshness in the air; the cerulean sea was glorious in the sunlight. Off to the westward, a smudge of smoke was gradually resolving itself into the shape of a ship which both men regarded with interest.

"She'll dock about nine," said Lee. "They won't be so expeditious here as in San Francisco. Give her thirty-six hours to discharge and load, and she'll be off again tomorrow night."

Soon after the two men had seated themselves, a man and woman were ushered out on the terrace. The man was instantly recognizable from Jocelyn's description as Diehl, the purser.

"Here they come," said Lee; "don't look around."

Obviously German, the man's fair skin now had a yellowish tinge and his clothes hung loosely on his frame. In health, it was clear, he was too fat for his years. The expression of his blue eyes was both dull and chronically suspicious. He kept glancing from side to side to see if anybody was looking at him. Lee could look without appearing to look. The girl was pretty in a conventional fashion, with an oval face, a graceful mane of curly dark hair, and fine Spanish eyes. She appeared to be completely infatuated with her unattractive companion.

"As Joss says, there's no accounting for taste," remarked Lee.

The couple was placed at the edge of the terrace two tables away. They were intensely interested in the approaching ship. The girl talked animatedly. The man gave a brusque, impatient order to a waiter.

When the ship finally swung around to pass the breakwater at La Guaira, it was revealed that she was no clumsy, lumbering tramp. She had a single funnel with a jaunty cup around the brim and a graceful rake. Her white upper works suggested that she had carried passengers before the war. Apparently she was well known to most of the breakfasters on the terrace. The name *Arcturus* passed from table to table.

"She comes in smartly," said Lee. "Fifteen knots, I should say."

"They have to have speed nowadays to escape the U-boats," remarked Welby.

"No U-boat will attack the *Arcturus*," said Lee dryly. At that moment the Stars and Stripes broke out at the ship's taffrail, glorious in the morning sun.

"Doesn't it make your blood boil," growled Welby, "to see them dare to raise *that* flag?"

"It's our ship," said Lee calmly. "You mustn't blame the innocent and unsuspicious owners for allowing it to fall into enemy hands."

At the near-by table, Diehl and his companion hastily swallowed their breakfast and departed.

CHAPTER TWENTY-THREE

LEE SPENT THE BALANCE of that day and the whole of the following day in lounging about the patios and terraces of the luxurious hotel. He often let himself be seen in the bar, like a man with nothing to do but kill time. He was not, however, so idle as he appeared. Several Venezuelans recommended to him by our Embassy came to him to receive instructions, and later came back to report.

Through this means he kept a close watch on the *Arcturus* while she lay discharging and receiving freight. He was assured that nothing was put aboard her but the legitimate products of Venezuela. Diehl, the purser, he was informed, sent his girl-friend back to Caracas and went aboard the ship. He did not appear again on shore. In fact, none of the crew or the officers of the *Arcturus* came ashore, though there was a gang of stevedores to load her. Only the captain made brief visits to the harbor office and the Customhouse, and immediately returned on board. If they had a wireless station somewhere near, it was not necessary to visit it, of course. They could communicate with it by the ship's wireless.

Welby during these hours was wandering through the streets of La Guaira and along the near-by roads like an idle-minded sightseer. He was looking for anything that might serve as a wireless mast or antennae. He climbed part-way up the mountain road to a point where he could search the roofs of the town, with powerful binoculars. He had no success. He saw Jocelyn D'Arcy, but neither could her scouts supply the desired information.

After dinner on the second night, "Major Halperin" was paged for a telephone call. It was Jocelyn speaking from her hotel in town.

"Major, could you and the Captain come down?"

By her extreme casualness, Lee knew that something was in the wind. "Immediately," he said.

They engaged a car with the top down. It was a night of stars. Mixed with the scents of the sea and the forest came the fragrance of frangipani drifting over garden walls.

"What a pity we can't relax and enjoy this," said Lee.

It was a seven minutes' drive only. They sent the car back. The "Waldorf-Astoria" occupied a gimcrack building with a big neon sign on the front, and inside an ancient smell of cold grease. Jocelyn, still wearing her uniform, was waiting for them downstairs. Her face gave nothing away. Indicating her costume, she said with the schoolboy grin:

"It's good camouflage. Softens all hearts!"

In order not to outrage Venezuelan notions of propriety, they held their little consultation in the lobby. Arranging themselves on an imitation leather settee, mission style, which faced a sashless window opening on the street, Jocelyn handed Lee a hastily written pencil scrawl.

"Left here by a messenger half an hour ago. He didn't wait and so I didn't see him."

The note was in English. Lee read:

Illustrious Señorita:
I have found the wireless of the Axis. I am now watching it and send this to you by one of my men. It is the last house on the Calle Estados Unidos on the right-hand side as you travel west. It is a two-story house and the wireless is on the second floor. From the roof of the house across the street I am watching the operator. Sometimes he is transcribing messages; sometimes sending. It appears that his masters have much to say to each other. So far as I can see, he is alone in the place.

Get your friends quickly. For your own safety, you should proceed first to the police station on Calle 19th Settembre to ask for a guard of two or three men. It is near your hotel. Show the police this letter. They will guide you to the end of Calle Estados Unidos where you will find me waiting at the door of the house.

Devotedly,

Francesco Bareda.

"Another trap?" suggested Lee.

"Bareda is above suspicion," said Jocelyn; "a high-minded *caballero* and strong for our side. He's a captain in the army."

"Sure. But did he write this? Do you recognize his writing?"

"It is the first time I have seen it."

"How could the *Arcturus* gang know that we are here in La Guaira?" asked Welby.

"I can't tell you how they know. But they may know."

"Anyhow, there isn't much risk in going to the police station."

"You are right there," said Lee, "and what a prize if we can capture the messages they have been sending back and forth all day! Come on!"

Having obtained directions from the hotel clerk, they set out. Calle 19th Settembre started just around the corner. One of the ancient Spanish streets, narrow and dark, it ran east and west, parallel with the harbor front. The crumbling buildings lining both sides were now used as offices and warehouses, and were deserted at night. None of the windows had sashes. Some, protected by iron bars, gave the passers-by glimpses of yawning black interiors; others were closed with heavy wooden shutters. Bars and tight shutters gave the street a dead and forbidding look. An occasional street light only pointed up the gloom. Yet Lee and his friends were warned by no sense of danger, because a short way ahead the lights of the police station were beckoning them on. Several men could be seen lounging in front of the door.

At intervals along the narrow Calle opened lanes which were no more than passages between the buildings. From out of the mouth of the second black lane came a rush of rubber-shod feet. A blanket was thrown over Lee's head and a hand clapped on his face, pressing the harsh wool into mouth and nostrils, and cutting off his cries. Slight sounds reaching his ears told him that his friends were being similarly treated. The attack had been planned with characteristic German thoroughness. Every man knew exactly what he had to do and did it silently. There was not enough noise to warn the men in front of the police station a hundred yards away.

Lee and his companions were hustled into the dark lane. Gags were tied over the blankets around their heads and ropes wound around their bodies, pinioning arms and legs. Hands felt over Lee's clothes and took his gun. Every spot in La Guaira is near the water. They were picked up and rushed through the lane, carried across the quay, down a few stone steps, and dropped in a boat. No alarm was raised behind them. The entire operation was carried out in three or four minutes. Lee heard the thump of the two other bodies as they hit the boat. Then the engine was started and water began to murmur under the bow.

After about ten minutes the engine was stopped again. They had left the harbor and were alternately lifted and dropped on long swells from the Caribbean. By this time, for lack of air, Lee's head felt as if it was about to burst and flames danced in front of his eyeballs. As he was about to pass out, he heard a voice say as from a great distance:

"They are too quiet. Better give them air."

He came back to find the sweet air of the sea in his nostrils and overhead the grave stars looking down. The blanket had been removed but he was still bound and gagged. He was lying in the bottom of a ship's boat. He could see half a dozen men crouched around the engine trunk astern. Those in the bow were invisible to him.

A long wait followed. The men in the boat lit rank cigarettes and talked in low tones. One slept with his head on his arms. Lee could not follow their talk, but he heard occasionally an English, a German or a Spanish word. The men belched, they scratched themselves, and yawned loudly. There was something terrifying in their complete disregard of the three bound figures on the floor boards. Their captives might as well have been dead already.

On one side of Lee lay Jocelyn; on the other side, Welby. They were bound and gagged like himself, but he could distinguish the flicker of eyelids. He cautiously shifted his body until the back of his hand touched Jocelyn's hand. He pressed it and received an answering pressure. Later he found Welby's hand. These signals stiffened their morale.

From far over the water came the sound of a deep-toned whistle. The boat's crew roused themselves. Amidst the sudden little jabber of talk, Lee heard the words: "She has cast off." All the faces he could see were turned in the direction of the sound. Soon afterwards the throb of a ship's propeller came faintly through the air. One of the boat's crew in the stern signaled briefly with a flashlight in the direction of the sound.

Time passed; the throb of the propeller slowly drew nearer. When it was almost upon them, the whir of an engine room telegraph sounded and the propeller stopped. In the stern of the small boat, a man rocked the fly-wheel until the engine fired. After a few dozen turns, he shut it off and the boat drifted alongside a steel hull that seemed to rise to the very stars. There was no hail from the vessel; none from the boat. Every man knew what he had to do.

The boat's crew held their frail craft away from the steel hull with boat hooks. Out of the sky over Lee's head appeared two hooks dangling at the end of tackle. Men attached them bow and stern to the boat, and a low-voiced order was given: "Hoist away!" There was the clank of steam winches from the vessel's deck; the tackle creaked and stiffened; the boat rose from the water. Hoisted high in the air, they swung in obliquely and were dropped in chocks on the boat deck of the ship.

When the boat came to rest, the engine room telegraph sounded and the ship quivered with the thrust of her engine. A man kneeled alongside Lee and, removing his gag and the rope around his body, said with a hateful laugh: "You can holler all you want now."

Lee did not holler.

Jocelyn and Welby were freed. The three of them were helped out of the boat. There were no lights on the boat deck. A score of men stood around, silently facing them. Jocelyn pressed close to Lee and her hand crept inside his like a child's.

"Steady on!" he murmured.

"They're so quiet!" she whispered. "Like shadows of men!"

"Come with me," said the man with the ugly voice.

He started aft. The captives followed and two more men brought up the rear. The trembling Jocelyn kept looking over her shoulder.

"They didn't bring us all the way out here to shoot us," said Lee cheerfully. "Would have been easier to let us suffocate under the blankets."

"What *are* they going to do to us?" she whispered.

"Keep a stiff upper lip, Joss. All is not lost."

They were led down a companion ladder to the promenade deck. Their conductor opened a door leading to a passage across the ship. Midway in the passage, light was streaming out of the saloon and they were told to enter. In the light, they saw that their conductor was none other than the unwholesome-looking Purser Diehl. The evil grin in his yellow face did not improve it any.

The brightly lighted saloon was empty. It was a well-found ship and the paneled walls and dark green upholstery suggested comfort at sea. Down the middle ran a long table under a green cloth, with a row of swivel chairs screwed to the deck along each side. At the forward end of the room a cushioned seat ran across from side to side with a row of portholes above it, each masked with a pair of little green curtains. Three cabin doors opened off at each side.

"You may sit down," said Diehl in his hateful, gloating voice.

"We prefer to stand," said Lee.

They stood warily with their backs against the paneled wall on the port side. Diehl and two members of the crew remained in the passage, grinning, feeding their hate. After years of hiding his feelings, the mean-souled Diehl could be himself at last.

After a moment, the door of the forward cabin on the starboard side swung in, and little Count Deduchin came mincing out on his high heels. Perfectly delighted with his dramatic entrance, he was coquetting like a woman. Lee and his friends, who had steeled themselves for anything, never changed a muscle. The Count was followed by one of the hulking bodyguards, who carried his hand significantly in the right-hand pocket of his coat.

"Ha, Mr. Mappin!" the Count cackled gaily. "We meet again!"

"The pleasure is yours," returned Lee dryly.

The little man laughed in his noiseless fashion. "Same old Mappin! Always ready with a quip! . . . Sit down! Sit down!"

"We will stand," said Lee.

The Count was obtaining an exquisite pleasure from the situation. Rising to his toes, ogling, turning his head from side to side, he glanced toward the passage to make sure his performance was appreciated out there. "Ah, my dear Mappin, I'm afraid you are under a misapprehension. Believe me, no danger threatens you. You are my guests aboard this vessel."

"In that case," said Lee, "tell your man to drop his gun. Our guns have been taken from us, as you know, and we are certainly not going to attack you with bare hands."

Deduchin looked at his servant. "You heard the gentleman, Mischa. Take your hand out of your pocket."

The slouching servant obeyed impassively.

"I'm hoping you'll make a fourth at bridge," said Deduchin with cloying sweetness. "This fellow," indicating the servant, "is impossible!"

Lee made no answer to this one.

There was a pounding on the door of the forward cabin to port, and a young male voice crying: "Let me out!

"You may unlock the door," said Deduchin to his servant.

The man turned the key, the door was jerked inward, and Raoul Duplessis ran out, a wild sight with his blond hair in a tangle, a great bruise covering one side of his face, and his shirt partly torn off him.

"Mr. Mappin!" he gasped. "I heard your voice! It's you! It's you!"

"As you see!" said Lee with a real smile. "And glad I am to see you alive!"

"Mr. Mappin," cried the boy beseechingly, "I am not a willing passenger aboard this ship!"

"I can see that," said Lee. "Neither am I!"

"Mr. Mappin, they told me after my letter had gone that it was used to decoy you to your death! Oh, God, how I have suffered!"

"Think no more of it, Raoul. I knew that you were deceived."

"And now they've got you on this vessel!" the boy cried in an agony. "And it's all my fault!"

"Not at all!" said Lee. "It's the other way around. I got you into this trouble."

"No! No! I was a fool ever to have taken service with this beast!"

The Count showed his beautifully matched false teeth. "Be more careful in your choice of words, if you please!"

"Go to hell!" shouted the boy. "You can't do anything worse to me than you've done already!"

The Count smiled and turned a ring on his finger. "And this is the thanks I get for bringing you and your friends together!"

"Beast!" cried Raoul.

"I'm sorry his beauty is a little marred," said Deduchin to Lee, "but we can't do anything with him. . . You may go back to your room!"

The servant moved threateningly toward the boy. Raoul stood his ground. "Keep your hands off me," he said furiously, "and I'll go in."

The servant halted. Raoul entered the cabin, slamming the door after him. The servant turned the key.

Lee's face was like a mask. "If we are your guests," he said, "may we be permitted to retire?"

"If that is your wish," said Deduchin, bowing. "I was hoping we might have a rubber or two before bedtime. But tomorrow is another day. From this moment your wish is law aboard this vessel."

Lee took him up quickly. "Most kind of you. We three would like to share the same quarters. And have the young man with us."

The Count raised his shoulders. "I am desolated that I cannot trust the young man with you. You have seen how treacherous and violent he is."

"Okay," said Lee, "I never thought you would."

The Count made believe not to hear this. "But for the rest, I am happy to say that we have a de luxe cabin big enough for three. It has a bathroom, too."

"We are obliged," said Lee.

"You must forgive me if I have to lock you in. It is for your own good. Until I have convinced you of my good will, I dare not take the risk that you might do harm to yourselves."

"You are too thoughtful," said Lee. "Believe me, we have no intention of giving you that satisfaction."

The Count held up a beringed claw in affected protest. "Incorrigible!" he said with an air. ". . . Mr. Diehl," he went on to the man at the door, "be good enough to conduct my friends to the bridal suite. And make it your business, if you please, to see that their every want is supplied."

"Yes, Excellency," said the grinning Diehl.

"Until tomorrow!" warbled the Count, waving his hand.

"Until tomorrow," answered Lee grimly.

The "bridal suite" opened directly on the promenade deck. It consisted of a commodious cabin with two single beds and a couch bed and the bathroom. At the door, Lee said coolly to Diehl:

"Bring me a bottle of good Scotch whisky, if you please. Also a siphon of soda and some cracked ice."

To his surprise, he got it.

When he left them, Diehl locked the door on the outside. Through the windows, they could see a guard pacing the deck.

Jocelyn came to Lee. "How good of you to think of me!"

"Pooh!" said Lee. "One can get quite a lot out of the little monkey by playing up to him."

"I think I should have died if I had been left alone in a cabin on this hell-ship!"

"Look," said Lee, "there's a strong bolt on the *inside* of the door. From that, I assume we are not to be bothered during the night."

CHAPTER TWENTY-FOUR

IN THE MORNING the farcical pretense that Lee and his companions were the Count's honored guests was kept up. Deduchin, the master of cruelty, judged that this would undermine the morale of his captives quicker than naked brutality. The fact that he had a pretty tough subject in Lee added to his pleasure. The door of their cabin was ostentatiously unlocked and the guard on deck removed.

"Let's go out," said Lee.

A blue-and-white morning at sea; the blue of that peculiar, pale intensity that only the Caribbean can show. Lee noted from the sun that the *Arcturus* was on her usual course, northwestward toward the Dutch islands. Jocelyn, pressing her hands hard on the teak rail, experienced a moment of weakness.

"So beautiful!" she murmured. "It's unbearable! Our last morning on earth!"

Lee clapped her shoulder as if she had been a boy. "Don't give up the ship, Joss!"

Welby joined them and Lee went on: "Sometime today, I judge, a crisis will arise. Just how, I don't know, of course. Anyhow, our course of action is clear; *we must have guns!*"

"But how?" said Welby gloomily.

"Listen! Whatever happens, the Count will be present to see the fun. Let us stick as close as we can to him. Wherever the Count is, big Mischa, his bodyguard, will be beside him. Welby, if we jump with lightning swiftness, can we bear down that big brute and take his gun?"

Welby cheered up. "It can be done."

"The Count will be armed also," Lee went on. "Joss, you must tackle him. Are you equal to it?"

She nodded. In action I'll be all right, duckling. It's this awful waiting for something to happen that gets me down."

"Don't be too rough with the Count," said Lee dryly, "or he'll come apart in your hands."

"Just let me get a chance at him!" she said.

"If necessary, we'll take cover in our cabin," Lee went on. "The walls are of steel and the windows too small to admit a body."

A white-coated steward approached to ask if they would breakfast in the saloon with Count Deduchin or in their own cabin. When they chose the latter alternative, a good and plentiful breakfast was brought.

"Eat hearty," said Lee. "It strengthens the nerves."

Jocelyn was much revived by the food. "With two good friends beside me, I can take anything," she said.

Out on deck again, Lee noted by the sun that the *Arcturus* had altered her course to the northward. On the bridge the Captain was taking a sight of the sun; unusual at that hour in clear weather. The deferential steward came to ask where they would have their chairs placed. After they were settled facing the sea, he brought an armful of American magazines.

"Home was never like this," said Jocelyn.

Better than magazines was the sight of young Raoul striding along the deck toward them, neatly dressed, shaven and combed. Only his bruised cheek testified to what he had been through.

"They brought me a clean shirt and told me I could come and find you," he said excitedly. "That is how the Count plays cat and mouse with us. He will be watching us and gloating over our despair."

"Are we despairing?" said Lee.

"No!" said Jocelyn and Welby.

The boy's blue eyes were bewitched by Jocelyn.

"This is Miss D'Arcy," said Lee.

Raoul had been through too much to be mindful of social con-
ventions. "How beautiful you are!" he said. "How sweet and how
terrible to find a beautiful woman at a time like this!"

Lee drew him away a little. "Whist! don't let's get theatrical,"
he said laughing, "or we'll all break down and grizzle!"

Raoul was instantly remorseful. "I'm sorry! But you understand
what a power a woman has at such a time. Oh God! my hands are
empty! I can't defend her! I can only die with her!"

"Are you so sure of dying?"

Raoul smiled. "How can we escape it? I feel that it will come
today. I have been kept alive so far only to give him the pleasure of
exhibiting me to you. He wants to be present while we are watching each other die."

"Well, if it comes to that," said Lee, "we'll cheat him by dying
with a wisecrack." Lee summoned the steward and ordered him to
place a chair at Jocelyn's end of the row. "Go and talk to her," he
said to the boy. "You will find that her heart is as warm as her face
is beautiful.

The overwrought boy dropped in the chair beside Jocelyn. Re-
gardless of the other two men, he caught up her hand and pressed
it to his lips. "*Je t'adore!*" he murmured.

Jocelyn laughed, but her eyes were very soft. "What, already!"
she said.

"I haven't much time," said Raoul somberly. He lost himself in
gazing at her.

From the other end of the row, Lee said cheerfully: "Let's get
down to earth. Tell us what happened since I saw you in San Francisco, Raoul. You can leave out the most horrible details if you
want."

Raoul passed a hand over his face and came back to reality.
"Not much to tell, Mr. Mappin. The Count became suspicious of
me, even before we left New York. I was so closely watched I was
unable to warn you of our trip to San Francisco. I have told you
what happened there up to the moment of my writing you that letter. I was a fool as usual. The woman who brought me my meals
seemed honest and kind and I trusted her. She was the wickedest

of them all. After my letter had been sent, she laughed at my simplicity, and told me my letter would be used to entrap you.

"When it began to grow dark, I was gagged and bound again, carried downstairs, and thrown into the same car that had brought me to that house. I was forced to lie on the floor of the car and the two servants held me down with their feet. I don't know what became of the woman. I suppose she belonged in San Francisco. We drove out of town. I couldn't tell the direction, but it must have been to the south because we immediately left the town behind. We must have been too early for the rendezvous with the rest of the gang, because we drove slowly and stopped to wait several times. The servants were always looking at their watches. During one wait they got out of the car and I was able to raise myself sufficiently to glance out of the window. We were standing in an odd-looking village, very neat; all the houses painted white as in New England."

"Pescadoro," put in Lee.

"We drove on very slowly and in a few minutes stopped in the open country and picked up Count Deduchin and the other two servants. I don't know how they got there."

"In the black limousine," said Lee. "They drove it over the cliffs and threw the chauffeur after it."

"Strange," said Raoul. "I didn't know what had happened because they talked their own language. But I had a feeling that murder had been done."

"Go on," said Lee.

"The three men crowded into the car along with the others. I then had four pairs of feet on my body. After driving for some miles further, we stopped in another village and everybody got out. This was a straggling little place on the shore of a creek or small river; from not far away I could hear the sea. All the windows in the houses were dark. The car went back. As it turned, I saw the license number and memorized it."

"Good!" said Lee.

Raoul continued: "A ship's boat with an engine in it was lying in the creek. There were several men in it. I was thrown in the bottom, Count Deduchin and his four servants got aboard, and we put out to sea. A couple of miles offshore we fell in with the *Arcturus*. The boat was hoisted aboard and the ship resumed her journey. As to what happened aboard her, I would rather not say."

Jocelyn silently pressed his hand.

Lee was restless. At intervals he rose and walked aft where he could search the sky. Upon one such tour, he summoned Welby to his side.

"I thought I heard something," he said, "but there's so much noise aboard the ship I can't be sure. Can you see anything? Your eyes are better than mine."

"I can see it," said Welby, "a mere dot. Must be flying at 25,000 feet."

"Okay," said Lee. "The wake of the ship will betray our position."

LATER COUNT DEDUCHIN came tripping along the deck, wearing his most apelike grin. Big Mischa followed, carrying a deck chair. Every eye watched the Count's approach. The horrible little creature had a morbid fascination for them. He was delighted by the tribute of their somber stares.

"Put it there," he said to Mischa, indicating the place beside Lee.

The servant eased him into the chair and he settled back with a sigh of content. "Mappin," he said, "this is what I have wanted ever since we met; the opportunity for a long, quiet talk with you."

"What about?" asked Lee grimly.

The Count did not reply directly. "Ah, you disappoint me!" he said with a shake of the head. "You and I have been engaged in a kind of contest, a duel if you like, a duel of the wits. Believe me, I regarded it as a privilege to be opposed by so clever and famous an adversary as yourself. I supposed that even when you found yourself outpointed you would continue to fight on gallantly. That's where you disappoint me. I have beaten you and you are sore!"

Lee's expression was good-humored. "So you regard me as beaten?"

The Count raised his shoulders. "It is not in my nature to triumph over you in vulgar fashion. We set out to deceive each other. I succeeded and you failed. Is it not so?"

"I don't quite follow you," said Lee

"Your object was to keep me from discovering that you were in the pay of the Federal Government. My dear fellow, I knew it from the beginning! And you never guessed that I knew!"

"That is not quite right," said Lee. "I always had that possibility in mind. How did you find out about me? From Lenkoran? He knew."

"No. There was very little communication between Prince Lenkoran and me. That was the course of safety. It was not until I took over that I was informed by my principals abroad that you were trying to investigate us."

"How do you and Lenkoran communicate with overseas?" asked Lee with an idle air.

The Count laughed silently. "Really, Mappin! You surely can't expect me to answer that!"

"If I am to be eliminated," said Lee, "what's the difference?

"No! That is the thing you couldn't find out with all your snooping! Others are ready to take up the work at the point where I leave off."

"Are you dropping it?"

"Yes. I am returning to Europe. After the war is over, of course, there will be important work for me in connection with the reconstruction of America, and I'll be back. I'll be back."

"I hope when that day arrives you'll take care of me," said Lee slyly.

"You won't have to wait so long to be taken care of, my dear Mappin!"

The nearness of Count Deduchin afflicted the two young people with a kind of nausea. They left their chairs and strolled away aft, arm in arm.

The Count watched them. "Love at sight!" he simpered with a smile that was like a glimpse of hell. "How touching!"

Lee said nothing. As he refused to be provoked to an outburst, the conversation languished. Finally the Count said with a spiteful glance:

"Aren't you curious to learn how I can return to Europe?"

Lee affected to start. "Sorry, I was thinking of something else. . . . And how will you return to Europe?" he continued with ironical politeness.

The Count's effect was spoiled. "Later in the day a vessel will take me and my servants off the *Arcturus*," he returned sulkily.

"A U-boat?"

"How did you guess it?"

"I heard there was one lurking in the neighborhood."

After another pause, the Count set out to goad Lee afresh. "You must admit that my espionage has been consistently better than yours, though you had the famous FBI back of you. The moment your female operative landed in La Guaira I was notified by wireless, and again when you and Welby came ashore from the clipper. That, I confess, was a surprise and necessitated a change in my plans. But I flatter myself I am ready for anything. My best stroke was the letter I wrote and signed Francesco Bareda. The touch about the police station was masterly, if I do say it."

The conversation, mostly supplied by the Count, proceeded by fits and starts. He didn't get much change out of Lee. Later he asked slyly:

"Aren't you curious to learn what is the mission of this vessel?"

"If you want to tell me you will," said Lee. "I'm not going to beg to be told."

"Well, I cannot resist the pleasure of seeing your face when I tell you. We have a rendezvous with a U-boat at noon. After I learned that you had come to La Guaira, I changed the meeting place."

"That means nothing to me," said Lee, "because I didn't know the location of the first meeting place."

"Of course, of course, but just to be on the safe side. . . . This plan has been in preparation for years and everybody concerned in it is letter perfect. The U-boat will transfer a huge charge of explosive to this vessel. It will be placed in the bow and covered with many bags of coffee. The ship is American and well known in these waters; her papers are all in order. At Cristobal she will be passed into the Canal with the minimum of delay. At Gatun, after she has been admitted to the lock, she will ram the upper gates; the merest touch will be sufficient. Not to bore you with too many technical details, I assure you that everything has been taken care of. The whole installation will be destroyed."

Lee turned a perfectly bland face to the Count. "How ingenious!" he said coolly.

An angry, brickish color showed under Deduchin's rouge. "Ah, you may make believe to put a calm face on it!" he said waspishly, "but you can't fool me! You are frightened, Mappin! A chill is stealing through your veins!"

Lee produced his snuffbox and, snapping back the lid, offered it to the Count politely. The little man angrily waved it away. Lee took a pinch with deliberate enjoyment. "Really, Count, you ought to go on the stage!"

The Count lost his self-possession. "You'll see! You'll see!" he threatened darkly.

"What is to become of the crew?" asked Lee.

The Count waited until he could compose himself before he answered. "At the moment of impact they will be gathered in the stern of the vessel. It is expected that they will escape in the confusion that will follow the explosion. They will scatter and meet again at a point where a launch is to be waiting in Gatun Lake. The launch takes them to the head of the east bay of the lake, where it is only a couple of miles of rough going down to Las Minas Bay on the Atlantic. There one of our vessels will pick them up."

"They will never make it."

"Perhaps not," said the Count carelessly, "but it gives them something to hope for."

"What about the black gang down below?"

The Count did not answer.

"They are to be sacrificed," murmured Lee. "And where will I and my three friends be at the moment of the explosion?"

This was what the Count was waiting for. He smiled at Lee. All the venom stored in a lifetime of frustration was in it.

"I see. We are to be confined below," said Lee quietly.

The Count's pale eyes greedily searched his face for a sign of fear. "Terrible," he said, moistening his lips, "to think of a beautiful young girl being snatched into eternity!"

Lee said nothing.

"Shall you tell her what is before her? Shall you tell her?"

"I don't know. I will have to consider that."

"I'll tell her," said the grinning Count.

"As you please," said Lee. "You will find that she has a man's courage."

The Count was disappointed in the effect of his bombshell. Showing his teeth, he stared at Lee, trying to think of something that would crush him. Out it came. "You can thank your President Roosevelt for this!"

Lee laughed. "Really Count, don't tell me that you are fooled by the German propaganda! An intelligent man like you! That's for robots!"

CHAPTER TWENTY-FIVE

LEE, WITH THAT SUDDEN SENSE OF LOSS that one feels at sea, became aware that the ship's engines had stopped. He glanced at his watch; it lacked a few minutes of noon. Presently Captain Miller came striding stiffly aft. It was Lee's first sight of him close to. This was a very different kind of enemy, a stalwart, seamanlike man with the habit of command, whose blue eyes glittered with the light of pure fanaticism.

Contemptuously ignoring Lee, he clicked his heels and, bowing to Count Deduchin, addressed him in German.

"Speak English," drawled the Count.

The Captain looked surprised. He said: "May I have a word with you, Excellency?"

"You may speak freely before Mr. Mappin. I have informed him of our plans."

The Captain disapproved. It was clear from his expression that he detested the mummy, but felt obliged as a good German to defer to a superior. He said curtly: "We have arrived at the appointed meeting place, Excellency."

"All right," said the Count with insulting indifference. "Then there is nothing to do but wait for the arrival of our friends.

The Captain's jaw stiffened; he bowed again and retired along the deck. The Count preened himself. Welby murmured to Lee:

"What a wonder somebody didn't slit the little bastard's gizzard long ago!"

217

A few minutes later, Jocelyn and Raoul came tearing along the deck. "Look! Look!" they cried, pointing astern.

Running to the rail, they all saw an upright rod cleaving the sea like a fin and leaving a narrow white wake behind.

"One of ours?" Jocelyn gasped out, wild with eagerness.

Lee shook his head. "German."

The Count, who had not left his chair, was glancing at his watch. "Right on the dot!" he drawled. "Aren't Germans wonderful!"

The sea divided, and between pouring cataracts a long black shape rose slanting-wise to the surface. They were astonished at the size of it, so much bigger than any picture suggested.

"One of the cruising type," remarked Lee.

The U-boat slowed down and came to a stop abreast of the ship, less than two hundred yards away. The sea was calm. A door in the conning tower opened and an officer stepped out, megaphone in hand. He hailed the *Arcturus* in German, and was answered by Captain Miller from the bridge. Meanwhile, a boat was being lowered from the ship. Manned by a junior officer and six oarsmen, it pulled over and brought the U-boat commander back to the *Arcturus*. Part of the forward rail was removed; other men lugged the Jacob's ladder to the edge of the deck and hung it over. Captain Miller came down from the bridge.

Soon the head of the visiting officer rose into view over the side. Fifty feet away, Lee and his group were watching. On deck, Captain Miller greeted the officer formally and waved his hand in the direction of Count Deduchin's chair. The officer came striding aft. He was a comely young fellow, whose pale face was set in a mask of tragic sternness.

"Why . . . why . . ." stammered Jocelyn, ". . . almost like one of our boys!"

"Why not?" murmured Lee. "That's the pity of it!"

The officer clicked his heels before the Count, saluted, and introduced himself in German.

The Count continued to loll in his chair. "Speak English," he drawled, with a sidelong look at the Americans. They understood that this insistence on their own tongue was only designed to torment them.

"Capitän Von Schramm at your Excellency's service," said the officer. "Is it your wish to board my vessel at once, or will you wait until the transfer of goods has been effected?"

"I'll wait," said the Count with affected disdain. "I fear your vessel lacks comfort."

The young officer looked at him sternly. Friend and foe, all men experienced the same desire to punch the mummy. The officer said: "Very good, Excellency. I am happy to say that you will not have to endure the discomfort for long."

"You mean that a meeting with a surface vessel has been arranged?"

"It is so, Excellency."

"So much the better," said the Count, looking away.

The officer saluted and started back for the ladder. He was not so wooden but he could steal a glance at Jocelyn as he passed her.

A scene of activity succeeded. Three more boats had been lowered from the *Arcturus* and were making their way toward the black U-boat; one had an engine, the others were propelled by oars. On board the ship, other sailors were removing the cover of the forward hatch and testing out a steam winch. On the submarine, also, a hatch had been opened on the deck and a small hoist rigged. Ominous-looking little boxes were being drawn up and piled on her deck.

"What do they contain?" asked Jocelyn.

"Contraband of some kind," said Lee carelessly.

Behind them in his chair Count Deduchin giggled.

Jocelyn was the first to see what was coming. "Oh, my God!" she gasped out, and clapped her hands over her face. It was like a big fish swimming on the surface of the water straight for the U-boat. In the next moment it was seen by all, and a wild confusion of shouts and screams broke out. "Torpedo! Torpedo!" The men on the small boats started pulling frantically back toward their ship. The sailors on the U-boat began to dive into the sea. Count

Deduchin scrambled out of his chair and came hobbling to the rail. His wrinkled face was devoid of all sense.

It struck, and the world seemed to be torn apart by the explosion. The U-boat opened wide and vomited a gigantic scarlet flame spotted with dark objects, including the sprawling bodies of men. Then a vast black cloud of smoke obscured all. There was the sound of solid objects raining on the sea, followed by silence. Presently the smoke was blown a little aside and there was nothing there but some insignificant floating debris and a spreading slick of oil.

Lee was the first to recover himself. "Now! Now!" he cried to Welby.

The big Russian, still dazed by the explosion, was standing with his hands on the rail, staring out. Lee and Welby leaped on him from behind, pulled him to the deck and searched his clothes. He had two guns which they secured. Gathering his strength, Mischa heaved and threw them both off. He rose to his feet with his head down like a bull. But behind him the door to the "bridal suite" stood open. Lee and Welby saw it at the same moment. Side by side, they charged Mischa and bore him staggering back through the door. He fell to the floor on his back. Welby pushed his feet out of the way; Lee drew the door shut and locked it.

Meanwhile, Jocelyn looked at Raoul and pointed to the Count. Raoul seized him by the shoulder and swung him away from the rail. The old man fell to the deck. His cap rolled off, taking his toupee with it; the false teeth flew out of his mouth. He made no attempt to defend himself, but lay still with his arms wrapped around his bald pate. Raoul was sorely tempted to kick his brittle ribs in, but he held his foot. He took a gun from the old man's hip pocket and offered it to Jocelyn.

"You keep it," she said.

Leaving the miserable remains of a man lying where it had fallen, the four of them then lined up with their backs against the cabin wall; three were armed. Lee said:

"I thought they would attack us in their first rage."

After a moment or two, the Count stirred as secretly as a turtle prepares to look out from its shell. He raised his naked head, looked around furtively, secured his toupee and his teeth, then crawled on hands and knees to his chair, climbed over the foot-piece and collapsed in a heap. There was something hideously comic in the sight. Jocelyn and Raoul looked at each other and burst out laughing.

The boats of the *Arcturus* were tossing, motionless and bloody, on the smooth swells. Oars had been smashed; men killed and wounded by flying debris. One boat had been completely smashed and was rolling awash. Two or three men were swimming from it feebly. Two other boats moved with an oar or two to pick them up. The silence persisted as if the one awful burst had killed sound.

Aft of the spot where the U-boat had sunk and further to the east, a second submarine, smaller than the first, parted the surface of the sea and came up into the air. Lee suddenly yelled:

"That's ours! That's ours! Cheer!"

Their eyes filled with tears and their throats choked up; all they could get out were hoarse, croaking sounds. Jocelyn was the next to find her voice.

"Boy! we're saved! we're saved!" she screamed.

Raoul flung his arms around her. "Then you are mine!" he shouted, mad with joy.

Laughing and crying together, Jocelyn fought to push him away.

A commotion arose in the bow and they ran to see what was happening. What was left of the crew of the *Arcturus* was running to train the bow gun on the submarine. They glanced toward the bridge for orders. Lee craned his neck to see what the Captain was up to. He was in time to see Miller climb on the rail of the bridge and dive headlong into the sea. He never came up.

This act threw the crew into confusion. Some were still for firing the gun; others yelled: "Leave it alone or they'll blow us to hell!" This was the larger party and the fire-eaters were shouldered away from the gun. Finally they all went to the rail and sullenly waited for the American vessel. When she came up close they held their hands over their heads.

The submarine was slowly approaching the ship. Her deck gun, attended by its crew, was trained on the *Arcturus*. The commander ordered one of the ship's boats alongside and jumped in with half a dozen sailors. The swimmers had been picked up. The boat made for the ladder, and in a minute or two the Americans were standing on deck with fighting faces and guns in hand.

"Where's the Captain?" asked the officer.

"Overboard," answered several voices.

He saw the group standing a little aft and came to them. Recognizing them as his own people, his set face broke up in a friendly American grin. "I am Lieutenant-Commander Wheelwright," he said "Is Major Halperin here?"

"Halperin?" said Lee blankly. "Don't know him."

Then he perceived that Welby was indicating himself.

"By Golly," he said. "In the excitement I forgot my own name!"

There was a general laugh which eased the strain.

Wheelwright said: "I wasn't advised until this morning that you had been carried off, sir. What's the situation aboard?"

"Officers and deck crew are all treacherous," said Lee. "And there's a man locked in this cabin who is dangerous."

"Okay, I'll put them in irons. I can spare men to navigate the ship."

"I have reason to believe that the black gang is loyal," Lee went on. "They were to be destroyed with the ship."

Count Deduchin was huddled in his deck chair playing dead. "What's this object?" asked Wheelwright wonderingly.

"That," said Lee, "believe it or not, is the big shot. A very important prisoner, Commander. His chief need at the moment, I should say, is to be protected from my friends here. I leave him to you."

"I'll take care of it, sir. My first orders were to sink the submarine and take this vessel into a Florida port. Is that agreeable to you?"

"We don't care where you take us," said Lee, "as long as it's the United States!"

CHAPTER TWENTY-SIX

FOUR DAYS LATER, Lee and his friends were back in New York. After he had gone home to assure the faithful Jermyn of his safety and to put off the army uniform, Lee's next act was to call at Police Headquarters. From Inspector Loasby he learned that, in his absence, Sergei Scharipov had been indicted for the murder of Prince Lenkoran and that preparations for his trial were being hastened. Anton Goroshovel and Nicolai Tashla were being held as material witnesses. Loasby had by now convinced himself that Scharipov was the murderer, and his good humor was restored. Lee obtained an order permitting him to talk to Scharipov.

At the City Prison he received the privilege of a private room for the interview. A guard waited within call. Scharipov in prison still preserved his neatness. It was a kind of passion with the man to build up so respectable a front that no one would suspect the workings of his devious mind behind it. Pince-nez, brushed mustache, sober, expensive clothes, a little old-fashioned in cut, everything contributed to the effect. His smooth, pale face, too, after years of practice, had become fixed in an ultra-respectable mask.

They sat down.

"Well," said Lee, "I've been doing a bit of traveling since I saw you."

"Yes?" said Scharipov, polite and noncommittal.

"To La Guaira," Lee went on, watching his face, "to investigate the activities of the *Arcturus*."

Scharipov's polite, listening air did not alter.

"Your friends were better spies than I was," Lee continued cheerfully. "I was shanghaied aboard the ship when she set sail. It was the amiable intention of your friends to blow me up against the Gatun lock gates."

"Why do you speak of them as my friends?"

Lee ignored the question. "But it worked out differently," he went on. "I had tipped off our Navy. When the U-boat came to the surface to put the charge of explosives aboard the *Arcturus*, one of our submarines blew her to smithereens and brought the *Arcturus* into port along with me."

Scharipov's face still showed no change. "Really!" he said. "I am allowed to read the newspapers here; I haven't seen a word of it!"

"Oh, you know the Navy," said Lee, laughing. "They're so afraid of furnishing information to the enemy, they'd suppress the baseball scores if they could. Some day, I suppose they will release the story."

"It was kind of you to bring me advance information."

"Not at all," said Lee. "I have an object in telling you."

"And what is that?"

"You have been indicted for murder and your trial will open in two weeks. The District Attorney's office is confident of obtaining a conviction."

A note of bitterness crept into Scharipov's even voice. "I am innocent," he protested. "The witnesses against me are all lying." He glanced sharply at Lee. "And you know it!"

"I produced the evidence against you," Lee continued calmly, "and I insisted on the indictment." After a moment's pause, he added: "I can have the indictment quashed."

"How?" demanded Scharipov. "Are you more powerful than the law?"

"You'll have to take my word for the how."

"So you're proposing a deal," sneered Scharipov. "What have I got to do?"

"I learned all about the operations of you and your friends except for two things. The first was the name of the treacherous inspector at Cristobal. I have persuaded Purser Diehl to give me that. I'm sure I could find out the other thing, too, eventually, but I have already spent too much time on this case. I want to finish it up clean."

"Give me some proof that you know 'all'!"

"Well, I established a listening-post in Prince Lenkoran's living room, and all conversations that took place there were written down. I listened in at your various conversations with your wife in Berkeley—that's how you came to be arrested—and I intercepted your letter to Captain Miller of the *Arcturus*. I know all about the relations between your organization and the German Government. That part I dug up at Count Deduchin's place near Philadelphia . . . Shall I go on?"

"Where is Count Deduchin?" demanded Scharipov.

"A prisoner in the hands of the FBI. He's a pretty sick man."

"And Miller?"

"When he saw that the game was up, he killed himself."

Scharipov's calm was beginning to break up. "Name your price! Name your price!"

"I want you to describe by what means Prince Lenkoran, and afterwards Count Deduchin, communicated with the German Government."

"I don't know that."

"You do know. You boasted of knowing in your letter to Miller."

"And if I do know, do you think I'm going to tell you?"

Lee smiled. "I do."

"I'll demand to see the District Attorney!" cried Scharipov excitedly. "I'll tell him that you proposed a deal with me to cheat the law!"

"It makes no difference to me," said Lee, shrugging. "I have you either way, murder or treason."

Scharipov hung his head. "If I tell you, do I go free?"

"Certainly not," said Lee. "You're an American citizen. You'll be tried for treason."

"And executed?"

"Undoubtedly."

"Then what have I to gain by helping you out?" he cried.

"Wouldn't you rather be tried for treason than for murder?"

"No! Death is death. What is it to me how it comes?"

"The news of this case will, in time, travel all over the world," said Lee gravely. "You have associates in every country. If they are led to believe that you murdered the chief of your organization for *money*, they will regard you as the vilest traitor in history!"

This was new to Scharipov. He raised a ghastly face. "For money?"

"After the murder the party funds disappeared," said Lee with a calm air. "Goroshovel can tell you something about that."

"I never touched it," stammered Scharipov.

"On the other hand," Lee continued, "if you are pictured to your friends as a daring saboteur who only by the narrowest margin missed dealing a stroke that might have brought the United States to its knees, they will exalt you as a hero!"

Scharipov's head went down again and he was silent. Lee gave him his own time. In the end he murmured: "All right. You win."

"Go ahead," said Lee, taking out his notebook.

"Prince Lenkoran established the wireless station several years ago," Scharipov began. "I don't know the exact date. There was a rich old bachelor died here in New York. He was the last of his family, and in his will he instructed his executors that after he had been put away, the family vault was to be locked and the key carried out to sea and dropped overboard. At the Day of Judgment, no key would be needed, he said. It was done with some ceremony. Prince Lenkoran read the story in the newspapers and that gave him his idea for the wireless station he was looking for.

"The vault is in Greenwood Cemetery; the family name is Redburn. Prince Lenkoran visited the spot and found it exactly adapted to his needs. It is more than an ordinary burial vault; it is a kind of little mortuary chapel excavated in the side of a hill. It has a ventilator in the roof. The Prince had the door opened by an expert German locksmith, and two keys were made, one for himself and one for Count Deduchin in case anything happened to him. Piece by piece, the wireless apparatus was assembled there. It was for sending and receiving. An electric line in the cemetery was tapped for the necessary current. The vault is not far from the northern boundary of the cemetery and everything was passed over the wall at night. That is why the Prince bought a house at Tuckahoe. It was not near enough the cemetery to arouse suspicion, but it was not too far away for him to reach the north wall quickly by car. They fixed the ventilator so it could be shoved aside and a telescopic wireless mast run up from below. Messages were sent and received only at night. I don't know where the two keys are now."

"That doesn't matter," said Lee. "If Lenkoran could have the door opened, so can we . . . I'll check your story, and if I find it true, I will immediately have the indictment quashed."

"Could you keep my name out of this part?" Scharipov asked, humble enough now.

Lee glanced with a kind of pity at the miserable wretch who had been faced with such a hard choice. He said: "When the whole story is published, nobody would blame you for choosing to tell me that much."

ON THE FOLLOWING AFTERNOON Lee was back at Headquarters. He had telephoned in advance of his coming. "Very important," he had said, and Assistant District Attorney Whittemore was waiting with Loasby in the latter's office. Lee faced them with a grave face, but anybody who knew him well would have distinguished a kind of wicked glitter behind the polished glasses.

"Gentlemen," he said, "all proceedings against Sergei Scharipov for murder must be dropped."

They stared. Whittemore spoke first. "But, good God, Mr. Mappin! you furnished the evidence against him!"

"That's right," said Lee. "But it's phony."

"*Phony!*"

"Welby planted the gun on him and I had already planted the bullet in the beer mug."

"*Where did you get that gun and that bullet?*"

"Picked the bullet up at the scene of the shooting. The gun is mine. I shot Prince Lenkoran."

WHITTEMORE AND LOASBY were unable to take it in. They gaped at Lee and each glanced at the other to see how he was taking it. As they seemed incapable of speaking, Lee went on:

"The killing was a nasty job, but my conscience is quite easy about it. I do feel badly, though, about the necessity of deceiving two friends like yourselves. I have written a statement of the whole circumstances, and I hope when you have read it you will see, as criminal investigators yourselves, that I couldn't have acted differently. Please remember that I was under the strictest orders of secrecy from the FBI. In time I hope you will be able to forgive me."

Lee paused. As neither of the others offered to speak, he continued, now with an undeniable twinkle in his eye: "My statement will enable the District Attorney to determine what action it is proper for him to take under the circumstances. The Inspector, of course, would be justified in ordering my immediate arrest, if he so desires."

"Don't be foolish," growled Loasby. "Let's see the statement."

Lee handed it over. "I must ask you both to consider the contents as confidential until such time as the Navy Department and the FBI see fit to release the story."

CHAPTER TWENTY-SEVEN

STATEMENT OF AMOS LEE MAPPIN.

Several months ago, the Ambassador of the U.S.S.R. in Washington warned our Federal Investigation Bureau of the existence of a secret agreement between the German Government and the organization of Latvian fascists. Not much has been published about the various orders of fascists outside Germany. They are numerous and scattered all over the world, including a good many in North and South America. They are united now under German leadership and their headquarters are in Harbin in Japanese Manchuria. The Latvians include the great proprietors who were evicted by the Russians when they took over, and exiled.

According to the secret agreement, the fascists of other countries were to serve as saboteurs for the Germans, since they naturally would not be suspected. The Russian Ambassador suggested that the well-known Prince Lenkoran might be the boss of the outfit in the United States, and that I soon established to be a fact. Nine years ago, when the present German Government assumed power, Prince Lenkoran, who was not Latvian but a Junker nobleman, was appointed as director and paymaster of German

229

propaganda in the United States; later the fascist
saboteurs were put under his orders. His reasons for
masquerading as a Russian are obvious. Russian
exiles were popular in our country.

The FBI requested me to procure evidence
against Prince Lenkoran because, as they said, I
moved in the same circles, and could come close to
the man without exciting his suspicion. I accepted
the assignment and Prince Lenkoran and I became
seeming friends. He was a bold and clever man.
Almost from the first, he was aware of what I was
after, but he regarded himself as so much smarter
than I that he felt himself in no danger. In nine years,
naturally, he had perfected a very ingenious system
of camouflage.

Learning that there was an empty apartment over
Prince Lenkoran's living room, I had Welby take a
top-floor apartment a few doors away. Passing over
the intervening roofs, Welby removed the skylight
over the empty apartment and lowered himself
through. We fixed the skylight so that it could be
taken off and put back without showing that it had
been disturbed. There was a fireplace in the room
above Lenkoran's living room. By knocking out a
couple of bricks at a time when there was no one at
home below, we broke into the flue from Lenkoran's
fireplace and hung a microphone down the flue. It
was bound with soft rubber so as not to betray us by
knocking against the sides of the flue. That was our
listening-post. It worked fairly well.

On the night that Lenkoran, in a spirit of bra-
vado, had me to dine with his three so-called Russians, their clumsy attempts to pull wool over my
eyes bored me, and I left early. It occurred to me
that the conversation might become interesting
after I had left, so I proceeded to Welby's apartment
and, returning over the roofs, put on the earphones

in the listening-post. I was disappointed; their talk that night had nothing for me. However, something, I will never know what, had aroused Lenkoran's suspicions. I had no warning of his coming until I heard him open the door of the flat I was in. As the skylight was over the little foyer, Welby and I were cut off from escape when the Prince entered the foyer.

The rooms were dark but of course he knew we were there when he saw the open skylight and the dangling ladder. It happened in less time than it takes to tell. We heard him feeling around the wall of the living room for a switch. Welby threw the light of his flash on him and I shot. Lenkoran had a gun. It fell from his hand when he was hit, but he had strength enough to stagger through the apartment door and lock it after him. He managed to get down the single flight of stairs, and, as you know, died in his own apartment.

I got out through the skylight as quick as I could, leaving Welby to gather up all the evidence, including Lenkoran's gun and the bullet which had passed through his body, and follow. I was just entering my own apartment when Jocelyn D'Arcy called me to tell me Lenkoran was dead. The girl, as you have guessed, was an operative of mine that I had placed near Lenkoran. I hastened back there. This, of course, was *before* she notified the police. Welby was waiting for me at the street door and I took him in with me. My object in making this secret visit was to secure for the FBI any evidence there might be in the place before the police were admitted to the case. I was under the strictest orders not to let the story break until I had secured sufficient evidence to smash the whole ring.

All the evidence I found in the apartment was the war chest of the saboteurs. This amounted to nearly three million dollars in United States notes of high denomination. I had previously taken the keys to the upstairs rooms from Lenkoran's body. We packed the money in the Prince's own suitcases and Welby carried it away over the roofs. The money is now in the possession of the FBI. Luckily, nobody ever noticed that Lenkoran had no hand baggage in the place. As I left the house, I snapped the padlock to on the flat upstairs and went home again. Soon afterwards, Inspector Loasby notified me of the killing and you know what happened after that.

There was a certain weight of evidence against the girl, and in order to avoid showing my hand, I had to allow her to be arrested and locked up until such time as I could produce another scapegoat. The death of Lenkoran was an accident which threatened to undo all my work up to that time. I had to go on playing the part of Lenkoran's "friend" and make believe to be concentrating on avenging his murder. This was for the purpose of recommending myself to his successor, whenever he should turn up. It proved to be Count Deduchin. Deduchin is a Latvian nobleman. The Germans had no other man of Lenkoran's caliber in this country, and after his death they were forced to entrust the direction of operations to Deduchin. He now says that he was aware of my real job from the beginning, but he may be lying. Deduchin is not the man that Lenkoran was.

In Scharipov, I had just the scapegoat I needed. By faking the evidence against him in what appears to be so shameless a manner, I not only secured the release of the girl (whom I needed in another direction) but I also obtained a hold over Scharipov. There was a vital piece of information that I lacked. Scharipov was in possession of it. By bringing him to the very edge of a trial for murder, I forced him to tell me what I wanted to know. My case against the saboteurs is now complete; that is why I can come clean with you.

WHITTEMORE AND INSPECTOR LOASBY were deeply impressed by the statement.

"A big case!" exclaimed the Assistant District Attorney.

"Quite!" said Lee. "Much bigger than the murder of an individual."

"Saboteurs! Did they get away with anything?"

"No! We scotched them in time. But it was a near thing!"

"What were they after?"

"That must be left to the discretion of the FBI. Sooner or later, the whole story will be told."

"For my part," said Whittemore, "I feel no resentment for the way you deceived me."

"Same here," growled Loasby. "You played me for a sucker twice over, first about the girl, then Scharipov, but I suppose I must forget it. You were always ribbing me about international complications and I never caught on."

"Thanks, both of you," said Lee. "I didn't expect you to let me off so easily. Some day I hope to have the opportunity to make it up to you."

SINCE WASHINGTON SUPPLIED ample support of Lee's statement, no "proceedings" were taken against him, and to the public the murder of Prince Lenkoran continued to be a mystery for the time being.

AFTER HE HAD CLEARED UP the difficulty with his two friends, Lee had Jocelyn and Raoul to dinner at his apartment. They arrived together in a starry-eyed condition. Jocelyn insisted on sending Raoul out of the room while she made her announcement.

"Duckling," she said defiantly, "the boy has talked me into promising to marry him."

"Okay," said Lee mildly. "Why not?"

Jocelyn had not expected this. She frowned at Lee uncertainly.

"Why fling it in my teeth as if I were a disapproving papa?" asked Lee.

"On the level, don't you think I'm a fool?" she demanded. "He's five years younger than me."

"What of it? After what you have been through together? It's the real thing. You can never be mistaken about that when you see it. And in spite of all the books that are written about love and the songs that are crooned, the real thing is rare. I consider you are both lucky!"

Jocelyn embraced him, and Raoul ran in from the corridor where he had been listening.

COACHWHIP PUBLICATIONS

COACHWHIPBOOKS.COM

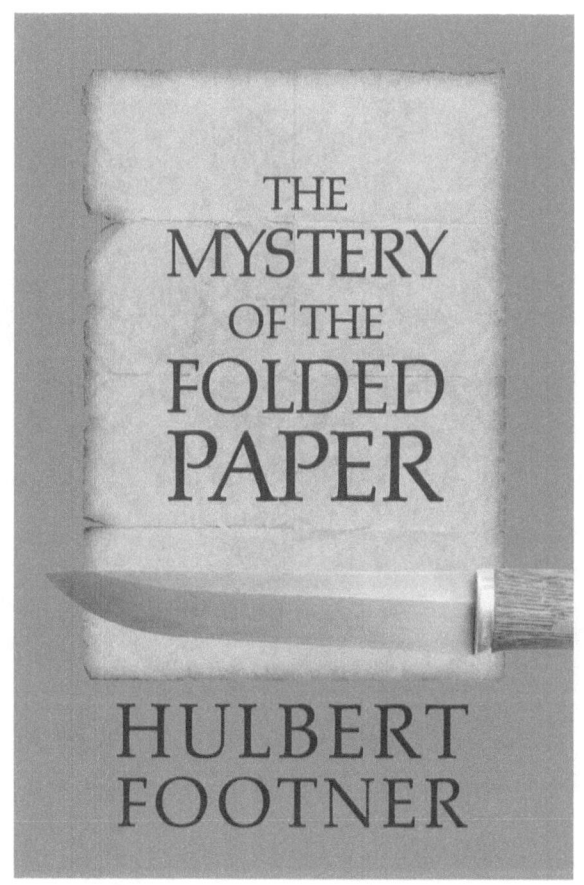

ISBN 978-1-61646-255-8

ORCHIDS
TO MURDER

HULBERT
FOOTNER

ISBN 978-1-61646-262-8

COACHWHIP PUBLICATIONS

COACHWHIPBOOKS.COM

WHO KILLED THE
HUSBAND?

HULBERT FOOTNER

ISBN 978-1-61646-256-6

COACHWHIP PUBLICATIONS

ALSO AVAILABLE

THE MURDER
THAT HAD
EVERYTHING!

HULBURT
FOOTNER

ISBN 978-1-61646-258-2

Coachwhip Publications

CoachwhipBooks.com

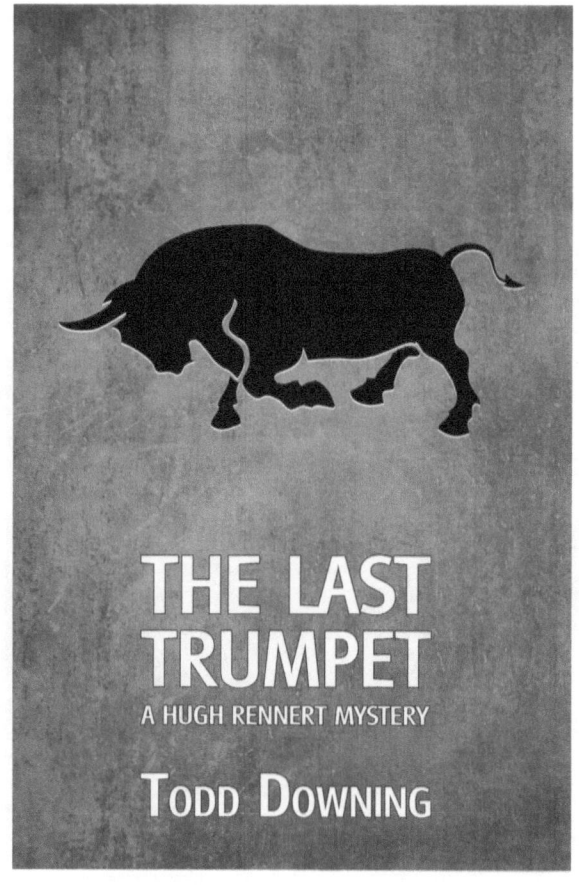

THE LAST
TRUMPET
A HUGH RENNERT MYSTERY

Todd Downing

ISBN 978-1-61646-152-2

THE QUINNY HITE
MYSTERIES

CHINESE RED · HERE LIES THE BODY

RICHARD BURKE

ISBN 978-1-61646-247-5

COACHWHIP PUBLICATIONS

COACHWHIPBOOKS.COM

MURDER OF
THE HONEST BROKER

WILLOUGHBY SHARP

ISBN 978-1-61646-211-6

COACHWHIP PUBLICATIONS

ALSO AVAILABLE

THERE IS
NO RETURN
THE ADELAIDE ADAMS MYSTERIES
ANITA BLACKMON

ISBN 978-1-61646-223-9